PURE HELL WITH A GUN

Newt was glaring at the man at the table, his eyes slitted. "What do you think you're looking at, dummy?" he hissed.

The man made no response. He just sat there, expressionless.

Newt crouched, looking into the man's eyes. "You wish you had a gun, dummy? Why I bet you'd try to shoot me if you did, wouldn't you?"

The man made no move. He seemed not to hear.

Newt pulled a second revolver from his belt and tossed it on the table. "How about that, dummy? There's a gun for you. All you got to do is pick it up and . . ."

Newt never saw what happened. One second the man was sitting there, not even looking at the gun next to his hand . . . the next second the room was full of thunder. Two shots, impossibly fast, roared and echoed from the walls, and Newt was cartwheeling backward, falling against the screen, clinging to the fabric with dead hands.

The silent one crouched down to pick up Newt's fallen gun and stepped through the doorway. More thunders sounded from beyond.

Then an abrupt and ringing silence.

DAN PARKINSON
DUST ON THE WIND

ZEBRA BOOKS
KENSINGTON PUBLISHING CORP.

ZEBRA BOOKS

are published by

Kensington Publishing Corp.
475 Park Avenue South
New York, NY 10016

First printing: January, 1992

Printed in the United States of America

Chapter One

Sully said the word was that the Johnnies had broke the line. Two companies of cavalry, he said. Or maybe more. Nobody seemed to know for sure, and with the rain falling like it was, there wasn't any way to see if it was true. From where we were, hunkered down behind deadfall in a gully that was already a foot deep in muddy water, we couldn't see much more than one another—just pale, frightened faces turning this way and that, ghostly faces shadowed by the bills of dripping caps, half hidden by screens of dead foliage, skeletal branches with twig fingers, fans of tall grass . . . and the rain.

At sunset the clouds had stacked up, with a cold wind behind them, and the rain came.

It was Sully who Sergeant Burroughs sent for orders, the way he usually did. On scout, reconnoiter, or as a runner, Sully was good. And Burroughs didn't know any special reason not to trust him.

But this time when he came back, crawling like a snake through the wet underbrush, he didn't have orders, only what he'd heard. "There ain't anybody back there to give orders," he panted. "Not that I could find, anyway. Captain's moved the company out, all but his foragers, an' they're pullin' back. They said there's Johnny cavalry past the line, clearin' breech for an advance. They said they don't intend to get caught out here surrounded."

Sergeant Burroughs glared at him in that way he had, like his teeth would stick out through his whiskers. "How about Ames? Captain wouldn't have pulled out without leavin' Ames for us to gather to."

"Lieutenant's dead, Sergeant," Sully said, still gulping for air. "Saw him, but he's dead. Minie ball took off half his head. Sergeant Coleman's dead, too, an' that corporal of his tucked tail an' ran, with the rest of 'em followin'. That's what the foragers said. They said if we got sense we'll pull out, too, while we still can."

Burroughs's mustache twitched like he had a foul taste in his mouth, and he looked around. Cornell was nearest to him, crouched down next to a black stump, holding his musket in white-knuckled hands, and then there were Reynolds and Jordy, looking like a pair of wet alley-dogs waiting for the butcher's wagon. Gathered around, here and there, were the rest of us who were still alive—Smith with his bayonet still afixed to his musket, Boley and Hobbs almost invisible in a stand of brambles, Tanner with a dirty bandage wrapped around his head, the McNeil brothers and little Talmadge Wade.

Burroughs looked at them all, then he looked at me and looked right through me like I wasn't there.

"All right," he said. "We're losin' daylight, so we pull back while we can still see. Stay low and stay close. Sully, you lead. Keep it quiet, and keep your heads down 'til we're past the ridge. You . . ." he looked at me again and there wasn't any doubt now that he saw me. The glare in his eyes was pure hatred. "You stay in front of me, where I can see you. And if you level that gun it better be at the enemy."

6

I didn't say anything. There wasn't anything to say, nor anybody there who would have listened. I just did what he said, and followed where Sully led off. And none of them except Sergeant Burroughs so much as looked my way.

The rain was cold, and the mud clinging to me was cold, and it was just like it had always been. Nothing to go back to, nothing to go anywhere for, no reason to move at all except that there was a man who would kill me — or try — if I didn't go where he said. Just like always.

Maybe it was my fault we were out there in that lonely woods, too far from battalion to know when the lines shifted and too far from company to have got word to withdraw. And maybe cut off so that we couldn't even get back. Maybe I was to blame for that. I don't know. But blame is something a man gets used to, and when he's had enough of it piled on him it doesn't matter if more comes along.

It got darker while we crept up that gully. The over-hanging, dead-looking trees, the low dark clouds peppering us with misty rain, they shut out the light so there was nothing to see except just the shadowy figure of Sully ahead of me and, when I glanced back, the gray-pale blotch that was Burroughs's face . . . watching me like he always did now.

A few hundred yards up that runneled slope the gully narrowed, pinching down to a tight little ditch where a tree had fallen across it. Sully came up to the tree, paused there for a heartbeat, then went up the bank and crouched there, hidden by the black stubs of exposed roots. Off in the distance, something rumbled, deep and low. It might have been artillery, or only thunder. I looked away and when I looked back Sully was gone. Then I saw him, bent low and finding cover, heading for the top of the ridge.

He was good. Burroughs knew that, and that was why Burroughs used him as scout and runner. Sully was one of those boys who could go over any fence, or under any gate, and not be seen doing it. The kind who could duck into a back alley and just disappear, or blend with a crowd on the street and never be noticed or remembered. Sully never talked about where he came from or anything about the past. For that matter, most of us didn't. But I knew Sully from the old neighborhood, from when we were just kids. He was one of a kind, and in the part of the city where we grew up there were plenty of his kind.

It was in his speech, in the way his eyes were never still. The waterfront, the old battery area, the dark streets around the Bowery—parts of the city were full of Sullys . . . and this one knew how to use his skills out in the wilderness, too.

Sully was what he was, just like me, and probably no better than me in where he'd been and what he'd done. Most of the rest likely were the same. We all came from the same cloth, one way or another.

But I was the one Burroughs found out about, somehow. So I was the one he watched, the way a man might watch a skulking dog that crosses his path in a dump. And if it curls its lip or lays its ears back and starts toward him, he'll shoot it. I didn't think for a minute that the sergeant would hesitate to kill me. Or that if he did, it would be like killing a man. It would be the way he'd kill a dangerous dog.

It had always been that way. Sergeant Burroughs was just the latest one walking through my dump. "Battery boys," they used to call us in the city, at least until we grew up enough to be given other names. Battery boys—products of the dark streets and back ways from Delancey and the Bowery down to the Corners and Canvastown. Dangerous, they called us.

8

Dangerous? We must have been. Some of us lived to grow up.

I knew what Burroughs thought. He thought I had crossed over the ridge to desert — to get away from him and what he knew. And his coming after me was why they were out there a mile or more past the lines. So it was my fault, and he wouldn't see it any other way. It didn't matter that he thought I might desert. I had already decided about that. But if I had been escaping, they wouldn't have caught me. Like Sully and his kind, I'd learned some things, too, where we grew up. Places like that, you learn, all right.

Otherwise you don't live to grow up.

I had grown up. I was one of the lucky ones. Billy Bean had noticed me. Liked the way I handled myself, he said, and there were things he could teach me, that would make me useful to him. He taught — he and others who worked for him — and I learned. Then I wasn't a Battery Boy anymore. There were other things to call me, when I worked for Billy Bean.

When Sully started up the ridge I moved up, coming out of the gully where he had, crouching behind the dead tree's roots. It was clearer there, but the daylight was almost gone and with the rain there wasn't anything to see.

Directly behind me, Burroughs said, "Go on, you. Move!"

The rest of them were all bunched up behind him, just coming out of the gully. I started to follow after Sully, then hesitated. Ahead were sounds that weren't part of the rain.

"I said, move out, you murderin' scum," Burroughs growled, and prodded me with the muzzle of his Spencer.

So I moved out. There wasn't much cover on the slope, just a growing darkness and the steady rain.

9

Sully was up ahead somewhere, out of sight, but I knew the direction. I kept low and moved fast and I could hear the others right behind me. Then I heard that sound again, close ahead, and I knew what it was. The creaking of wet saddle leather, the clink of metal trappings. Cavalry, coming down the slope right on top of us.

There was a flash of light and a roar like thunder, and we saw them—tall silhouettes against the light, mounted men with guns in their hands. And they saw us, too.

There wasn't time for dodging, or even for thinking. Another explosion shook the ground beyond them, closer this time, and everybody opened fire all at once. A bullet from Burroughs's Spencer burned air an inch from my ear, and a horseman just ahead of me went down. The one next to him came charging down on us, a revolver in his hand firing as fast as he could cock and trigger it. I hit the ground and let him go over me, then rolled and fired my Springfield and he doubled over. Again there was a deafening explosion, not fifty yards away, and another one on the heels of it, even closer.

Someone screamed, "Artillery!" The shout was drowned out by another round that showered mud and rocks all around us, and in the echoes of it came the distinctive thud of howitzers being fired, beyond the ridge. From our own lines. I tried to stand up, and was thrown on my face by a blast behind me. Something heavy landed on me and in the light of another blast I saw what it was. Sergeant Burroughs was staring at me from an inch away, but he didn't see me. He was dead, sprawled on top of me, pinning me down. At least, part of him was. The barrage was a constant pounding now, horses and men going down everywhere, thrown around like rag dolls by blaz-

10

ing gouts of mud, stone, and shell fragments.

I guess I pushed away the remains of Burroughs. I guess I got my feet under me and tried to run, because I remember being upright when it seemed I had forgotten something. Then I was down again, on my knees, and the gun in my hand wasn't an empty Springfield .58. It was Burroughs's Spencer carbine, and I was using it. A reb rider came charging out of the smoke, swinging a saber, and I shot him out of his saddle.

I saw Cornell and Tanner go down, and little Talmadge Wade. There was a glare, and I saw Smith out in the clear — his bayonet still afixed. He was dancing around like a maniac, shouting and spinning. Then a howitzer round exploded at his feet and he wasn't there anymore.

A wild-eyed horse ran past, going uphill, its rider clinging to his saddle. I brought the Spencer up, but as I leveled it they disappeared, dropping out of sight. Darkness descended and I wondered vaguely how a rider and horse could just disappear like that. Then in another glare I saw the horse, struggling to its feet, riderless.

Something as hot as Hades erupted right in front of me, and I closed my eyes tight. My face was on fire, and I could smell burning hair. Still, I realized that I was moving, and I kept at it. Uphill, stumbling, the world a crazy quilt of blinding light and darkness, of deafening roars and echoes, of gouts of earth thrown upward to fall back with the rain.

And smoke. Everywhere, thick and stinking . . . smoke. Like when torchers fired that tenement on Canal Street and all the buildings around it caught fire. There had been burning people then, too. Some said Tweeds did that. Others said it was drunken sailors.

11

I knew who it was. I saw them.

I had just about decided that I might make it to the top of the ridge when something hit me from behind, something that lifted me off my feet and sent me tumbling . . . sailing and tumbling into darkness.

I awoke to stillness. Not silence, but a cold, dark stillness that smelled of fresh mud and falling rain. A darkness full of hurt. For a time I didn't know where I was, couldn't remember how I came to be there, couldn't remember anything except that I had not been alone . . . but I was now.

Or thought I was. In the darkness, very close, a voice as thin as winter wind said, "Oh God, it's cold."

I couldn't see him. I couldn't see anything, but I knew where he was. I eased around, reached out a hand, and touched him. His breath hissed through his teeth and his voice was ragged with pain. "Don't try to move me, boys. Don't touch me. Ah, God have mercy, it hurts so much!"

I backed away, or tried to. Pain washed over me when I moved. My leg, my back, my face . . . searing, singing pains, and my head felt as though it would explode. I lay in the cold mud and waited for it to ebb.

I could hear him, near me. His breathing was shallow and rapid, full of faint hissing sounds. Then he found his voice again. "Did we make it, Tom?" he asked. "Did we get through?"

"I'm not Tom," I told him. "Shut up."

I doubt he heard me. He was hearing voices, all right, but they were no voices that I could hear. He said, "Tom, I don't think I'm gonna make it home. I'm all busted up inside. And cold . . . God, it's cold these days. Bad for the crops, like Pa would say. Tom? Is Pa still tryin' to patch that roof on the barn? He ought to leave that for us . . ."

I knew him for a reb by the way he talked. Even gasping, half whispering, his words had that slow, sloppy way of coming out that said South. That, and something else. Like a musical quality. Like there was a faint, steady rhythm inside him and the words he said rode upon it like words do in a song.

I thought he'd given up, and it was all right with me. I didn't care about hearing him, but he started again. "No, that's right. Pa died, didn't he. Mary's letter says so. I wish we'd been there, Tom. *One* of us should have been there when he died."

He was out of his head, talking to ghosts, and I didn't want to hear him. He meant nothing to me.

My pains were sorting themselves out. Becoming individual pains that I could count. My leg ached like the very devil, and I felt like my whole back was laid open. My face and hands felt burned, and every heartbeat pounded in my head like cannon fire. And the other fellow was there, and I could hear him and that irritated me. I wished he would go away. Go away, or just die.

Still, he lay there, gasping for breath. I tried to shut out the sound. I didn't need him there. He didn't matter. I couldn't remember when anyone had mattered to me, or whether anyone ever had. People don't matter. I knew that. They only matter when they are a threat to you, or if they have something you want. That's all.

There was lightning somewhere — not artillery now, only lightning — and I had glimpses of the surroundings. I was in a hole, with rubble all around. A shell crater. I was on the slope of it and the reb lay in the bottom, with rainwater pooling around him.

"We shouldn't have left Texas, Tom," he said. "We got no business here, you know. Lordy, it's ugly here."

13

I tried to shut him out. He meant nothing to me—no threat, no gain, nothing.

"The sky here is always smoky," he said, straining to get the words out. "In Texas it's blue . . . so blue sometimes it makes you want to laugh right out loud. And the green, Tom! Remember? So many different colors of green? Then wildflowers in the spring . . . and the redbuds in bloom so bright, they . . ."

"Shut your damned mouth!" I was tired of hearing it, and suddenly it hurt to hear it. All that crap about colors. I knew about colors. Mud splattered on sooty brick, that was colors. And the smoke of chimneys, and when it rained the rain was dull gray. Soot and gutter slime and rotting clapboard, back-alley filth and open sewers, those were colors. Those, and the glare of fire when buildings burned.

And blood. Out here in the wilderness, or back home on city streets, the color that mattered was the color of blood.

"Did you know Mary is gonna have a baby, Tom?" The thin voice sounded far away. "That's why I should have stayed home. She worries so. We're gonna give it my name, Tom. My name. David Allen Austin . . . Junior. If it's a boy. Then when he grows, I can tell him, 'Be proud son. You have a fine Texas name, from good Texas stock. You got kin.' Oh, Mary, honey . . . don't worry, Mary. I'm comin' home soon . . . it'll be all right."

He lay still for a long time, then, and I thought he had died. But then there was the faint gasping again, and the voice, no more now than a whisper. "All the colors. All the pretty colors. Like that rainbow at Lone Oak that time. At the depot, they were all out front, just lookin'. I asked if they had a shipment for the Austin place, an' the man . . . Mister Colter . . . he said, 'What's your hurry, son? Take time to look

14

at the rainbow. God put it there for you to see."

He sounded bubbly, as though he needed to cough but couldn't. "I'll be there soon, Mary. Then you and me . . . and the baby . . . we'll go out an' look at the rainbow."

What color is a rainbow? Vaguely, I tried to picture it. I saw arches of ash and smoke, of fire and blood.

Blood. I knew I was bleeding, in a dozen places, but it didn't seem like so much. The worst hurts now were the ache in my head and the burns on my face.

Why didn't he leave me alone? The damn reb, he had me thinking about rainbows, trying to see them in my mind. I saw them there, but they were dirty gray things, not like he said. Gray like the pall of smoke on Canal Street, that time. Or the chimneys on Delancey any time. I tried to raise my head, to curse him for a fool, but it didn't seem worth the effort. He didn't matter. Nobody mattered. I felt tired, and it was hard to move.

Canal Street. Sergeant Burroughs would have known all about Canal Street. And the Bowery and Delancey Street and all the rest. He'd been a copper before the war. A damned harness bull, probably. Like the one that was going to break my legs, then kill me. He bragged about what he would do to me. That bull didn't break any more legs, though. Not mine or anybody's. I had graduated from the streets by then, and Billy Bean had taught me to use a gun.

That was what Burroughs found out, somehow . . . that I had killed a copper. And since he knew, then others did, too. But that didn't matter, either. I wasn't going back. There was nothing to go back to.

"All busted up," the whispery voice said in the darkness. "Horse rolled on me. Tom, if I don't make it, you . . . but you can't do anything, can you,

15

Tom? They killed you. I forgot. Ah . . . good lord. Mary, you just don't fret yourself. I'll find a way. I'll be there, honey . . ."

The rain on my face felt cool, and good. I closed my eyes, and the mud was a soft bed. The softest I had ever known.

There was light when I woke up. The sky was still cloudy, but the rain had gone, and first dawn was peeking under the clouds in the east, giving everything a strange, rosy cast.

It hurt like blazes to move, but I needed to. I was alive, for whatever that was worth. That's the difference between dead people and live ones. Live ones move.

The Johnny Reb wasn't mumbling anymore, or moving. He just lay there in the muddy water. I glanced at him. A young man, maybe twenty or twenty-five. Near my own age, and about my size. His uniform was cavalry, and there was hardly a mark on him except the mud. The horse that rolled on him hadn't marked him . . . just killed him. His boots looked as if they would fit me. Maybe some of his other things, too. My own clothing was in ruins. I was more naked than not.

I crawled to him and started taking what I needed. He groaned when I moved him, and I realized he was still alive. But that didn't matter. He wouldn't need those things again. I was getting his coat off him when his head turned and water sloshed across his face, washing away some of the mud. I looked at his face, and had a shock. It was like looking in a mirror . . . like seeing myself there, stripped and dying in the bottom of a shell crater. We could have been brothers. We might even have been twins, but for the marks on my own face that weren't on his — scars from the streets, from fighting and surviving. The badge of

16

Delancey Street.

I didn't like the feeling I got, looking at a face so like my own face, dying in the clammy mud. His eyelids twitched, as though they would open, and I didn't look any more. He didn't matter, anyway. Nobody mattered. When I could, I got my feet under me. Every movement was agony, but there didn't seem to be any really serious wounds. The deepest was the bullet burn on my leg, but it would heal. I was dizzy and light-headed, but that would pass, too.

I looked around. At first there wasn't a living thing to see, just a shell-pocked slope above a dead forest, where dead men and dead horses lay scattered here and there. Almost at my feet was a Spencer carbine. Burroughs's Spencer, I knew. I knelt to pick it up, and the weird, whispery voice came again, from the crater. I turned, and the dying reb was looking right at me.

"It'll be all right now," he whispered. "You see, I *am* coming home." His eyes shifted, looking past me, into distance. "There you are," he husked. "I wondered when you'd show up again. Lordy, but ain't you a sight."

I turned. Not fifty yards away, a saddled horse stood head-down, nibbling at the grass. But there was something else, hanging in the air beyond it, bright against the slate-gray clouds to the west . . . a rainbow. A full, arching, brilliant rainbow made of every color a man could imagine. Colors like I had never seen. It stood there in the sky, its ends anchored on far places, and it made me dizzy to see it. It was like it had been set there just for me.

Look at me, it said. Use your eyes and look. I am how the world is. Not mean and drab and bloody. Not hopeless. Not wretched. But like this! I am how it is . . . how it can be for a man with eyes to see.

17

Look at me!

Behind me, so soft that it might have been the wind, the reb's voice said, "Thank you, Lord. I can go home now."

I didn't look back at him. I just looked at the rainbow standing there where the battlefield ended and distance began. Like an invitation. I looked, and found myself walking toward it.

Chapter Two

A patrol out of Fort Benton picked up the wagon tracks a mile above Rocky Creek and followed them to the ford. There had been guerrilla activity in the area, and they were taking a hard look at everything that moved. But this time it looked innocent enough. Locals. Civilians with four farm wagons piled high with hay from the flats above the Missouri, headed for Willow Bend to feed the stock. The patrol watched as the wagons splashed across the ford one by one, floating askew in midstream while gaunt dray animals struggled for purchase in the belly-deep current.

The last wagon was crossing when they rode down to the ford for a closer look. The patrol sergeant, a grizzled career soldier of middle years, leaned on his saddlebow, studying the splashing wagon and the others beyond, on the far bank. Six men in all he saw—rough-dressed farmers, all of them old men. Sometimes it seemed like that was all there was left in Missouri . . . old men. Three of them held the leads of the wagons that were across, while the rest worked to ford the fourth wagon. Bed-deep in the current, it was as much as they could do to keep it from swinging downstream and taking its horse with it.

A hundred yards away, the three on the far bank stared back at the blue-coated men who had appeared behind them. There was no friendliness in their gazes, but neither was there any particular hostility. People in these parts generally weren't fond of Union soldiers, but they were resigned to their presence. Except for scattered bands of guerrillas—Anderson followers and remnants of the Quantrill bunch, and a scattering of deserters, stragglers, and plain outlaws—this part of Missouri was out of the war and through with it. It was all they could do to get a crop up and made, and put food on their tables.

Half afloat in the current, the wagon lurched as its wheels found solid bottom. Its horse, driver, and two helpers struggled to get it ashore.

"We goin' across, Sergeant?" One of the troopers asked.

The sergeant glanced aside, where the sun sat atop the hills, then looked again at the fording wagon and those beyond. "No need, I guess," he said. "They aren't hurtin' anybody."

"Don't know what they might have under that hay, though."

The sergeant shook his head. "Whatever's there is wet," he said. He cupped his hands to his mouth and raised himself in his stirrups. "You there! You men!"

On the far bank, an old man in worn, dark clothing handed his lead rope to another and walked down to water's edge. He limped as he walked. Hands at his beard, he called, "Seek the Lord's mercy, soldier. We have little enough left."

"You got anything in those loads that I can't see?"

The old man shrugged visibly, then cupped his hands again. "Come take a look if y'all want to. We got hay for our stock."

"No contraband?" the sergeant called.

"Land, we surely might!" the answer came back. "Could be that we got the national treasury of Macedonia, hid right under this here hay. We just might all be rich men by mornin'. Y'all want to jaw about it, or come over an' look?"

The sergeant frowned, hacked, and spat. "Just askin'," he called. "You see any riders between here and the hay fields?"

"Have now," the old voice answered. "Y'all."

"He wouldn't say if he had," one of the soldiers muttered. "These people ain't about to tell us anything."

"Maybe not," the sergeant agreed, again glancing at the lowering sun. They were a long way from Benton, and it was late. Reining back from the creek bank, he raised his hat in ironic salute toward those across the stream, then turned his mount and headed northward, the others following him.

"They wouldn't tell us any more if we were over there with them," he growled, for any who wanted to hear.

Across the creek, the men got the final wagon onto dry ground, then looked back at the soldiers disappearing among the thickets. One of them turned to scowl at the limping oldster in the dark coat. "Took a mighty chance there, Preacher, proddin' them soldiers like that. They might'a just come on over, just for spite."

The old man didn't even look at him. "All things

21

are in the Lord's hands," he said. Scuffling along the line of hay wagons he stopped at each one, cautiously, and tapped on its siderails. Each time, he was answered by a muffled voice.

"Let's git on up the road," he said to the others with him. "These fellers gonna need some fire an' comforts 'fore they catch their death in that wet hay."

Willow Bend was a tiny settlement tucked into the hills, four miles southwest of the ford. Evening shadows lay deep in the valley when the hay wagons rolled in, each in turn halting at the side of a stone building that served as store, post office, hospital, and community center. From each wagon, men crawled forth, helped by rough, gentle hands. They were hurried into the building, some walking under their own power, two or three being helped by others.

When the wagons held nothing but hay, the preacher told their drivers, "Get on over to the barn and tend to this forage an' the critters. Doc Samples can take it from here. God bless ye all."

Inside the building, lamps had been lighted and the preacher looked around, counting noses. The little back room was crowded. There were the seven young men he had brought in — stragglers, lost, hungry, and hurt, trying to get home. The doctor and four elderly women were among them, tending them.

Doc Samples glanced around. "You brought in a load this time, Preacher. How many seem bad?"

"Mainly just them two yonder." Preacher nodded toward the back wall, where the women were peeling wet clothes off a pair of pale young men and helping them into cots. "Young feller over there's

22

got a festered arm, but he's walkin'. An' that'n yonder, I don't know about him. Seems all right, but maybe he's out of his head some way. He don't say a word, just stares."

The doctor took a quick look at the two in the cots, then at the arm of the one sitting by the door. "Not too bad," he said. "We'll get this cleaned up, son. Saber cut?"

"Yes, sir," the injured one nodded. "It was healin' 'til a day or so back. Yankees near caught me, an' I fell down. Opened it up, an' it's been rilin' some since."

"It'll be all right," the doctor said. He looked around, gazing at the other young man the preacher had noted. A tall, dark-haired individual with an old bandage on one thigh. The sheen of burn scars on his forehead and cheeks softened other, older scars beneath. He wore remnants of a cavalry uniform of unusual cut and color. The young man had sat down on a bench at the table, and now he simply sat there, reacting to nothing. The doctor waved a hand at him, then stepped closer, stooped, and looked into his eyes.

He straightened. "Any of you know this man's name?"

Around the room, other refugees shook their heads. One said, "Cob and me, we found him, three days east. He'd rid a good horse to death, an' was just sittin' there by a patrol road. We brought him along. That ca'tridge gun yonder, that's his. Didn' have no pack."

"That uniform's Texas," another allowed. "Hood's Cavalry. They a long ways from here, though. This'n come a piece."

The doctor stooped again, placing his hand on

23

the silent one's shoulder. "We'll take care of you, son. Give you some vittles, an' a change of clothes. Some of the boys will see if they can't get you all safe to the Territories. It's all we can do."

He watched the eyes closely, wondering what was going on inside that head. The young soldier seemed to see him, all right. It just seemed as though he didn't care. Not about anything. Frowning in thought, the doctor lifted his hand from the man's shoulder, still watching his eyes. He snapped his fingers, almost at the soldier's ear. The eyes blinked, but remained remote.

"Not his ears," the doctor murmured. "You might be right, Preacher. Whatever it is, it's inside his head. Not much anybody can do about things like that." He straightened and turned away. "Concussion, possibly. Maybe a systemic infection, centering there. Lord, who knows? Well, we do what we can." He shrugged. "There'll be supper directly, boys, and we'll see about fresh clothes, so you can get rid of those uniforms. I'll treat those that need it the best I can, and you can all get some sleep. Come morning, we have to get you on your way. Not safe for you here."

The women brought in pots of food, and stacks of clothing. Gathering the stragglers' coats, they compared sizes, emptied pockets, transferred personal items to fresh coats, and carried the old ones out for disposal. After a time the doctor took Preacher's arm and walked him outside. In the still darkness beyond the door, he said, "We had a scare today. Hope nothin' comes of it."

"Soldiers?" Preacher asked.

"Jayhawkers," the doctor said. "Half a dozen, like a raiding party. Mean-looking bunch. They rode through, looked us over, then went on up the hill. I was afraid they'd catch you all, comin' in."

"Didn't see 'em," Preacher said. "How about this batch, Doc? Will they make it?"

"All but two, I'd say. The boy with the festered arm might have trouble with it later, but I'll tend him for now. The two in the cots . . . well, one of 'em won't see morning. The other . . . I don't know. Maybe he'll get where he's going, though it isn't likely. Sorry."

"Not your fault, Doc. It's the war. How about the other'n . . . the one that's out of his head?"

"Hard to tell, Preacher. I don't have any notion what ails him. The brain's a mysterious thing. He feeds himself, though, and he got into those clothes. Somebody said he's come a long way?"

"If he's Hood's, he has. A mighty long way."

"Well, then, maybe he'll make out." He raised his head, looking upward at the cold, indifferent stars. "Lord, I hope they all make it. I wish they would. Just get on home, wherever they came from, and maybe some day forget all about what they've been through."

"It's in God's hands," the preacher said.

It was past midnight, the little valley of Willow Bend resting dark and silent beneath a sliver of moon, when the riders came down from the hill. Muffled hooves raised hardly a sound as they circled the settlement, satisfied themselves that there was no danger there, and dismounted outside the stone building.

"Not much of a place, is it?" one said. "Worth a look, though, 'cause of those wagons. Will, you and Newt make the rounds. Anybody you find, bring 'em here. We'll be inside."

25

Two of them set off on foot, while the other four paused outside the side door to light a hanging lamp. Then, with handguns drawn, they kicked in the door and filed inside, looking around at the startled faces just coming awake in the lamplight. The leader took a long look, and grinned. "Well, lookee here. Just like we figgered, gents. Johnny Rebs. This place is a landin', sure enough."

The one holding the lantern lifted it higher, feral delight glowing in his eyes as he counted. "Six . . . seven of 'em. My, my. We gonna use us some rope this trip, Colby."

Colby waved his gun. "All right, you southern gentlemen. On your feet. Over there in the corner. All of you, where I can see you all at once."

In silence the men got to their feet, obeying the gun. All but two. One had been sitting at a table, asleep on his crossed arms. This one sat up, but did not stand. He simply looked at the intruders, one after another, then seemed to ignore them.

In the cots, one man had not moved at all. One of the gunmen prodded at the blanketed form there, then peered closely. "Here's one we don't get to hang, Colby. He's already dead."

"Might just hang him anyhow," Colby snorted. He waved his gun at the man sitting at the table. "You! What's the matter with you, you deaf? Get up an' get over there with the rest of 'em."

The man didn't move. He seemed not even to hear.

"Maybe he *is* deaf," a gunman suggested. "See them burns on his face? He might have busted eardrums from whatever done that."

The door opened, and people came in . . . several

26

old men and four old women, all herded by a pair of men with guns.

"This the lot, Newt?" Colby asked.

"Every last soul."

"Come right on in, reb-lovers," Colby growled. "Come sunup we'll be doin' some hangin' out yonder. You behave yourselves, we might be satisfied just to let you watch. Maybe. Right now, I want food for my men and me, and we'll see what else you all got that we want."

The captives were herded into a corner. Newt looked across at the lone man sitting at the table. "What about that one, Colby?"

"Him? He's a dummy. Don't know a thing we're sayin', I reckon."

"The man has symptoms of a head injury," one of the captives said. "Leave him alone."

Colby looked at the speaker. "Symptoms . . . of a head injury? What are you, a doctor?"

"I am. These men are in my care."

"Not anymore, they're not. We got a special kind of *care* for these Johnnies."

With their prisoners contained, the intruders spread around the room, lighting other lanterns, searching here and there. Two of them went through into the forward room, then came back. "There's some things in yonder, Colby," one said. "It's a store."

"Go ahead and see what we can use," Colby said. "Newt, we'll keep an eye on these folks while the boys get us a bite to eat." He eased back against the wall beside the door and relaxed there. Four of them went through into the store, carrying lanterns.

Newt was glaring at the man at the table, his eyes

27

slitted, "What do you think you're lookin' at, dummy?" he hissed.

The man made no response. He just sat there, expressionless.

"Let it go, Newt," Colby said. "Dummy or not, he'll swing just like the rest of 'em when there's light."

"He's starin' at me!" Newt rasped. "I don't like it." He crouched, looking into the man's eyes. "You don't like this, do you, dummy? What do you want to do, fight me? Maybe you wish you had a gun? You suppose that's it?"

Colby looked away. Newt was like that. He couldn't let a thing alone. So let him have his fun.

"You wish you had a gun, dummy? Why, I bet you'd try to shoot me if you did, wouldn't you?"

The man made no move. He seemed not to hear.

Newt pulled a second revolver from his belt and tossed it onto the table. "How about that, now, dummy! You see that? There's a gun for you. All you got to do is pick it up an' . . ."

Newt never saw what happened. None of them did, exactly. One second the man was just sitting there, not even looking at the gun next to his hand . . . and the next second the room was full of thunder. Two shots, impossibly fast, roared and echoed from the walls, and Newt was cartwheeling backward, falling. A third shot, and Colby's bull neck exploded just below his jaw. He fell atop Newt.

While the others in the room gaped, the man at the table—the dummy—stood, crouched to pick up Newt's fallen gun, and—still crouched—put two shots through the screen hiding the front room, just as it bulged, someone starting through. The screen was torn loose as the gunman beyond it fell, clinging to the fabric with dead hands. Without a glance at him, the silent one stepped over him, through the doorway. More thunders sounded from beyond.

Then an abrupt and ringing silence.

Ten shots had been fired—ten shots in the space of six heartbeats. Ten shots had rolled like chain-thunder, and six hearts no longer beat. In an acrid, smoky silence reeking of spent black powder, the "dummy" came back through the screen, carrying a pair of smoking guns. He dropped them on the floor, stooped, and picked up Colby's unfired revolver, a sleek .36 Colt. He thrust it into his belt, picked up the coat and hat the women had selected for him, put them on, and went into the front again. In a moment he was back, a tote of supplies on his shoulder.

The doctor was kneeling beside the first two dead Jayhawkers, looking at them. Both had died instantly. The leader's spine had been severed below his jaw. The other, Newt, had two bullets in his heart. The holes in his chest were a finger's width apart. When the strange one appeared at the portal, the doctor looked up. "Son, I've never seen anything like . . ."

"Get out of my way," the other said. He picked up the Spencer carbine beside the broken door, and went outside where there were saddled horses. He chose one, climbed aboard stiffly and wheeled the animal, drummed his heels against its sides and reined for the road.

Behind him, speechless people came from the building, wide-eyed in the moonlight.

Preacher scratched his beard, stifling a cough. "Lord a'mercy," he rasped, "I never seen the like of that."

Behind him, one of the old men said, "They're all dead in there, Doc. All six of them Jayhawkers, dead as doornails."

Doc Samples didn't reply. He strode to the corner of the building and looked where the young man had gone. He had only a glimpse of him where the trail curved southward, then he was gone. But an odd thought lingered, tugging at him, not wanting to go away without an answer.

The doctor had never seen Texas cavalry, but he had seen cavalry. Odd, he thought, that a man who had worn the uniform of Hood's Cavalry should be so . . . awkward, the best word seemed . . . in his handling of a horse. As though he were not really used to riding. And when he had spoken, his speech was odd—clipped and brusque. Doc had heard such accents, but he couldn't remember where or when.

Chapter Three

The gun that Billy Bean gave me when I was ready to earn my keep for him—I was sixteen years old and had made my scores with him in the Tenderloin and on the East Side—was a .36 caliber Beals, modified by one of the immigrant craftsmen he used for such purposes. It had a grooved cylinder pin, so that in a fix it didn't have to be reloaded one chamber at a time. The cylinder could just be dropped from it and a fresh, full-loaded one put in. All in the space of a breath, with practice. The craftsman had added a lug so that the gun could be carried in any position—under a coat, in a boot or wherever—without the cylinder pin working itself loose.

Billy Bean provided the gun, and he provided a teacher. I never knew the man's name. He was just called Dutchman. But if there was anything he didn't know about handguns and how to use them, then I guess nobody else did, either. He taught well, and I learned fast. "Aptitude," he called it. He said I was a natural . . . a born shooter. And the Beals was a shooter's gun.

Guns like that could make the difference when rival factions vied for control of neighborhoods—or

31

sometimes even whole districts. That was the business that Billy Bean was in. He wasn't the top man, of course. There were others he answered to, but we didn't need to know who they were, and one of the things you learn is not to know any more than you're supposed to . . . or if you do, don't let on.

I'd hear a name now and then, and sometimes there were meetings where fancy rigs showed up and Billy told us which ones to let through . . . meaning that those were the only ones that got through. I knew enough to know that Billy's associations went right into City Hall and up to Albany. And more important, there were connections inside Tammany Hall, though those were very private. It wasn't the Tweed bunch that Billy did business with, and I knew that. The Tweeds had coppers to enforce for them. Billy and his associates had us . . . me and others like me.

He was a careful recruiter. He knew the streets and he knew who showed promise, and the way to graduate from Battery Boy to Bean's Boy was to do a favor for Billy Bean. If you were one he had his eye on, you'd get the chance. Someone would let you know what you could do to make a score with Billy.

My first score was simple. All I had to do was stand guard in the shadows beside the livery door of a greengrocer's market, with a hickory club in my hand, and not let anyone past who might interfere with those doing business inside.

I saw the two coming when they were still a block away, and when they passed a street lamp I knew them. A pair of toughs I had seen on the streets, when the Tweeds were out. They paused at the archway, drew knives and started in. Then they saw me, and one of them said, "Move along, boy. You've no business here."

I didn't say anything, but I moved to block the door and let them see the club I had.

The second one grinned. "One of Billy's boys," he said. They rushed me then.

I took a knife cut on my shoulder, and a scratch below my right eye, but they went down and stayed down. When Billy Bean came out, with several bodyguards, one of his men stooped to look at the knifers, then looked up and nodded. Billy Bean looked at me with that way of his—as though he could see right into your head—and said, "These men are dead."

"I know," I told him. "I meant for them to be."

It wasn't long afterward that I got the Beals, and the Dutchman taught me to use it. And after that I worked for Billy Bean.

The .36 Colt I had now, taken from a dead marauder in Missouri, was as near to a Beals as I had seen since leaving New York. It had the same nice balance to it—if anything, it was lighter and quicker. It didn't have the quick-pin cylinder replacement, but I'd never found use for that even when I carried the Beals. The Dutchman had never been impressed with that feature, anyway. "You don't face gangs with these," he'd said. "You face one man, or two or three. If six shots aren't enough, then more would just be wasted."

To the Dutchman, the measure of a gun lay in speed—which a well-balanced handgun gives you if you have the knack for it—and accuracy, which a handgun doesn't give you. But there are ways to get it. I knew how to learn, and he knew how to teach.

"Don't aim," he would say, over and over. "Don't

33

even think about aiming. Don't look along the gun barrel. Don't even look at the gun. You look at just one thing. The target. Your hand knows what your eyes are looking at. Let your hand aim the gun. You just look and shoot . . . fast! Don't hesitate. Don't think about shooting. Just shoot. Your hand knows how. Let it. The faster you are the better you are."

"Look at the target," he'd say. "Not the man, the target! The target is inside the man. You can't see it, but you have to know where it is and look at it. The target is his heart, or the spine in his neck, or the part of his brain that's between his eyebrows and the tops of his ears. The target is always in the middle. The heart is midway between the front and the back of him, midway between his armpits. Sometimes it's a little to the left, but midway is close enough. It's the size of his fist. In the neck, below the jaw, the spine is in the middle. In his skull, the part of the brain you want is as big as a hen's egg, and in the middle. You look there and you shoot."

It was how the Dutchman saw things, and he taught me to see the same way. Not men, just shapes that contained targets. In the middle of the skull, in the middle of the neck, in the middle of the upper chest.

And when a target is seen it must be hit — fast and first. Otherwise the shape that contains it might kill you.

I used to wonder how the Dutchman had learned his art, but I didn't need to know. Sometimes when I thought about it, I didn't even want to know. It didn't matter to me. Only what I could learn from him mattered.

34

My wounds had healed, all except the pain in my head that came and went—a dull, throbbing pain behind my ears that sometimes swept over me like a dark mantle, closing in. There were times that I couldn't remember, like pieces of time that just didn't exist. They came with the pain. The throbbing would begin, then close in around me, and then the sun would be higher than I remembered. Or lower. Or instead of day it would be night. Sometimes I would be where I had been, sometimes I would come out of it somewhere else entirely. It was as though time had stopped, then started again at some other point, and I was there when it started.

As though I had lost a few minutes, or hours, or maybe days. Time gone, except for vague, hard-to-place dreams that I remembered mostly just as colors. Like the colors in a rainbow.

I didn't remember coming to that place where the reb stragglers were being tended. I was just there, and it seemed I had been looking at colors but I didn't know what the colors meant. Or cared. I was tired, so I slept. Then there were toughs, taking the place over. Like when a bunch of tweeds or a squad of harness bulls would sometimes show up in a quiet neighborhood and throw their weight around, just to prove they could.

I'd seen that happen, any number of times. The thing to do was to count them. In the streets, you know what you need to know. Like how many bulls there are, and exactly where each of them is. Once you know that, you can ignore them. Unless they push it too far. Then you do what you need to do.

I counted those men, and knew where they were, and I ignored them . . . as long as I could. Why they were there didn't matter. What they planned for those other people didn't matter. But that one, he just had to push it. He had to make himself a threat. When he did that, then they mattered.

Those six likely thought of themselves as dangerous men. All they were was yokels. They wouldn't have lasted an hour on the Bowery.

I had come away with different clothing, a horse, and a good revolving handgun. The clothing was better than what I left. It wasn't a uniform, or any part of one. Just britches, a shirt, and a worn old coat, like a drayman or a shopkeeper might wear. The horse was a horse. The gun was a Colt revolver that was as comfortable as my old Beals.

The horse lasted me two days, then it stepped in a hole and broke its leg. I'd seen horses go down — dray horses in the city, caisson horses in the army — and I knew what to do about it. The target I saw was a little place inside the animal's skull, just forward of its ears . . . in the middle. The Colt in my hand was as true as I thought it would be. See, point, and shoot. Like the Dutchman said. It only took one shot.

I went on, then. I wasn't sure why, and didn't have any idea where I was going, but I wasn't like the dead horse back there. I was alive.

When you're alive, you move.

I had just sort of followed the sun, for a few days. The country was open and wild, and if there were people around I didn't see them or try to find them. Until my food ran out, I didn't need people. And after it did, there weren't any around to find.

Lonely, some of the soldiers in the outfit I was in had called open country. No buildings, no streets, no crowds, no noise except the racket of birds and livestock, and the sounds of our own feet on dirt roads.

Some of them kept talking about it, like they couldn't get it out of their heads. All those miles of open country, just *being* there. Some of them were always nervous about it, especially at night. I think a lot of them welcomed the enemy when we met them the first time. There they were, out there across that valley, looking back at us and getting ready to kill us if they could.

They were a crowd of people, fixing for a fight. That was something anybody from New York could understand.

We had our fight, and we learned something about ourselves—the downtown companies of the Second New York Infantry. Some of us figured out what we were there for.

To me, until then, being a soldier was just another job for Billy Bean. Up in Albany, the politicians had decided that New York needed to make a showing in the field, to offset all the talk about how South Carolina had started this war, and Massachusetts and Virginia were using it as a fight for power, and New York was sitting back and raking in all the profit from it.

So the Second New York was authorized, and when the Tweeds decided to raise a brigade Billy Bean's friends weren't to be outdone. Street politics is all it ever was, but a lot of us went and put on uniforms. You don't say no to Billy Bean when he wants a favor.

There were a lot of different units in the Second New York. There were fancy-dress companies from uptown, and from Albany and White Plains, volunteer Zouave units sponsored by restaurants and opera houses, even a company from the Bronx with its own flag. Cannoneers and wagoneers, foragers from upper Long Island and the Hudson Heights, and a drum corps financed by Wall Street traders.

The whole outfit didn't come together until we were in the field, so I never saw all of it at one place. But when we met the enemy, we—those of us out in front, boys from Delancey Street and the Battery, from The Corners and the Bowery—we learned why we were there. We were cannon fodder. We were there so that the enemy would be tired before the fancy-dress outfits had to meet him.

And because Billy Bean had collected three hundred dollars a head for us as substitutes for uptown gentry who could pay to avoid the draft.

Just like always. And like always, we fought. Some of us went on from there and fought again, and I was thinking all that time about getting back to New York. I had things to do there. And even if I hadn't, the idea of going anyplace else never crossed my mind. Not until Sergeant Burroughs showed up, and learned about me.

That was a man I wouldn't have minded killing. I probably would have, except that somebody else did it first—our own cannoneers.

And now I was out here—somewhere—and still going.

It seemed like three days since I'd killed the horse, though it may have been four. The country all looked alike—uphill for a while, then downhill, then uphill again. Trees and brush, thickets and clearings and now and then a stream of water in the low places. I knew people lived in country like this, raising their own food . . . or going out and shooting it. I had seen plenty of animals that could make

38

meat. But why anyone would choose to live out here was beyond me. Nothing out here to buy, or sell. Nothing worth stealing, or worth defending. Nothing to lay claim to unless a man just decided to look around and tell himself, all right, everything I can see around here belongs to me.

A man could do that, I supposed. Pick a place. Any place. And just claim it. But what would be the sense of that? What would you do with it once you'd claimed it? Sit on it and wish somebody would come along so you could chase them off? Or that somebody would try to take the territory away from you, so you could fight for it and feel justified in having claimed it? Feel like it mattered, because somebody else wanted it?

I had been thinking about that as I walked. There was nothing anywhere out here but land, and what good was it? Why would a body want it? Still, what else was there here to want? I was tired and hungry, and needed a rest, so I stopped on a hilltop where I could look out and see miles of valleys spreading beyond. Distances . . . everywhere, just more and more damned distances.

What good is this? I wondered. Does it matter? Would it matter if it belonged to me? On impulse I stood and turned full circle shouting at the top of my lungs, "This is mine! All of this! Every damned bit of it belongs to me!"

I did that, just to see if it would mean anything. To see if it would matter. I did it, then felt like a pure fool because nothing happened at all. The land didn't change. Nothing changed. I said it was mine, and there wasn't anybody there to argue about it, and the land didn't care one bit.

"This is all mine!" I shouted, and nothing came

39

back but slow echoes, lazy country echoes drifting down on the wind—echoes that said, "So what?"

It just didn't matter. Just like always. Nothing mattered. Maybe I thought once that I mattered, when Billy Bean gave me a gun and the Dutchman taught me to use it. But I learned. When the big boys decided to play at war, I wound up right out there among the cannonfodder. Just like Sully and them. Just like those Johnnies that were taking our howitzer fire right along with us.

Well, I hadn't lost much back there. I never had much to lose. I just lost track of times and days.

The pain in my head started again there on that hill, and closed in around me, and when I came out of it I was somewhere else. Maybe a day had come and gone, maybe not. The land all looked pretty much the same. But I was hungry—so hungry that my belly hurt and I felt weak in the knees.

Maybe it had been a day, another day missed, passed by as though it had never happened. And all I remembered was an impression of distant colors. Colors like the bands in a rainbow.

I was sitting on a rock ledge, with a rising slope behind me and the deep green of a forested valley falling away ahead—ahead where the sky above climbing blue hills was a blaze of crimson, banners and flags of pink and purple waving lazily against it like pennants above a Tammany parade on Broadway.

The colors pulsed and dazzled and I knew I was weak in the head, seeing such things. Or caring enough about it to keep looking. But as I watched, the colors deepened and the hills darkened beneath them, and I was pleased that I had found a reason for caring how it looked. The sun was down, not just coming up. So it was evening, and I was looking west.

That mattered. It mattered because unless it mattered, there wasn't any reason for me to still be there, looking at it.

That reb in the shell hole, he'd rambled on about taking time to look at rainbows. But he was a fool. I knew I was no fool. Fools don't last long where I came from. It irritated me, though, that I might *act* like a fool—like I had on that hill, shouting at the country. Head injury, the bumpkin doctor back there said. Concussion. Out of his head, someone said. What they said didn't matter . . . as long as I knew they were wrong.

I looked away from the darkening colors of the sky. I dismissed them in my mind the way I'd dismiss a beggar on Canal Street. If you don't want to see a beggar, you just don't see him. It's easy. There's no beggar there. And there were no colors there, and it didn't matter what the sky looked like. There were no colors.

No colors . . . but one lingered. A color that was not a color, but a smell. Like the smell of the Coach and Lantern on Delancey, sometimes on a warm evening when the double doors stood open and there was breeze enough to subdue the other smells of the street.

A smell like food being cooked. Like meat roasting.

My legs felt weak when I started down the hill—weak and trembly, echoing the ache in my belly. How long since I had eaten? I didn't know. I hadn't thought about it. The light in the sky had dimmed to a pale scarlet, just hanging above the dark hills to the west. Not bright anymore, I thought, gazing

41

at it. But when I looked down, I still saw it in my eyes, and could see nothing else. The path was steep—and it was dark.

I had just noticed that when suddenly there was no path at all. I took a step and there wasn't anything to step on. I was falling. I hit something hard, and blacked out again.

Chapter Four

The dogs found the stranger, and set up such a clamor that Wendell and Mason took a lantern and went to see. They brought him back to the camp, carrying him between them.

"Here's who made that racket," Wendell said as they entered the firelight. "Looked like he fell over a ledge up yonder an' rolled against a tree."

They set him down by the fire, with his back propped against a wheel, and Justine knelt to look at him. At first he seemed knocked out, but when she peered into his eyes they held on hers, and followed when she moved. "Just dazed," she decided. "Had the wind knocked out of him. Did you look around?"

"Looked." Mason shrugged. "Wasn't anybody else around, nor any sign of a horse. But he had these guns." He held them up to show, then put them in the wagon. A short-barrel butt gun of some kind, and a shiny revolver.

"Not likely he's a marshal," Wendell said. "Might have been followin' us, though."

Mason shook his head. "If he was followin' us, he picked a sorry way to do it. Look at his boots. They're wore plumb through."

Justine looked at the man's eyes again. They seemed all right. The pupils were the same size, and became smaller when she led his gaze toward the fire. "You took a fall, mister," she said. "You hurt any?"

He didn't respond, though she had the feeling he heard her.

"Can you tell me who you are?" she asked. "Or how come you're way off out here without a horse to ride?"

He made no answer, but she saw his eyes focus on the cookpots hanging over the fire.

"Maybe he can't talk," Wendell said.

"Maybe he don't speak English," Mason suggested. "He might be a foreigner."

"Well, whatever he is, he's hungry." Justine backed away, getting to her feet, her hand on the wagon wheel for balance. "Get me another tin, Mason. And a cup." She looked down at the man. "Do you suppose you can feed yourself, mister? Or do we have to feed you?"

He shook his head slowly, wincing at the movement. "I'll eat," he said.

"So you *can* talk. That's good." Moving carefully, favoring her bad leg, she went to the fire and ladled stew into the tin that Mason handed her. She added bread, broken from a fresh loaf, filled a cup with coffee, and turned to take them to him. He shifted, wincing, to sit more upright. When he raised his eyes there was a hint of curiosity there — a look Justine had seen most of her life . . . when people noticed. He had noticed.

"That's right," she said. "I'm a cripple. Now eat."

44

Satisfied that the stranger was accepted in camp, the dogs had gone off into the darkness, to continue their patrol. Wendell and Mason cast curious glances at the stranger as they tended their supper duties, but they kept their distance. Justine would know what to do about him. Justine usually knew what to do, about anything.

At the edge of the firelight now, she leaned against an elm bole and watched judiciously while the man by the wagon ate. He was ravenous, wolfing down food in the odd, tight-throated manner of one who has not eaten for some time. As though his gullet has forgotten how to swallow, she thought.

When the tin plate was empty she went and took it from him, filling it only halfway this time. "This'll be enough for now," she told him. "If your belly is shrunk, too much at once will just make you sick. Finish this, then we'll have a chat while your innards work on it."

He took the plate, glancing up at her. There was distance in the glance. I'll eat your food, the look said, but I have nothing to talk to you about.

She shrugged and limped away, feeling his silent eyes following her, knowing what he saw — a woman whose forty years and more showed in her face and her hair. A tiny woman, less than five feet tall and skinny-gaunt. A woman whose walk made it clear that one of the legs beneath her long skirt was crippled and distorted. A woman making evening camp in the mountain wilderness with a tandem-hitch wagon and two black-haired young men half her age.

Maybe he was curious. Most would be. Yet

there was something in his manner that said he didn't care one way or another, about much of anything. As though nothing beyond himself mattered enough to him to even wonder about.

Past the wagon's tailgate, Mason snapped his fingers and dug a hand into his coat pocket. "Near forgot, Justine," he said. "Thought you might look at this. It's his."

It was a folded wallet, stained and worn.

"I didn' take it," Mason said. "It fell out of his coat when we picked him up."

She nodded, accepting. By lantern light she looked at the contents, then replaced them.

Back by the fire, the stranger had finished his food. He sat for a time, sipping coffee, then got to his feet. He was taller than either Mason or Wendell, and there was a quick-eyed furtiveness about him — an alert, animal-like quality that seemed as natural to him as the traces of old scars on his face. A dangerous man, her intuition told her.

And a puzzle. Somehow what she saw didn't quite fit with what she had just read. Still, he might be useful. It was worth thinking about.

For a moment he seemed unsteady, but only for a moment. He looked around, and his eyes fell on the two horses grazing in a roped enclosure at the limits of the firelight. He turned, searching, and Justine knew instinctively what he was looking for. She came around the wagon, keeping her back to it. Both of his guns were inside, and she knew that Wendell and Mason would have him covered by their rifles in an instant if it seemed necessary.

"Those are draft animals," she said. "Not saddle mounts. We don't have any riding gear."

He looked at her blankly for a moment, then squatted by the fire and poured himself more coffee.

"You want to tell me about yourself now?" Justine asked.

He looked around, expressionless, but said nothing.

"Well, I'll do the honors, then," she said. "I'm Justine Fremont. *Miss* Justine Fremont, though at my age I don't suppose it makes much difference. Those two are my brothers, Wendell and Mason. Half brothers, really, but family. Now, it's your turn."

He glanced toward her, then away, saying nothing.

"Don't want to talk? Then I'll tell you about you," she said. "You had a horse, but you lost it, quite a ways back. Those are riders' boots on your feet—what's left of them—but you've been walking for quite a while. You're lost, I'd say. Probably haven't the vaguest notion where you are, and you sure don't know the first thing about how to forage for yourself. Food all around you, for the takin', and you nigh starved. Am I right so far?"

Shadowed, wide-set eyes studied him, missing little. She was making progress. He didn't answer, but at least he shrugged.

"Still not saying?" she prodded. "Then I'll try a little harder. How about I tell you that you're on the run, a straggler from a Texas outfit serving the Confederacy, and you're trying to get home before somebody hangs you or shoots you?"

She had his full attention now. His eyes were distant, looking past her more than toward her, but there was a tension there. He was listening.

She pressed on, allowing an expression of guarded sympathy. "I'm sorry about your father dying. Yes, I read the letter in your wallet. The one from your wife . . . I assume that's who Mary is? Your wife? Anyhow, that's how I know who you are, Corporal Austin . . . Corporal David Allen Austin."

She waited for a reaction, and got none except that distant, unyielding silence. Irritated, she tossed the wallet to him. "All right, if you don't want to talk, don't talk. It's up to you. We've fed you, and taken the time to care about you, and if you don't want to say a simple 'thank you,' that's your concern, not mine."

"Why?" he asked.

"Why what?"

"Why did you give me food?" The question was blunt and terse, the expression suspicious. He was looking at her now, and there was a hostility there.

"Because you were hungry," she said.

"What do you expect to get from me?"

"I told you. A simple 'thanks' will do."

He gazed at her for another moment, then dropped his gaze. "Then thanks," he said, almost a whisper.

"That's more like it," she allowed. "You're welcome to share our food. You can sleep by our fire if you want to. There's a trail a mile from here, and come morning we'll be on it, heading south. If you want to ride along in the wagon and give

48

your feet a rest, I expect you'd be welcome. But don't take it into your head again to steal from us, Corporal Austin—like you were thinking of just then—or you might not ever get home to your Mary."

The look in his eyes now was . . . puzzled. The way a hawk might look, she thought, if it were threatened by a pigeon. Again the premonition was there: be careful, this man is dangerous. Still, she sensed no immediate hostility in him. Suspicion, yes, and a kind of sullen aggressiveness—as though he expected at any moment to be . . . what? Attacked? Swindled? Betrayed? Maybe he expected all of that. But she found no real hostility, only an icy reserve that he wore like an impenetrable shell.

And that faint puzzlement. She felt a need to shake him, somehow. To make him know that she was serious. "My brothers," she said, pointing. "They're half Indian, and they wouldn't like it if you did us wrong."

"I don't see why we brought him along with us," Wendell said quietly, frowning at the rolling wagon twenty yards ahead. "That fella's got all the charm of a rattlesnake. Shoot, he acts like he's about half crazy."

Justine had left Mason to drive the wagon, when she got out to walk for a time. Sitting up on the hard bench made her bad leg ache, and she had found that walking a mile or so—even though it was awkward with the makeshift crutch Wendell had made after she lost her good one—eased the

49

pain.

"I don't think he means us harm," she said. "He's just a lost soul needing a little help."

"If he doesn't mean us harm, it's because we don't have anything he wants." Wendell shifted the rifle on his arm. "I don't like him, Justine. He gives me the willies."

"He's unusual, I'll grant you that." Justine sighed, glancing around. Steep wooded slopes rose on both sides. They were far south of the Cherokee nation now, deep into Choctaw lands, and the Kiamichi Mountains shadowed the trail. "He isn't what he seems to be, either, though I don't know what he is. But I intend to find out."

"You keep lookin' back," Wendell said. "You think those marshals are after us? You think they're following?"

"Oh, I don't think they'll come after us," she said, "but we could run into them, or others like them. They'll be riding the trails. And they might be trouble. I'd just as soon not have any more trouble."

"I still don't see how they could just . . . kick us out like that. We didn't do anything wrong."

"It's the war," she said. "That, and that agent, Fry. Getting me proscribed, that was his doing."

"Well, it isn't fair. Just because some of those boys in your school . . ."

"It wasn't my school," she pointed out. "It was an agency school. The agency says what happens there."

"All right, but you'd taught there for nearly fifteen years, Justine. Just because some of those fellows went off with Watie to fight for the South, well, shoot, that wasn't your fault."

"I was born in the South, Wendell. That isn't my fault, either, but it's enough to get me proscribed in the Nations."

Ahead, the stranger sat on the wagon's tailgate, resting against a box of books. He seemed half asleep.

"That's another thing," Wendell said. "Do you really think that jasper is from Texas?"

"That's what his letter says."

"Yeah, but do you believe it? He doesn't seem right . . . to be from Texas, I mean. He acts peculiar. One minute it seems like he's coiled like a rattler, the next it seems like he doesn't care about anything in the world. What kind of person acts that way?"

"I don't know," she admitted. "He doesn't sound like a Texan, either. He hasn't said a dozen words, but he talks like an Easterner."

"Easterner? Like those Agency inspectors two years ago? They were Easterners. He doesn't sound like them. Should have left him where we found him, that's all. Just left him, like a stray dog."

Justine stifled a smile. Wendell talked tough, but he could no more ignore a stray dog—or a stray anything else—than she could.

When a mile or so had passed, Mason reined in and waited for them. "That's mighty windy trail ahead," he said, stepping down from the wagon box. "I'd like to run on ahead and have a look, just in case."

"I'll drive," Justine said. "You go on and have a look. Meet me up ahead someplace." She frowned, looking at the rising slopes ahead.

51

"Wendell, you go, too. Two pairs of eyes will be better than one."

Wendell helped her up to the box, then backed off, looking worried. "I don't know, Justine. You think you'll be all right? I mean"—he indicated the rear of the wagon—"with him?"

"I'll be all right," she said positively. "You go on. Find us a place to noon, and I'll be along directly."

They both hesitated, but the habit of obeying their sister was deeply ingrained. Justine was Big Sister. She had raised them alone since their father's death, sixteen years before. What she said do, they generally did. With worried frowns, they turned away, one to each side of the trail, and in a moment they were gone—vanished like ghosts into the rising forest.

She started the team, and was settling the reins into her hands when a voice behind her asked, "How did they do that?"

Startled, she looked around. The stranger was directly behind her, looking past her, gazing at the wilderness. She looked where he was looking. "How did they do what?"

"They disappeared. Like first-rate filchers, but there's no buildings. How did they do that?"

"Oh, that. Well, those boys grew up in the woods. They know their way around out here. It's their natural surrounding."

For a time, nothing more was said. She looked around finally, and felt a cold chill. He had found his guns. He had them in his hands, checking their loads. But he put them away, then—the Colt in his belt, the short rifle laid aside, though ready to hand.

The trail wound upward, curving this way and that, the slopes towering above. When Justine looked back again, the man was gazing absently at the scenery, his expression a mixture of curiosity and disdain.

"This is pretty country," Justine said. "More mountainous than where we came from, but it's pretty."

He gazed this way and that, judiciously. "What's it good for?"

"Good for? Why, I don't know. Maybe all kinds of things. I just said it's pretty. Don't you think it is?"

"No."

"Well, you're welcome to your opinion. What kind of terrain do you think *is* pretty?"

"What kind of what?"

"Terrain. Country. Land."

"I don't know. I never thought about it."

How very odd, his speech, she thought. And it reminded her of something else she had noticed. The man seemed to avoid looking people in the eye — as though he would rather look past them or through them than look at them. But when she had caught and held his eyes, there had been an abrupt ferocity there . . . instantly confrontational. It was in his look and in his manner. As though he has only two attitudes, she thought. Complete disdain, or raw aggression. As though he must always display one or the other.

"This is all empty," he said, and she tried again to place the brusque, clipped manner of his speech. "There's no people. No buildings."

"Oh, you like towns, then? You like people?"

"No. What does pro-scribe mean?"

She glanced around. How much had he heard? "It's just a word they use," she said. "It means . . . well, it means several things. It means to denounce, to condemn, to prohibit something that somebody does . . . and to banish, to send away."

"Shyster talk," he said, dismissing the words. "Somebody put the cue on you. Why? You rub a boss, maybe . . . or pinch somethin'?"

"What?"

"What did they nail you for?"

"What did they . . .? If you mean, what did I do to deserve proscription, nothing. It's just the war. I'm a teacher. A school teacher. Or at least, I was. At one of the Agency schools for the Cherokees."

"Why?"

"To make a living . . . and maybe to do some good for somebody. But when some of the Cherokee went off to fight for the Confederacy, the Agent had to blame somebody, so I guess he blamed me."

"You send 'em?"

"I had nothing to do with it. But I was born in the South, so they—Fry and the review board—they decided to assume I was a Southern sympathizer."

"I was in the war. I didn't see any Cherokees."

"It's a big war."

"You said your brothers are Indians."

"That's right. Half Cherokee. Their mother was a member of the Cherokee tribe."

"Why them and not you?"

54

What does he want, she thought, my life story? Well, maybe if I give him some answers, he'll give me some. "My mother died when I was just a little girl," she said. "The same disease that crippled my leg, killed her. We were in Texas then, but when she was gone, my father wanted to move away. He was a minister of the gospel. We went up to Saint Louis, and he was offered a missionary ministry in the Nations, with the Cherokee. We moved to Tahlequah. Guwist—the boys' mother—was the mission's secretary. Really a remarkable woman. A great help to my father, and a friend to me. My father fell in love with her, and they were married. That's . . ." she looked around, and stopped. The wagon was empty. The man was gone. But there were horsemen on the trail behind, overtaking her. Three riders, all armed. The instant she saw them, she knew what they were. Territorial marshals.

The one closest, the one in the lead, was looking off to his right and as Justine looked back he pointed and said something to the other two. They reined their mounts off the trail and into the woods to the west. The leader looked after them for a moment, then spurred his horse and drew alongside the wagon.

"Haul up, Lady," he ordered. "You got some questions to answer."

Chapter Five

He was a burly, thick-chested man, and the stamped brass badge on his lapel showed no trace of patina. It was new. By this, and by his general appearance, Justine knew him for what he was. The entry of an Indian brigade into the rebellion — on the side of the rebels — had brought immediate retaliation to the Indian nations, largely in the form of swarms of newly appointed marshals with wartime powers rooted more in the War Department than in the Bureau of Indian Affairs.

Bullies and toughs, mostly, she had heard. But with the power of the law behind them. The decision by some Cherokees to go to war had brought plague upon the Nations, and the man facing Justine now was part of that plague.

"Get down," he said, and watched coldly as she clambered down from the wagon box, awkward because of her bad leg. On the ground, she steadied herself against the iron-tired wheel and reached for her crutch. The man pulled a gun, pointed it at her, and said, "Turn around here and keep your hands where I can see 'em."

She turned, and he lowered his gun.

"What's your name?" he demanded.

"Justine Fremont. I don't know what you want . . ."

"What are you doin' way out here? What's in the wagon?"

"Nothing. Just personal possessions. Why have you stopped me?"

"Saw a feller jump off this wagon and run for the brush," he said, ignoring her question. "Who was that?"

"Just a man who'd lost his horse. I was giving him a ride."

"His name?"

"Ah . . . Austin, I think. David Austin. That's all I know about him."

"Why did he run when he seen us?"

"I haven't the least idea. I didn't even know he had, until I looked around. Look, Marshal, whatever you want is . . ."

"Shut up," he growled, squinting at her from his saddle. "You're a cripple, ain't you?"

"I am crippled, yes. I don't see what . . ."

"Shut up." He thrust his gun away, and swung down from his horse. "I'll have a look in this wagon. You go ahead of me. Move."

Awkwardly, she started toward the rear, hobbling and clinging for support.

"I said, move," the man barked. A large hand pushed her from behind and she fell, sprawling. Biting her lip, she got to her feet again, and stood beside the open gate of the wagon. The man stepped past her and peered inside. He pointed at a crate near the tail and asked, "What's in there?"

"Books," she said. "Readers. I'm a teacher."

"Books?" With a scowl, he leaned into the wagon, got a hand behind the crate and heaved at it. It slid outward, fell and broke open. He kicked it, scattering the books. "Books," he said. "What else you got?"

"Nothing, I told you. That other crate, that's slates and chalk. All the rest is just personal belongings."

Abruptly, he turned and slapped her with the back of his hand, across the face. "I don't like to be lied to," he growled. "And I don't like to waste my time. If you're a teacher, what are you doin' way off out here? I want to know who you are, where you thought you were goin', and who that jasper with you is. And I want to know . . ."

He didn't finish it. The man—the stranger—came from brush behind him, charging like a bull. He hit the marshal from behind, slamming him into the wagon gate, doubling him over. A hard hand came down on his head, crushing his face against the wood bed, while another delivered short, quick blows to his kidneys. The marshal gasped and howled.

With the marshal's hat—and the hair beneath it—crumpled in his fist, the man lifted him upright, swung him around and kicked him in the crotch, then braced himself and swung a hard uppercut into his belly. The marshal sagged, and his assailant turned him again, bent him over and rammed his head against the iron tire of the rear wheel. The marshal slumped to the ground and the man backed off a step and delivered a kick to the ribs that lifted the inert body and rolled it half under the wagon.

Methodically, the man stooped, grabbed the marshal's booted feet and dragged him clear, then stomped a worn boot heel downward into his face.

Justine found herself tugging at the man's coat, trying to pull him away. "Stop it!" she shouted. "Stop! You're killing him!"

He hesitated, then turned, seeming puzzled.

"Leave him alone!" she panted. "My God, look what you've done to him!"

He looked at the motionless, bloody form on the ground, and shrugged. "Yeah." With total indifference, he slid a toe under the unconscious marshal, rolled him over, stooped and took his gun from its holster. He tossed it into the wagon, ripped off the brass badge and looked at it for a moment before throwing it into the brush. "Harness bull," he said.

Justine watched in disbelief as the man she knew as David Austin knelt calmly by the fallen marshal, looked at his boots, and pulled them from his feet. He sat, then, pulled off his own worn boots, cast them aside and put on the marshal's. When he was done, he stood and stamped around, getting the boots settled.

Justine found her voice again. "How could you do that? How could you . . . beat him like that? I've never seen anything so brutal. You've half killed him!"

"Sometimes half's enough," he said. "Just so they don't come back on you." He squatted, picked up one of the readers and gazed at it, ruffling its pages. "What's this?"

"What do you mean, what's that? It's a book."

"What kind of a book?"

59

"McGuffey's Reader," she said, feeling dazed. "It's for learning to read."

He stood, tossing it aside. His glance at her might have been concern, that she wasn't hurt, or it might have been only a glance. He went to the marshal's ground-reined horse, which backed away from him. He leaped, grabbed the dragging reins, and the horse reared, pawing air above him. He staggered back and drew his gun.

"No!" Justine shrieked. Hopping and hobbling, she rushed past him, pushing his gun aside. "Whoa," she said to the panicked horse. "Here, now. Whoa down. There, that's a good boy. Easy . . . easy . . . there, now. That's better." She crooned and caressed the horse, calming it, while her fingers controlled its headstall. When it was gentled, she turned toward the man, her eyes blazing. "What's the matter with you? You were going to shoot this animal!"

"It tried to fight," he said.

"It was just afraid. Don't you know anything about horses?"

"Then you tend to it," he said, turning away. "I'll get the others." With a glance at the bloodied man on the ground, he stepped over him and walked off into the brush. She heard sounds from nearby, and a moment later he was in sight again, returning, leading two saddled horses.

When he had them all together, beside the wagon, he said, "I want the best one. Which is it?"

She stared at him. "You really *don't* know about horses."

"What's to know? Which one is best?"

60

Shaking her head in disbelief, she hobbled around them, looking them over. Finally she indicated the one the lead marshal had ridden. "The one you tried to shoot, I'd say."

"All right." Taking the leads on the other two, he led them around to the rear and tried to tie their reins there. With white-rimmed eyes, they stared at the bleeding man almost under their feet and skittered back. He tugged cruelly at the reins, forcing them to stand. Then he tied them.

He crawled into the wagon and emerged with the carbine and a bulging sack, which he slung across the saddle of the marshal's horse. He took its reins from Justine and climbed aboard, awkwardly. Justine had started picking up books, putting them into the wagon, but now she stopped.

"What do you have?" She pointed at the sack. "What are you doing?"

"Food," he said, tersely. Hauling at the reins as though to bit-strangle the animal, he backed it away and turned it, spreading his heels to get it started up the trail. As though by afterthought, though, he hesitated and turned. "Get up there and drive," he said.

"But what about the . . . the marshal? I can't just leave him like that."

"Yes, you can," he rasped. "Drive the wagon."

Again he backed the horse, and Justine blazed at him, "Don't saw the reins that way! Don't you know how to ride?"

For a mile or more she drove, the reined saddle horses coming along behind, the stranger following. Where mountain slopes veered away, the trail dipped into a narrow little valley. To the west, clouds hugged the forested tops, and there was distant rain. Halfway across the valley she forded a rock-bottom stream, then glanced back and saw that the man had turned off, westward. She reined in, leaned around the wagon bow and shouted, "Where are you going?"

If he heard her, he didn't show it. He kept going, and within minutes he was out of sight, going away.

When he was gone, Justine lifted her reins and drove on, confused and still trembling, her mind full of the beating she had witnessed—the sheer, methodical brutality of it. The man she had called David Austin—from a name on a letter he seemed not to even know he had—the stranger had mauled and maimed another man as swiftly and efficiently . . . and with the same absolute indifference . . . as a butcher might quarter a beef.

She was shaken by it. What kind of man was that, who could do something so . . . words failed her. She had never seen or even imagined anything like it.

She thought about going back, but instinct told her that what was done was done, and the best thing she could do was to get far away from it and not look back. She thought about turning the two saddle horses loose, then realized that if she did—and those marshals recovered them—they would come after her. Somewhere ahead, Wendell and Mason would be waiting. They would rest there, but not for long. She decided the thing to do was to travel far and fast.

Corporal David Allen Austin—or whoever the man was she had called by that name—had taken most of the supplies, and in return had left her with a predicament. Two stolen horses, and somewhere some rough men who were certainly angry enough—if they were still alive—to do her serious harm if they could.

The sun was hidden behind high clouds stacking up in the west, when Justine rounded a bend in the trail and found Wendell and Mason waiting for her. Both of them had stripped off their shirts and hung them in their belts, and as they stood waving, each holding his rifle, she thought about what she had told the man. Her half brothers looked as much a part of this land as did the pine trees, the spreading redbuds and the dogwood sprays on the hillsides. Their faces and shoulders sun-darkened below thick manes of raven hair, they looked Indian.

At eighteen, Wendell was the older of the two, and bore a resemblance to his mother. High cheekbones, deep-set eyes, and a wide, humorous mouth beneath a proud nose—sometimes she could see Guwist in his smiles and in his somber, reflective moments.

Mason was sixteen and, though he also had the look of Cherokee, sometimes he surprised her with abrupt resemblances to her father. Just at odd moments, at certain angles, it was as though the Reverend Thomas Fremont had reincarnated—with black hair instead of silvery-brown, and without the whiskers he had worn—but nonetheless himself.

The Reverend Fremont had been a fortunate man, to have won the love of two good women. He had been unfortunate in losing each of them after a few brief years—Eleanor to the paralyzing fever and Guwist to the pox. But from Guwist he had two fine sons—and from Eleanor, someone to care for them after he, too, was gone. That someone was Justine.

To the boys, Justine was Big Sister.

An hour had passed by the time she had answered their questions—about the stranger, and about the two saddled horses behind the wagon. When she told them about the marshal, and what the stranger had done, Wendell's eyes went dark and angry.

"Knew we should have left him where we found him," he said. "That jasper is trouble, for sure. I'm glad he's gone."

Mason, though, was stifling a chuckle by the time she finished talking. "I wish I'd seen that." He grinned. "Lord, that must'a been a sight."

Neither of them seemed disturbed at the acquisition of the horses, though. And when Justine—looking westward, where storms stood—decided that they should go a few more miles before making night camp, each of the boys chose a horse and swung aboard.

Full dusk was on the hills when they stopped for the night, on a shelf above a running stream that came down from western distances. Full dusk, and the sweet smell of rain carried on the breeze. Wendell went off to secure the stock where the graze was best—hobbles and a picket line would keep them until morning—and Mason was building a fire when he stopped abruptly, listened, then picked up his rifle.

"Somebody coming," he said.

Moments later, a dark figure on a head-down horse came into view, riding along the stream's edge. By the wagon he reined in and stepped down. "I got lost," he said.

Justine stared at him, shaking her head in disbelief. Then she pushed past him and retrieved the sack of supplies from his saddle. As far as she could tell, everything he had taken was there. "You got lost." She sighed. "Well, where were you to go?"

"Texas, I guess," he said.

"I don't see why," she told him. "I don't know who you are, but I know you aren't the man that letter went to. You're not David Allen Austin, and you've never been in the cavalry, and you certainly aren't from Texas. So why did you decide to go there?"

He looked at her, his eyes shadowed in the gloom, then turned his head away. "Maybe to see the rainbow," he said, almost a whisper.

Justine studied his face, puzzled. She had thought of it as a hard face—a cruel, predatory face. But now, just for an instant as he turned away, she sensed something more. There were scars beyond the visible scars on this man. There were deep, hidden scars, as though the hard shell in which he hid was made of scar tissue. "I don't understand," she said.

"Neither do I." His voice was distant again now, contained and remote, as though he regretted having spoken at all.

"But you want to go to Texas?"

"Might as well. Nowhere else I need to go. But I don't know where Texas is."

65

Wendell and Mason stood nearby, listening. Now Mason shrugged. "We could take him along, Sis. That *is* where we're headed."

"I say not," Wendell objected. "I say send him away. He's nothing but trouble for us."

Justine ignored them. To the man she said, "That letter you were carrying . . . you hadn't even read it, had you?"

"No."

"Why not?"

He hesitated, still looking away. "Didn't seem to matter. It's not my letter. It's some reb's."

"Yes. David Allen Austin's. Did you kill him?"

"He died, but I didn't kill him. He spent all night dying. So did I, maybe, but he got it done. I didn't."

"And you had his letter, but you didn't read it."

He said nothing.

"Do you have a name of your own?"

"Does it matter?"

"I suppose not, but I think I know why you didn't read the letter. You can't read, can you?"

He turned toward her, his face no more than a shadow but radiating challenge as surely as if she had seen his eyes. "I can read." he said. Then, more softly, "I read a little. Street signs, things like that. And numbers. I can read numbers. But I don't know how to read script."

She glanced around at her brothers, trying to make a decision. "I could help you with that, I suppose," she said.

"Why?"

"Because that's what I do. I teach."

"Nobody does anything without a reason," he

66

challenged. "What do you want from me?"

"I honestly don't know. Maybe nothing more than to help you, because you are so damned helpless."

"Helpless?" He sounded stunned. "Me . . . helpless? Lady, nobody messes with me. I take care of myself."

It was her turn to not respond. She simply stood there, letting him sense the irony of his own words. Maybe where he was from, he could take care of himself. But not here. And he knew it.

"You? Help me?" he demanded. "What good are you to me? Yokels!" He hissed it at her. "Two yokel kids and a crippled old woman!"

She sensed Wendell and Mason bristling in the gloom, and stilled them with a raised hand. "Oh, you're wrong about that, Mister No Name," she told him. "I'm not the cripple here. But maybe *you* are."

Chapter Six

I don't know what I expected to find, out there in those hills where rain clouds hid the higher slopes. Nothing, probably. But it was the direction I had been going, and at first I saw no reason to change.

And there was something about the view ahead that held the eye. Maybe it was the way the clouds lay out there, with the sun swallowed up behind them, and everything else about to be. It was a dimness. Like smoke over tar roofs, on a day when the air is heavy and smells of stale grease. Smoke and sea mist make a kind of false darkness, that veils everything except just what is close. Back when I was young and dumb, sometimes I would hide on those roofs and pretend that the blind faces of buildings around—dimming in the smokes—were nothing but parts of a wall that didn't have anything on the other side of it. Just nothing at all.

It was nice, that wall. Comfortable. It kept everything in, and kept all the nothing out. It kept the world close and tight, and small enough to be understood. I could see the world that way, and I could make it do what I wanted because I was above it and I could see it all. I could hurt it more than it could hurt me.

In a world like that one, I could be boss. I could say who got what and who went where, who was protected and who was not, and even how the payoffs would be split. In that world, if it had been more than just smoke dreams, I'd say how it would be. If anybody didn't like it that was their problem. If they wanted trouble I could send a squad to change their minds. Or maybe I'd go myself.

In that world, I could get even.

My best roof in those days was the O'Connell Mercantile roof, overlooking Bowery Street. It was the tallest building in that part of town, six stories of stone and brick. From that roof, on a dim day, the people on the street below were little, scurrying things going this way and that. Little quarreling creatures that didn't mean anything at all—that were just there. Like lifting a sewer cover to watch the rats below scurry from the light.

Down on the streets, I was just one of those rats. But on the roof, I was the one with the lid.

Stupid kinds of thoughts. Kid thoughts. Notions about things that never would be. In the city, that kind of thinking gets you nowhere. I learned that soon enough. In the city you think about what's real—who has what and how to get it, when to fight and when to run, the best places to hide when you need to, who has the muscle and who has the smarts and how to sense when they make a mistake that you can use.

The darkness to the west made me think of that, and I followed it. I kept thinking, there can't be this much nothing. There has to be something out here.

I could imagine that there was a city over there somewhere, just past those hills. A city . . . a place where I could burrow in, where I could listen around and find out who was who, where I could get anything I needed, one way or another.

It was stupid, thinking that way. Like I was a kid all over again. There wasn't anything out there except more of the same. Just endless, up-and-down country. Empty, useless spaces too big to mean anything.

In the city, you know where you are. Every sound you make has echoes, and they come back to you, fast. The way echoes should. Walls and fences are like mirrors of sound. You can hear your shoes on the pavement. Out there, what echoes there were took a long time coming back.

I didn't like so much emptiness . . . so much nothing. It reminded me that even though I was traveling, I really wasn't going anywhere. I was just moving, aimlessly. That had seemed right when I turned my back on that war. It was somebody else's war, not mine, and I didn't even have the money that some uptown draftee had paid to have me take his place.

Just go, and keep going, was all I had thought about then. Like I was sick somehow and that was all the thinking I could do. Maybe my head *had* been scrambled, like that hick doctor said.

I wasn't scrambled anymore, though, and it seemed I should be going someplace. It made no sense, just moving, unless I was bound for someplace.

70

Texas, the woman said. She had read the hand-written letter, and thought it was mine. She thought I was David Allen Austin, from Texas, so she assumed that was where I was going. And I seemed to keep thinking about Texas, as though it was a place that mattered to me.

I had heard of Texas. Sailors off ships at the Hudson River docks talked about it. They said Galveston was like New Orleans, but easier to get to. Traders at the bidding blocks on Wall Street— back before the rebellion started—used to say there was opportunity in Texas, and speculators and boat captains hawked land schemes on the streets.

I knew about the wallet, and the letter inside. They came with the coat I took off that dying reb in the shell hole. The letter was handwritten script, all the shapes run together and different from the shapes that make words on signs. It didn't mean anything. But the crippled woman with the wagon thought it was mine, and told me I had a wife in Texas, named Mary. That was what the reb had babbled about. Mary. Going home to Mary. Mary and the baby. Home to Texas. And I remembered a place. Lone Oak. Did I remember that, or just imagine it? Did I imagine Hunt County, Texas?

Colors and rainbows and Texas.

I wondered what it would be like, to have a wife waiting for me somewhere . . . even to have a somewhere, that I could go back to. The reb in the crater had a somewhere, before he died. He wouldn't be going home, but he had seemed so certain—there in his last minutes—that he would.

There was a notion that kept coming back, the way sometimes a dream will come back. The no-

71

tion was that maybe I might go to Texas, if I knew where it was. I knew I wasn't going back to New York any time soon. There'd be too many of them waiting for me there . . . too many people who knew too much. But maybe I might go to Texas.

There would be towns there, and where there is a town there is a way to get by.

Maybe at least I'd find a post office or a tele-graph wire. Billy Bean owed me money, and I intended to collect. He might not like paying, but he would pay. I saw who set that tenement fire. I'd seen some other things, too.

It got darker, and there were gusts of wind with rain in them. I had followed the line of a valley until it ran out, then I just sort of wandered, keeping to the low places, below the murk of clouds. I came to a creek and followed it, but after a while it seemed like I was going the wrong way. It was only a feeling. Without the sun to see, out here, there was nothing to show direction, and there surely weren't any streets. Still, it didn't seem right. But I had a stream to follow, which was better than nothing, so I kept moving.

It was just starting to get dark when I heard voices ahead, and saw the spark of a fire being made. It was them. The same crippled woman and the two dark-haired country kids.

I had gone in a circle.

It turned out, though, that they knew where Texas was, and were going that way. And the woman—after she blew off about me not being able to read handwriting—said I should come along with them.

As though she had a choice. I go where I want, when I want. But she said it, so the matter never came up. Still, there was plenty she wanted to talk about. In some ways she reminded me of the Irish tenement women along Delancey Street and around the markets. Always talking. You couldn't help hearing them, but you didn't have to listen. And I tried not to. What she said didn't matter.

I realized that she reminded me of somebody else, too. When I was just a kid — a Battery Boy — there was a night when I got careless and caught a knife in the gut. There was a woman in a carriage, an uptown woman who had no business being in that neighborhood at that hour, but she found me and took me to a place where there was a doctor to patch me up.

The woman's name was Mrs. Jessup. She was pinch-faced, graying, and had the saddest eyes I had ever seen. I never knew why she bothered to help me. Most people wouldn't have. But in an odd way, Justine Fremont reminded me of her. That wasn't why I jumped that yokel marshal who was roughing her up. I jumped him because I had already jumped his buddies, and it wouldn't be smart to leave him able to come after me if he found out about it.

But, then, maybe Justine's resemblance to Mrs. Jessup might have had something to do with it, too. Things like that are complicated.

I waited around until they had supper ready, then helped myself, only half aware of Justine rattling on at me. Talk. Just talk . . . about how she wanted to be a teacher again, and was hoping some relatives down in Texas could help her start

73

over, about how it was good to see children learn, about how learning wasn't just for children but for anybody who needed it, about how there were all kinds of ways to look at life, and education opened up new doors for people.

The talk was irritating, and I paid no attention for a while. But she just kept prodding at me with her words, then started to sound angry. She said, "You could at least have the decency to look at me when I speak to you."

I did look at her then, because she had put her finger on something I'd noticed about country people. Something I didn't like at all. They have a way of looking straight at someone, eye-to-eye, as though they don't know any better.

"Why?" I asked.

"Why, what?"

"Why should I look at you? Lady, you talk about teaching folks, but there's things I could teach you about getting along, and that's one of them. Don't go looking at people, unless you're ready for trouble, because that's a sure way of finding it."

"Looking at people?" She seemed amazed . . . or amused.

"That's right," I said. "Where I come from, you keep your eyes to yourself. People don't like to be looked at, not unless they're spruced for Easter or saying lines on a stage. A man doesn't look at a man on the street unless he's ready for a fight."

"I'm not a man," she pointed out, still sounding amused.

"No, you're not," I told her. "You're a frail old woman, and that's the kind who gets found dead in some back alley with their purses emptied. From looking at people, and getting noticed. You do that, you wouldn't last a minute where I'm from."

"And just where is that?"

"Delancey Street, mostly."

"Delancey Street . . . that's in New York City, isn't it?"

Stupid questions like that don't deserve answers, so I didn't bother. Instead, I glanced across the fire at her brothers, and they lowered their eyes. They understood what I'd been talking about, even if they didn't know why. To look in the eyes of a person is to get involved with that person. And on Delancey Street, getting involved is something you don't do unless you're sure you can do something to him that he can't do to you.

Indians, she had said. The two kids were half Indian. I could see they were half something. They had black hair and black eyes, sturdy builds and dark, square faces—like some of those Chinamen down around the East River docks. Not like all of them, but like some of those that the sailors called Tartars—strong, brown men who would work all day and half the night for pennies. There had been real trouble at the docks one time, when Big Jack Foley tried to bring in a gang of them to use as longshoremen.

The two brothers kept their peace for a minute or so, then the older one—Wendell—looked up and stared right at me. He understood what I'd said, all right. He was trying it out. His stare was pure challenge.

"What are you looking at?" I asked.

75

"You," he said. "What's your name? Your real name, I mean."

It wasn't any of his business, but he was a hick and probably didn't know that. "Bodie," I said. "Hands Bodie."

"Hands?" he was still staring, with that yokel directness. "What kind of a name is 'Hands'?"

"It's what people call me. At army muster I was listed as Callahan Bodie. Hands is good enough. Why do you want to know?"

"I don't like you," he said. "I like to know the name of people I don't like."

"That's enough, Wendell," the woman said.

"I just want to be sure he knows that." Wendell shrugged, still staring at me. His look said, here I am, tough guy. What are you going to do about me?

Maybe out in the sticks, a thing like that can be ignored. But not where I'm from. In the city there are only two ways to take a challenge. Meet it head on, or turn and run. On the streets, you don't negotiate. I don't know what the kid expected, but a face full of hot coals wasn't part of it. I scooped up a handful of fire, threw it at him, then stepped across the flames and knocked him down. When he started to get up, I kicked him. Behind me, the woman was yelling.

"Had enough?" I asked Wendell, then heard the click of a sidelock being cocked. The other kid, Mason, stood an arm's reach away, raising his long gun to his shoulder.

"If a gun comes to point on you, you've lost your edge," the Dutchman said. So don't give any gun the chance to line up on you. I could have killed the kid right then. My hand was on my revolver and he didn't have a chance and didn't even know it . . . but he wasn't a Tweed or a bull. Just a dumb country kid defending his brother. I sidestepped, got hold of his gun and pivoted, taking it away from him. Then I thumped him with it, just enough to put him down, and stood over Wendell again. "Answer me," I said. "Have you had enough?"

"Enough," he said.

Their sister was all over me, whacking at me with tight little fists, trying to push me away. "Let them alone!" she was yelling. "You're hurting them! Get away from them!" She was about as dangerous to me as a bedbug, but every bit as annoying. I pinned her arms at her sides, picked her up—she wouldn't have weighed a hundred pounds carrying a field pack—and sat her down on the wagon gate. She tried to bluster and I said, "Oh, shut up. I didn't hurt them."

"You hit them. You . . . you brute! You savage! Why did you . . .?"

"I said, shut up." I turned her loose and stepped away. Across the fire, the brothers were picking themselves up, glaring at me. I glared back until they dropped their eyes.

"I'm going to Texas with you," I told them. "Maybe by the time we get there, you boys will be smarter than you are now." I glanced at Big Sister. "That goes for you, too, *teacher*. There's things it wouldn't hurt you to learn."

"Why did you jump me like that?" Wendell growled, his black eyes glinting in the firelight.

"You know why. You think about it. That's

77

your first lesson. You challenge a man, you better expect him to jump you. And the next one might not go easy."

"I didn't say a word . . ."

"You didn't have to. You challenged, and you knew it. Now you know what it means."

"Why did you hit Mason? He didn't . . . challenge you."

"Mason's lucky. If he'd lined up that gun on me, he'd be dead." I looked at the younger of the brothers. "You keep that in mind, kid. If a man's carrying a handgun and you want to point a rifle at him, you'd better be behind him or out of his range. Otherwise he'll kill you."

"You can't be that fast with a . . ." He stopped and his eyes went wide, staring into the bore of the Colt. It was a dumb thing to do, drawing like that, letting them see what the Dutchman had taught me. A few others had seen that trick, but they were dead. Still, I knew these two didn't actually see it. They just saw an empty hand sprout a gun, and it made the point.

I put the Colt away and squatted by the fire to finish my supper. "How far is it to Texas?"

For a while nobody answered, but Justine finally said, "Just a few more days to the river. Texas is on the other side."

"What's this here?"

"What?"

"All this here, where we are. What's it called?"

"This is the Nations. I told you that."

"That's what you call it? The Nations?"

"It's part of the Indian Nations. This is Choctaw tribal land. We're in the Kiamichi Mountains."

"Any towns around here?"

"Not that I know of. Not until we get into Texas. Why?"

"I need to find a town and mail a letter."

"To family?"

That struck me funny, in a way. There were plenty of things I might call Billy Bean, but "family" wasn't one of them. "I don't have any family," I told her. "Haven't had since I was six years old. Where is Hunt County?"

"Hunt County, Texas? I don't know, exactly. We're heading for Pleasant Hill, and I suppose Hunt County would be somewhere west of there. We'll find out. Can you read a map?"

"No."

"Lord," she said. "No wonder you got lost. You don't know much of anything, do you?"

"I know how to get by."

The look on her face was one of contempt, and it spoke as clear as words. Maybe in New York City you know how to get by, she was thinking. Out here, all you know is how to beat up people, steal horses, and how to get lost.

Chapter Seven

The old linen map that Justine had, the same one that had guided her father nearly two decades earlier, indicated a low-water ford on the Red River southwest of Kiamichi Pass. But there was no low water there now, and no crossing. Heavy rains upstream had turned the Red into a surly, swirling brute. A quarter-mile-wide swath of roiling, mud-red waters blocked the old trail's end. Flood debris lined its sand-clay banks, and the skeletons of cottonwood trees rolled lazily in their voyage downriver.

"We'll have to go west, I guess," she said. "Upstream. There should be other crossings." She studied her map. "There's a town or something west of here, I think. On this side. The map says, 'Chase Landing.' Maybe there's a ferry or something there."

"Maybe someplace we could get supplies?" Wendell was rummaging in the back of the wagon. "We're low on things. Flour, jelly . . . that Bodie eats like two people, and he sure hasn't added anything to the pot."

"I don't know what's there. This is such an old map. It just has a name. But we can't cross here, so

I suppose we'll find out." She hobbled around the wagon, leaning on her crutch, getting the aches out of her legs. They had stopped on the high bank above the river, on the inward curve of a long bend. From where they were, miles of sullen river were visible in either direction. She glanced at the position of the sun, shading her eyes against the glare. They could rest the animals here for an hour or so, she decided, and still have enough daylight left to make several miles before evening.

It would have to be upstream, if the map was at all reliable. Downstream, to the east, the old linen warned of "marshes and bogs," and below that something called "falls."

"We'll let the stock graze here for a bit," she decided. "Where is Mr. Bodie? I haven't seen him all day."

"With any luck, he got lost again," Wendell grunted.

"That's enough of that," she snapped. "Where is he?"

"I don't know." Her oldest little brother backed out of the wagon, frowning. "I haven't seen him, either. He's probably back there someplace trying to kill his horse."

Mason had been down by the river, looking at it, but now he returned, in time to hear. "I haven't seen him, either," he said. "But he's getting better, you know. With horses, I mean. I've been teaching him things."

"Have you?" Justine nodded. "That's nice, Mason."

"Nice for the horses," Wendell said flatly. "As far as Bodie's concerned, I wouldn't waste my time tryin' to help him. He's not worth it."

81

Justine shook her head. "A little charity wouldn't hurt your disposition any, Wendell."

"Charity? Ha! Tell that jasper about charity, not me."

Mason chuckled. "He probably doesn't know what the word means."

"Probably not." Wendell grinned. "I bet he thinks 'charity' is robbing a church."

"That's enough," Justine said. "Just tend to the horses, and try to be friendly with Mr. Bodie. Nobody is all bad, you know."

"I'd rather try to get friendly with a badger," Wendell muttered. "It'd be a lot safer."

Mason was shading his eyes, peering upstream. "I wish we had a better map," he said. "Or somebody to tell us the way to Texas."

"That's Texas right over there." Wendell pointed across the river. "It's just that we don't know how to get there from here."

"We'll find a crossing," Justine assured them. "Go on, now, put the horses out to graze. I want to make a few more miles today. We'll be leaving in an hour."

"What if Mr. Bodie doesn't show up by then?"

"We'll go without him," Wendell said, unhitching the draft animals. "With any luck, he'll never figure out which way we went."

"I doubt if he'd know," Mason said, seriously. "I don't think he can read trail at all. I tried to show him some deer tracks yesterday. Plain as the nose on your face, but he couldn't see the sign. He tried, but he just couldn't make them out. Then he got all crusty when I said he ought to learn sign. He said *I* didn't know anything about sign. He said he could trace a runner from Five Points to the Bronx and

82

tell you what garret he'd holed up in, just from heel marks in pigeon droppings."

"I don't know what that means," Wendell said. "What's a 'runner'?"

"I don't know. Or what a garret is, either. He still couldn't see the deer tracks, though. How about I scout back a ways, see if I can find him?"

"If he's lost, let him stay . . ."

"I think you should," Justine said. "But don't go far, Mason. We'll be moving soon."

"I'll just look around a little. If you go on, I'll catch up." Carrying his old rifle, he headed into the woods on foot. Moments later, a birdcall sounded.

Wendell cocked his head, listening, then put two fingers in his mouth and repeated the call. His answer was another birdcall, this one different. It was the call of a bob white hen leading its chicks.

"That's Mason," Wendell said. "Somebody's coming, but it's not Bodie. Somebody else. Several of them."

For a moment, Justine felt dread. Then she realized how unlikely it was that the patrol marshals would come this far. Nonetheless, this was wild country and caution was a good idea. She hitched herself up onto the wagon's tailgate, found one of the handguns that Hands Bodie had left there, and held it on her lap. Wendell was nowhere in sight, but she knew he was nearby. So was Mason.

Long minutes passed before she heard the sounds of riders approaching, coming down the Kiamichi trail. Minutes more passed before they were in sight — five rough-clad men on well-tended horses. At sight of the wagon they stopped, then came on, their eyes taking in the grazing stock, the wagon . . . and Justine. Almost as one, they removed their

83

hats. They approached slowly, stopped several yards away, and the nearest one said, "Howdy, ma'am."

"Good afternoon," she said.

The man seemed at a loss for words. He was the oldest of the five, by the gray at his temples and the sharp-etched lines around his eyes, and he seemed embarrassed. Finally he said, "Ah, are you all right, ma'am?"

"Quite all right, thank you. We stopped for a rest."

"Yes, ma'am." He looked around, seeing no one else but not questioning that there were others here. It wasn't likely that a tiny, middle-aged woman would be here alone. Especially not with two grazing draft horses and two saddle mounts in plain view. He shrugged and gazed at the Red River. "Thought we might cross over," he said, lamely. "Maybe not here, though, by the looks of it. Ah . . . you wasn't meanin' to cross that wagon, I suppose?"

"Not here," she said. "I am hoping for a better crossing upstream."

"Yes, ma'am. Ah . . . sorry, ma'am. Joslyn's my name. Pete Joslyn. That's Rudy there, and Wilson, and Jim and Hank. We're . . . ah, we're just passin' through."

"I see," she said. "My name is Justine Fremont. The rest of my party are about, somewhere."

"Yes, ma'am. Lookin' us over, I expect. Was I them, I would. Can't be too careful, is my motto." He glanced around, then back. "We'll move along if you want us to, ma'am. Strangers make folks edgy sometimes. Other hand, though, we're about ready to sit a spell and boil up some coffee, and we'd be proud to share with you an' yours." He grinned.

"You can keep that shootin' iron in your hand if you want, and no exception taken."

"That's gracious of you, sir." Justine felt her ears go pink as she realized she had been pointing the revolver directly at him. She turned it away, then set it aside, found her crutch, and climbed down. Intuition told her there was no danger here. These were decent enough young men. Rough and ready types, probably, but they meant no harm. "Wendell!" she called. "Come get a fire going, so we can have coffee!"

The men were dismounting when Wendell stepped into the open. All of them froze for a moment, and the red-haired one—Rudy, he was called—said, "I god, Pete, that's a Injun."

Justine waved him close. "Gentlemen, this is my brother, Wendell Fremont."

They stared at him, then Rudy smiled sheepishly. "How do, there, Wendell. For a minute there, I took ye for a Injun."

"You were half right," Wendell said, suspiciously. "What brings you gents to these parts?"

Pete glanced at the puzzled-looking Rudy and whispered, "Mind your manners!" Then, to Wendell, "Just passin' through, goin' home to Texas."

"From the war, I guess?"

Pete shrugged. "The less said about that war, the better. It's nigh over, anyway, back east. Let's just say we found ourselves out of work an' figgered we'd get on back home to Texas. Y'all?"

"We've been living in the Cherokee nation," Justine said. "But now we're going to Texas . . . if we can get across the river. There are people at Pleasant Hill who were friends of my father."

"Ought to be crossin's upstream," Pete said.

" 'Course, most times this is as good as any, right here. It just gets bad when the river's up, is all. Cherokee nation, huh? Y'all have any problem with the special marshals? They're thick as thieves up that way. We stayed shy of 'em, ourselves. Worse'n Jayhawkers."

"No problem." Justine turned away, stifling a shiver. "Wendell, let's lay a fire over there by the bank."

She wasn't surprised that Mason had not come in. He would have stayed close by until he saw that there was no threat from the newcomers, then he would have gone on, looking for Hands Bodie. It was Mason's way. Once he set out to do something, he would concentrate on that until it was done.

She worried about her brothers, sometimes. Wendell always seemed to be carrying the weight of the world on his young shoulders, always hoping for the best and expecting the worst. In his moodiness he was like their father. Mason, on the other hand, was what the Cherokee called a "wind dancer." A free spirit, always curious, always searching for who knew what, always expecting the best . . . and vulnerable because of it.

Before their father's death, she had promised him that she would look out for the boys.

It was the kind of promise no one could keep, beyond childhood. They had their full growth now. They were what they were, and they went where they would go, and she had learned that there was no holding them back. If Mason set his mind to go looking for Hands Bodie, then that was what Mason would do. To plead otherwise would have been a mistake.

When the fire was burning and the pot was on to

86

boil, Justine got out her old linen map and spread it on the tailgate. Pete Joslyn looked at it and shook his head. "Ma'am, that chartin' must go back ten-fifteen years. Things look a sight different now, yonder in Texas."

"I'm not surprised," she said. "It's more than twenty years old. It was my father's when we left Texas. I wasn't much more than a little girl. We never went back to Texas. Not 'til now." She studied the linen, tracing marks with her finger. "What is this place, up the river on this side?"

He puzzled over it. "Chase Landing? Can't say I ever heard of that." He turned. "Boys, come take a look at this." When the others gathered around, Joslyn pointed. "It's an old map. Here's the river, and here we are, about here. Anybody know what's upstream yonder, where it says Chase Landing?"

"Never heard of it, myself." Rudy shrugged. "Wilson, you come from down yonder. What is that place?"

Wilson rubbed his grizzled chin. "Used to be a place about there, long time ago. My daddy'd haul goods yonder sometimes. I believe it was a franchise store somebody put up, for tradin' with the Injuns. But if that's it, I don't know what's there now. Last I heard, maybe that was where that Walsh bunch holed in, after they got run out of Grayson County. That was several years back."

No one else seemed to know about the place, so Justine rolled up her map. "Well, I guess we'll just head that way and see. I thought maybe it was a crossing."

"Might be," Joslyn said. "We can ride along, if you'd like company. We're goin' the same way."

Wendell was hovering nearby, cradling his old rifle. "It's a free country," he said. "But I don't know that we need any more company. We've picked up too much, already, seems to me."

"Wendell!" Justine hissed.

Joslyn's eyes narrowed. "No offense intended," he said. "It's just that sometimes more is better, when folks are travelin' though."

Wendell shrugged, though his dark eyes said he wasn't backing off. "It's up to Big Sister."

"Y'all had a problem with somebody, I guess?" Joslyn asked.

Justine shook her head. "Not really. We found a man a few days back, lost and hungry. He has been traveling with us, but Wendell doesn't think much of him."

"Where is he now?"

"Back there, someplace. He comes and goes. He might be lost again. Our brother, Mason, has gone to look for him."

Rudy cocked his head. "Wouldn't have been a big, spooky jasper on a dark sorrel, would he? Dark hair and kind of strange talkin'?"

"That sounds like him. Did you see him?"

The men exchanged glances. "Maybe so," Pete Joslyn said. "Few miles back. Funny-actin' jasper, like Rudy says. Talks like he's got nails in his mouth, and acts like he's spoilin' for trouble. A real odd one. Don't meet a man's eyes, though I had the feelin' he was watchin' every move we made."

"That's him," Wendell grunted.

"He wanted to know where he could find a telegraph wire."

Justine blinked. "A . . . telegraph wire?"

"Sure. We didn't know where one of those is, so we pointed him over to Yellow Hill. It's a Choctaw

88

Agency place. They might not have a telegraph, but there's bound to be a post office."

"Oh, mercy," Justine breathed. "Yellow Hill? Where is that?"

"Just yonder a ways," Joslyn said. "West an' a little north."

"And Mason's out looking for him," she said.

"Mason can take care of himself," Wendell assured her. "Don't worry about him, he'll catch up."

Backtracking, it took Mason less than an hour to find Hands Bodie's tracks, where they came down from a shoulder and onto the trail. The prints told him that Bodie had met other riders there, then had turned west. The others would be the men now setting coffee-camp with Big Sister and Wendell.

But where had Bodie gone? The trace was clear, almost due westward down a ravine, and he started to follow it, then on impulse turned up the shoulder of mountain, backtracking. He was curious where Bodie had been before rejoining the trail.

The sun lay low on pine-clad slopes by the time he had his answer. Bodie had been searching the area west of where they had passed, combing it, it seemed, sometimes going in circles. It was as odd a pattern of tracks as Mason had ever seen. Then he found another sign, and it struck him. He grinned, understanding what the city man had been doing. There were deer in the area—their tracks were plentiful—and Hands Bodie had been trying to track one . . . or maybe several.

"My land," Mason muttered. "First he sneers at what I try to teach him, then he takes off and tries to learn it by himself."

89

His curiosity satisfied, Mason set off cross-country, strong young legs carrying him at a tireless, mile-eating trot. When he came again to the ravine where Bodie had turned west, he knelt for a moment, sharp eyes identifying the sorrel's tracks in evening light. The man was headed due west.

At a pace that would have tired a horse in these hills, Mason followed. Evening was deepening over the ridges when he came out of the hills and saw a pretty valley ahead, a valley where a narrow dirt road wound down toward a little town.

A couple of barns, some sheds, and several snug bread-loaf houses in the Choctaw style, with a low, wood building in the center and planted fields on all sides—not much of a town, but Mason decided to have a look. It was where Hands Bodie had gone.

He passed a few people on the way in, brown-skinned people who looked him over curiously, wondering what a Cherokee was doing this far south. At a rail in front of the central structure, Callahan Bodie's stolen horse stood head-down, and Mason stopped to look it over. He lifted one foot after another, clicked his tongue, and fondled its ears while he inspected its mouth. It was tired, but in better shape than he would have expected, considering the way it had been handled.

"That Bodie," he muttered. "When's he gonna learn about horses?"

A Choctaw man in a plaid coat and straw hat passed, then stopped and turned. "Kinda far from your nation, aren't you, youngster?"

"Yes, sir." Mason nodded. "We're traveling through."

"That fella in the store . . . he one of yours?"

"He fell in with us a few days ago. Back a ways. Then he wandered off, so I came to find him." He felt the man's curious gaze on him and added, "He's kind of peculiar."

"Peculiar? How?"

"He gets lost."

The man turned slightly, and only then did Mason notice the brass star on his lapel. Nation police, he guessed. "Well, I'm glad that's all it is," the policeman said. "From the looks of him, I was afraid he might be a wilder. Don't get many of them through here. Don't want any."

"Where is he?"

"Inside."

Mason went in, pausing while his eyes adjusted. From evening gloom, he stepped into shadows and lamplight. There were a few people inside—two white men and some Choctaws—all just quietly standing around, but all obviously keeping an eye on the man who sat alone at a table in the corner. He had an oil lamp, several sheets of paper, and a pen and inkwell.

When Mason entered, Bodie glanced up at him, his eyes saying nothing.

"Hi, Mr. Bodie," Mason ventured. "I was worried about you."

The cold glance came again, this time quizzical. "Why?"

Mason shrugged.

"Can you write?" Bodie demanded.

"Sure, I can write."

"Come over here."

Mason came.

"I need to write a letter," Bodie said. "How much to write it for me?"

91

"How much what?"

Bodie stared at him in disbelief. "Money," he said. "How much money to write a damned letter for me?"

"Is that what he's been tryin' to do?" a man muttered. "Shoot, I'd have . . ."

"Shut up!" Bodie snapped. The room went silent.

Mason sat down and picked up the pen. "I don't want your money, Mr. Bodie. Just tell me what to write."

Bodie glared at those around the room, waiting for them to back away. Then he lowered his voice. "It's a letter to Billy Bean," he said. "William T. Bean. Say . . ."

"Where?"

"What?"

"What's his address? It ought to be on here."

"Oh." Bodie scratched his jaw. "Say, Last Hope Tenement, on Mulberry Street, New York City."

Mason wrote it, then looked up. "What do you want to say?"

Bodie glanced around again, assuring privacy. "Say: Billy Bean, you owe me three hundred dollars for soldier service and fifty-eight dollars for unpaid earnings. I want my money. Sign it, Hands."

Mason wrote dutifully, then looked up again. "Will he know where to send your money?"

"No, I guess he won't," Bodie admitted. "Say he should send it to me in Texas."

"Texas is a big place, Mr. Bodie. You ought to tell him where."

"I don't know where . . ." the man began, then paused in thought. "Tell him to send it in care of David Allen Austin, at. . . ah. . ." he searched

92

his memories, then nodded. "At Lone Oak. That's in Texas."

Mason wrote.

Bodie stared at the paper, tapping the table with big fingers, frowning. "Why should he send me money?" he muttered.

"Well, if he owes it to you . . ."

"Shut up. Write: Do not fail me in this, Billy. I saw who burned the Gates of Hell."

Mason's eyes narrowed. "You saw what?"

"Write it."

"Yes, sir."

When the letter was done, Bodie folded and sealed it, and took it to the countered corner where a printed sign said, UNITED STATES POST OFFICE, CHOCTAW AGENCY. He paid the postage, watched the postmaster—who was also storekeeper, post agent, and Federal registrar—put his letter into a box, then glared at the man threateningly. "How long will it take?"

"What?"

"My letter. How long before it gets to Billy Bean?"

The postmaster shrugged. "Clear to New York City? Damned if I know. Might be a week before we get a packet out to Salina. Might be a month or so. Maybe more than that. Couple of weeks, once it gets to the railroad."

Bodie glared at him. "That's not very fast."

"There's still a war on, some places," the man reminded him.

Bodie gritted his teeth, turned, and stalked from the room, Mason Fremont tagging after him. Outside it was dark, the only light the glow from windows and the silver wash of a high moon.

Bodie loosed the reins of his tired horse and put an awkward foot in the left-side stirrup. Mason had taught him that, at least — to mount on the left — and was still amazed that anyone wouldn't have known.

"Where you going?" Mason asked.

Bodie paused. "Back. Back to your wagon."

"You'll never find it." The youngster shook his head. "Come on, follow me. But don't ride. Walk and lead that horse. It's about done in."

Chapter Eight

I couldn't figure why that kid had followed me. Afraid I was lost, he said. So what? No skin off his nose — unless there was something in it for him, something to be gained by keeping me in tow. But I couldn't see what it would be.

It crossed my mind that he knew I had some money coming, and maybe figured he could get it off me. The problem was, he had already followed and found me before he knew that. He didn't know about that, until he wrote the letter for me.

And why did he write the letter? What did he want? Nothing, he said — like he saw I needed help, so he helped, just out of kindness or something.

Horse manure. I knew about *acts of kindness*. Where I grew up you learned early to be real cautious about accepting acts of charity. Favors done were favors owed, and people kept lists and there would always be someone coming along to collect.

When Billy Bean picked me out for special training — to be one of his good friends, he said, showing his teeth in a big smile — he didn't charge me anything for the favor. He got me a place to hole up, and some warm clothes, and gave me a modified Beals revolver and the Dutchman to teach me how to use it. And he didn't charge me a penny.

Not then. The payments came later . . . and kept on coming.

I worked for Billy Bean. I did errands for him — dark errands in dark places, where a lot of people got hurt. At first I was a collector, collecting on favors he had done for others when those others balked at the tab. Billy had a whole gang of collectors, of several kinds. There were a dozen or so that I thought of as bone-breakers — huge, thick-armed men with hands like ham hocks and nothing between their ears except skull. Billy used the bone-breakers very much the way the Tweeds, who owned City Hall by then, used harness bulls.

Plain, head-on, brute enforcement.

Then he had a few shadowy assassins for special jobs, and a front team of lawyers and paper-doctors, and nobody knew how many human ferrets like Sully, men who were never seen, but through whose eyes Billy Bean saw everything that went on downtown.

And there were Billy's "Good Friends." We were his bodyguard sometimes, and his errand boys at other times. He liked us because every one of us was very good at something.

Very good.

Billy had a big, narrow house on the Bowery, which was his headquarters, and we worked out of there and only he knew what each of us was supposed to do, and where. We all had a whole set of private orders from Billy himself. One of my private orders was to report straight to him if anyone in his employ started talking to anyone else about his assignments.

None of us talked much to any of the others. Doing that was a good way to join the sausage coming out of Billy's slaughterhouse on Pearl Street. The whispers were that not all of the hides soaking at Billy's tannery were animal hides.

There were rules, but it was prime work for a graduated Battery Boy. We lived all right, we slept warm, we ate well, and we had money in our pockets . . . and if we wanted to go into Five Points sometimes and raid the tenements there for some sport, people there knew better than to try to fight back. Billy took care of his own.

At least, until something better came along.

I knew now what kind of opportunity Billy had seen when the call came for a New York contingent to fight the secessionists. At three hundred dollars a head, he'd probably collected several thousand dollars in draftee fees. And even better, he could recruit a whole new gang of enforcers whose faces weren't known. And get rid of those of us who had been around a while. All favors called in, all debts paid. We went off to be cannon fodder, and I doubt if he expected any of us to come back.

I wasn't especially angry with Billy about that. I wanted my money, and intended to get it, but I couldn't fault him his methods. That's how things are done in the city. If you didn't know that, and play it that way, then you were just one of the herd, and the only thing the herd was good for was to pay taxes, pay tithes, pay protection, pay rent, pay to be left alone, pay special assessments, and eventually pay to die.

That's what the city is all about, in a way. A city is a contained herd, and the herd is the feeding ground for those who know how to use it.

Feel sorry for the herds? Sometimes, before I

learned better, I thought about that. After that up-town woman—Mrs. Jessup—took me in that time, I'd had some thoughts about the "plight of the common man" and the "power of kindness" and the "sorrow of the human condition." Mrs. Jessup talked that way, and I had thought about it.

But not for very long.

There was a street corner just at the west side of Five Points, where I passed sometimes walking from the Battery to the Bowery. It was a route where a lot of people walked because in summer it was up-wind from the tanneries and the bone mills, and from the school sink off Astin, where people dumped their waste—chamber pots, sludge from the vats, anything that would go down a pipe and a lot that wouldn't. On that corner, most days, there would be an old, bald-headed blind man begging for pennies. It was how he lived, I guess, on those pennies and the few others that his old, white-haired wife made scrubbing floors at the Two Lions.

She would leave him there at daylight, then come for him in the afternoon, when her work was finished. They probably lived in one of the tenements. Brickbat Mansion, or the Bones or the Gates of Hell, or one of the others. I never thought much about it, just that it was odd to see such old people in that part of town. Most people around Five Points didn't get very old. Those two were there, though. They were sort of fixtures, like the garbage that littered the streets or the stinking sewage that seeped from the stone bulwarks beyond the school sink, to run down the alleys.

But the old woman must have had a weak heart. I was walking by when she collapsed, and I stopped to watch. There must have been a thousand people along there, all hurrying by, and the old woman was just taking the blind man's arm to lead him away when she grabbed her chest, turned gray and stumbled, then fell. She sprawled on the paving stones, and didn't move again. There wasn't any question that she was dead. Just like that, she was gone.

But what I noticed was all those other people.

There they were, two old people down in the street, the old woman dead and the old man on his knees beside her, moaning and blubbering, running his hand over her face while tears dripped from his blind eyes. What did the people do? All those others? They looked away like they hadn't seen anything at all, and just hurried on by.

It was no surprise. It's what people do. They turn away and don't see. They all have their own concerns, and it's best not to look beyond your own concerns.

But I remembered Mrs. Jessup, and how she fretted about what happened to people. Maybe living uptown, like she did, it was easier to care. Living up there, she could worry from a distance. I was closer to it, though, and I knew the rules. Feel sorry for the herds? Not in that city. The bosses and the bulls and the gangs, they had the right idea. Herds are herds and nothing more.

The old woman died and the blind man wept and nobody did anything. Not me, even though I watched, because there wasn't anything to do. And not anybody else, because they didn't watch. They didn't look, so they didn't see, so there was nothing there.

I guess the meat wagon came along and took the old woman. The meat wagons were always busy in those neighborhoods. Dead horses, dead dogs, and dead people . . . they all have to be taken away. I wondered sometimes who paid for the meat wagons. Probably City Hall, I thought, although Three-Finger Sloan thought the rendering yards and the bone mills financed them.

I had a session with the Dutchman that day, and I said something to him about the old woman falling down dead. But it didn't mean anything to him.

He just looked at me with those cold, gunsight eyes — seeing the center of my chest, the center of my neck, and the center of my head — and said, "You got a problem?"

"What problem?" I stared back at him, daring him to make something of it, letting him know that even though he was the teacher, I was bigger than him.

"You think such things matter, kid, then you got a problem," he said. "You think too much, it slows you down. It gets you dead. Don't think about what don't matter."

"Like what?"

"People," he said. "Like people. They don't matter. Nothing matters, and nobody matters, unless . . ." All of a sudden there was a gun in his hand, pointed at me, and the hammer was falling. It clicked on an empty chamber. "Middle of the head," he said. Then he put the gun away and stared off into some distance past the stained brick wall. "Now you understand what matters? I mattered to you just then."

"Your gun mattered, Dutchman. Not you."

"Oh?" He raised one eyebrow. "Tough nut kid, right?"

"Tough enough," I told him. I didn't like that

cold-eyed bastard anyway, and pointing that gun at me had made me angry. I had a notion to show him a thing or two about that.

But he turned away, went to a side door, and said, "Club."

The bone-breaker who appeared there filled the doorway except right at the top. He was a foot shorter than me, but he'd have outweighed me by twice.

"Kid needs to learn," Dutchman said. "Teach him."

The tough came at me like a storm-wave crashing against the ramparts below Battery Street. He wasn't fast, but he didn't need to be. It was a small room, and he filled it. I ducked, dodged, danced around, and got in several good licks that would have put an ordinary man on the ground. It was like hitting a side of beef. It didn't even make him blink.

Then he scored. A forearm the size of a lamp post caught me across the side of the head, and I must have bounced off three walls before I sprawled on the floor. I rolled away from a kick that would have collapsed my ribs, got to my knees and grabbed him around the legs, trying to bring him down. I couldn't budge him. It was like trying to throw a tree.

I saw the final blow coming. His big fist drew back and there was nowhere to duck. But it never came.

"Club," the Dutchman said. "That's enough."

The bone-breaker shoved me aside like a stick-doll, turned, and left the room. I was shaking when I got my feet under me.

"Does *he* matter to you?" the Dutchman asked.

"I'll kill that son of a bitch," I swore.

"Oh?" The eyebrow went up again. "Then why didn't you? You could have, you know." He turned away, seeming to forget all about it. "Let's go to work, kid. You still got a lot to learn."

"You still got a lot to learn," the Indian kid said as we started up a rocky draw in the moonlight. "How come you keep fighting that horse, Mr. Bodie? Just lead him. He'll come along."

I shook my head, trying to clear that troubling, hazy ache that had crept back in, and looked around. I had no idea where we were, but the kid seemed to know. He was leading, setting a course cross-country that he seemed sure of. I tugged at the leads again, and the kid said, "That isn't doing any good. Do you want me to lead the horse?"

"I don't need your help," I told him. "Stupid animal doesn't know anything."

"He knows how to be a horse," he said. "What you really ought to learn—no offense intended—is how to get along with horses. It might come in handy, sometime."

The kid was right, and I knew it. The kid . . . I knew his name. Mason. Maybe I should think of him by name, I thought. He hasn't done anything to me. He's even been helpful. Why? What's the matter with these people out here?

I think that was the first time it dawned on me that maybe it wasn't them that were wrong. But I didn't want to think about it then.

Call the kid by name. Why not? "Mason," I said.

He looked around. "What?"

"What's in it for you if I learn things, like you say?"

He didn't answer for a while, like he was thinking

about it. Then he stopped and turned toward me. "I don't know." He shrugged. "But you don't like something for nothing, do you?"

"There isn't any such thing."

"Yeah, I figured you felt like that. All right, then, maybe if I do you a good turn, maybe some day you'll do me one. Is that better?"

"Not much," I told him. "I want it clear what you expect, if I let you help me."

"I swear I never saw anybody like you," he said. "All right. What I want is for you to stay with us until we get where Big Sister wants to go. And if we run into trouble, you're on our side. Is that good enough?"

I nodded. That made sense. He wanted a bodyguard. "All right. Start teaching."

He came and took the horse's lead, and set out again. The horse seemed content to follow, and I saw why. He wasn't trying to bully it . . . just lead it. It chose its own places to step, but they were in the right direction.

He glanced back. "You see?"

I nodded, following along.

"Cast your bread upon the waters," Mason said, not talking to me, just to himself.

But I answered him anyway. "Yeah, I've heard that kind of talk. It's preacher words. 'Cast your bread upon the waters.' Right. So some mullet eats it, and you do without."

"Jeez," he said, not turning around.

He did seem to know where he was going, though. All I had to do was just follow along.

That day when I saw the old woman die, and when the Dutchman set the bone breaker on me . . . I realized later that it was that day when I

103

really started learning. And everything I learned from the Dutchman, I learned well. But that evening I was still pretty shaken and angry, so I went up on the McConnell's Mercantile roof to cool off.

It was a good choice. There were a couple of street thugs up there when I got there, tough kids from one of the gangs that roamed the neighborhood. They didn't know me, and they didn't intend to share the roof. But then, neither did I. It gave me a chance to let off some steam. I don't know whether the one who went over the edge died in the fall. It didn't matter. Pretty soon I had the roof to myself, and I felt better.

The breeze was cool, coming off the Hudson, and it carried away the stink and the noise of the street below. I stayed up there until maybe midnight, and now and then the wind cleared away the smoke haze so there were stars in the sky. Uptown, you could see stars most nights. But down here it was rare. I was looking at stars when I heard a scuffing sound and realized there was someone else up there.

I was getting myself set for another fight when moonlight drifted across and I saw the person there. A girl. It was hard to see, but I had the impression of a willowy, slender shape dressed in a shift and a shawl. Shadowed, wide-set eyes in a face mostly hidden by tattered fabric. She had come up the hatchway, and was standing beside it, staring at the sky.

Dim lamplight came from the open ladder hatch, and the moonlight came and went as scud drifted across the sky. It was confusing. In an odd way, I wasn't sure whether there was really someone there or not. I could see her, but vaguely—as though my eyes were playing tricks.

There was another moment of moonlight, and she turned her head, looking directly at me. I don't know whether I saw her face, or whether all I saw was shadow patterns and imagination, but it was a face I knew I wouldn't forget. Even as I saw it, she cringed back, startled, and a roar like thunder came from behind me. I turned. Across the street below, and a block or so away, the front of a street-level shop erupted outward, a gout of fire and debris. There were shadows of people running, and shouts drifted upward.

I wondered who had been bombed, and why, but it was none of my business. Things like that happen. It's how it is in the city.

"Blasting powder," I said, over my shoulder. "It's all right, it isn't near . . ."

But there was nobody there. The ladder hatch stood open, dark now, and I was alone on the roof.

I was tempted to go after her, but the fireworks down the street caught my eye. It must have been a grog shop that exploded, because it was burning brightly now, and it was how distilled spirits burn—wisps and waves of floating fire billowing from the blasted shop front . . . flames that were red, and blue, and yellow and pink and purple. Flames that flowed and drifted in the night air. There was no telling what was in that grog shop, but it burned pretty. It lighted up the street.

I walked through wilderness now, following an Indian kid named Mason and a led horse, and I didn't know where I was or where I was going. But

105

I thought about those city flames. I knew something now that I hadn't realized then.

Those flames were every color of the rainbow.

Chapter Nine

Wilson rode in an hour after dark. He had been out ahead, scouting, when they stopped for night camp. The other four had come in when Wendell made the evening fire, but Wilson had stayed out, getting a look at the trail ahead.

He didn't look happy when he came in. "Place a few miles up," he said. "Saw the lights from a ridge. There's folks there."

The rest just waited. He would say what he had to say.

"Might be a comfort if we could find us a crossin' down this way," he said, pouring hot coffee into a tin cup.

"Think the Walsh bunch is still around these parts?" Pete Joslyn asked.

" 'Less I hear different." Wilson shrugged. "That's a hard bunch, Pete. They filled a sight of graves in Grayson County few years back. Best not to tangle with 'em if we can help it."

Justine and Wendell listened, exchanging glances. "I'd as soon avoid trouble, Mr. Joslyn. If we can."

"So would we, Miss Justine. If we can. At least 'til we get into Texas. Then we can choose the kind of trouble we want."

It was a strange response, but Justine kept her peace. It was none of her business. She had heard them talking among themselves of "the upsets yonder, with the war windin' down like it is," and comments like, "lot of sides to be chose up. Best bet's to get in early so a man knows who he's sidin' with."

They were talking about Texas, she knew. Troops were still in the field there, in the remote places, but more would be going on than battles. War and politics, she recalled her father saying. War and politics stir the pot, and the conflicts just go on and on. Where wars and politics trod, the order of daily life was disrupted. Where tradition and structure had been, was vacuum. Where law had assured peace, chaos could ensue.

"The worst of war comes after the war," Pastor Fremont had said. "The devil loves a battlefield, after the battle's done, for that's when folks have to claim again what was theirs before, and for each thing to be claimed there'll be a hundred that say it's theirs."

What would people fight over? Anything. Money, love, prestige, land, water . . . anything that might be desired certainly could be fought about. And would be, if these men riding with them were right. They seemed decent enough men, she thought— even charming, in a rough way. But were they hurrying back to Texas to protect what was theirs, or to take what might be up for grabs?

Only they knew for sure, but instinctively she supposed that they would be open to opportunity until a clear purpose presented itself. They were, after all, unemployed.

But then, wasn't everyone?

"What's so funny, Big Sister?" Wendell asked.

108

"Just private thoughts," she said.

An overhead moon cast a serene glow over the brushy landscape and shimmered on the murmuring width of the Red River. But to the west the sky was black and starless, with distant flares of lightning.

Pete Joslyn leaned against the wagon's near side, a rolled cheroot dangling from the corner of his mouth, his posture that of a man content and at rest. An easygoing man, Justine thought, glancing at him. At ease with himself and at peace with the world. It was an impression she had formed early, reinforced by Joslyn's quick grin, his casual, soft-spoken manner, and the lines on his face. Laugh-lines, she thought of them. The sort of little wrinkles that come naturally to a man who sees the humor of things.

Only two things about him seemed out-of-keeping with the impression of a gentle, laconic, good-natured individual—his eyes and the way he wore his side gun. The gun was low-slung, as ready to hand as though it were a natural part of him. And his eyes were those of a hunter. Lazy-seeming eyes, wide-set and hooded, they belied the lazy lines around them. They were quick eyes, that seemed to miss nothing.

He reminded her of a big cat, totally at ease but nonetheless formidable.

The others with him were all younger men. Wilson—if he had another name, she hadn't heard it—might have been in his thirties. Rudy, Jim, and Hank were of an age, it seemed. None of them were much older than Wendell.

As the lightning rippled in the west, Joslyn puffed on his cheroot and observed, "Might be a long wait for the river to go down. It's the season."

Wendell added wood to the fire and looked westward. "We can't wait here, anyway. We're short of supplies. Need to find a town with a store."

"Well, we're not far from a town," Wilson repeated. "But it's not a place I like very much."

"That would be Chase Landing, I suppose," Justine said.

Joslyn shrugged. "It's about where your map says." He looked around, his hand dropping instinctively to hang near the butt of his revolver. "Y'all hear something?"

Wilson had frozen in a half crouch near the fire, and Justine noticed that all of them — including Wendell — were gazing northward. She hadn't heard anything. "It might be Mason," she suggested.

Joslyn squinted, looking for movement. "Your other brother?"

Wendell shook his head. "You'd never hear Mason coming, unless he wanted us to . . ." he paused. "Or unless he's found that jasper again. That'n is about as quiet-movin' as a bull coon in a briar thicket."

As though in response, a birdcall sounded from the darkness. The trill of a night-bird seeking its nest.

Wendell sighed and lowered his gun. "That's Mason," he said. Cupping a hand at his mouth, he made the carrying sound of a loon. In the darkness, there was silence for a moment, then the sounds of scuffing pebbles and breaking twigs. "He's got that jasper in tow."

Wilson eased into his crouch and reached for the coffee. An amused grin tugged at Pete Joslyn's cheeks. "You don't sound real taken with your straggler, youngster."

"I guess you'll find out for yourself," Wendell grunted.

110

At the edge of firelight, Mason appeared, walking, carrying his old rifle and leading a tired horse. Behind, another, taller figure appeared, coat thrown back to expose the butt of a handgun at his belt, hard eyes measuring the men one after another.

By the fire, Rudy came to his feet, staring. As the man approached, he squinted, then stepped forward. "Mr. Austin? My lord, is that David Austin yonder? I swear, I . . ." then his voice trailed off in confusion.

"You know him, Rudy?" Joslyn asked.

"Ah . . . well, I thought he was somebody from back home. But maybe not. You ain't Mr. David Austin, are you, mister?"

The newcomer pinned him with cold eyes, not responding. His gaze shifted again to the others. To Justine, it seemed he was measuring them . . . or marking them, somehow, as one would mark a target for a shoot. He fairly bristled with challenge, with unspoken threat. Like a new dog come stiff-legged to a pack, she thought. Then she remembered the marshal, and the sudden violence of this man.

With a gasp, Justine pushed herself upright and hobbled forward, getting between him and the rest. "These gentlemen are our friends," she said. "I'll introduce . . ."

"You," he growled, his eyes on Pete Joslyn. "Get your hand away from that gun or I'll kill you."

"He means it," Wendell hissed. "Be careful."

"Stop it!" Justine demanded, trying to hold Bodie's eyes. "Just stop this, right now."

Behind her, Pete Joslyn's drawl had steel in it. "Don't know what's itchin' you, stranger, but only a fool talks killin' unless he's ready to try it."

The tension between the two men was like a physical force, and Justine held her breath. Then she saw the city man relax—just a little—and knew that Pete Joslyn, behind her, was doing the same.

"Hoo-ee," someone breathed.

Justine took a deep breath, clasping her arms to keep from shaking. "What in God's name was that all about?" she demanded, staring first at Bodie, then at Joslyn.

The Texan shrugged. "Ask him."

Bodie was staring at Joslyn. He seemed . . . the only word Justine could think of was, puzzled. "You," he said, "You'd have tried me, wouldn't you?" The idea seemed to amaze him.

"Tried? I'd have killed you, come to that."

Justine hugged herself, wide-eyed, feeling the lightning-like tension surge again. But it was only for an instant, then it faded.

Bodie turned his gaze to Rudy. "Where do you think you know me from?"

"I . . . I guess I thought you was somebody else," Rudy stammered. "Somebody from back home. Hunt County. But you're not . . ."

"David Austin?" Bodie's question was hardly more than a whisper. "David Allen Austin, from Hunt County?"

Justine's eyes widened as she saw his features in the firelight, and recalled the name on the letter he carried. She stared, feeling a shiver go up her back. His face . . . she had never seen such a strange expression. As though he were seeing things, or hearing things, that only he could see or hear.

"That's who I thought you were," Rudy said. "But now I don't. Who are you, anyway?"

"His name is Bodie," Justine said. "Callahan . . ."

"My name is David Allen Austin," Bodie over-rode her.

"You're not David Austin," Rudy declared. "I know better now."

Bodie glanced at him, then gazed at Justine. "Odd thing," he said quietly. "I don't believe I ever did know who I was. Not for sure. And it never mattered."

"You're not David Allen Austin!" Rudy insisted. "You looked a little like him, just for a minute there, but you ain't him. You can't be him."

Bodie glanced at him again. "I don't see why not," he said, slowly, as though he were trying to imitate the Texas drawl of the others. "Nobody else is."

The muted lightning flared again, in the western distance. Bodie gazed at them, noticing for the first time that the flares seemed to come in groups, lighting the distant storm's front in staccato dances that gyrated here and there among the high-banked clouds. And there were colors there—reds and yellows, silvers and greens, brilliant against the black of stormy sky.

Colors that were almost like a bright, dancing rainbow.

"I never seen such a spooky jasper in my whole life," Rudy declared, riding alongside Pete Joslyn. Morning sun came roseate through the willows and dogwoods, and danced on the muddy waters of the Red River fifty yards away. "I was afraid for a minute there . . . last night . . . that you'd have to gun him down where he stood. Bracin' you like that! I never seen the like."

"He's a strange one, right enough," Joslyn muttered. He glanced back, where Justine's wagon was just rounding a curve in the river trail. The Indian-looking kids — her half brothers — rode aflank of the wagon, and the man who called himself David Austin was following along behind, stiff and awkward in the saddle.

"How come him to decide he's somebody that I know damned well he ain't?" Rudy wondered. "He does call to mind Mr. Austin, but he ain't him. An' bracin' you that way . . . what kind of man acts like that, Pete?"

"Like how?"

"Well, like a curly wolf . . . or a rabid one, more like. You ever seen the likes of him?"

"Not out in open country," Joslyn admitted. "But I've seen the type, I guess."

"Yeah? Where?"

"Back east, when I went there before the war. That trip Stoney and me made for Old Man Cole — I've talked about that."

"Yeah. Old man was set on findin' his lost nephew or somebody, wasn't it?"

"Grandson. One of his daughter's boys, that was lost as a baby. Rawhiders carried him off. They'd do that, sometimes, back then. Steal babies an' sell 'em to sailors that might get a price back east. The old man never stopped looking, not 'til the day he died. But nothing ever came of it. That one time, he sent us all the way to New York City on a tip. Thought the boy might be there. We searched, but we didn't find a trace. Saw some sights, though. And I recollect the street gangs down in the south end of that town. Like wild animals. Called themselves the Shirt Tails or the Devil's Twisters, or the Battery Boys or such. Different gangs ran different parts of town. Different streets, different neighborhoods. I remember them."

"That's who this fella reminds you of?"

"Yeah. It's the way he talks, the way he acts. Like he's just spoilin' for trouble . . . or expecting it and trying to get the jump on it."

"What if he'd drawed down on you, Pete? Would you have killed him?"

"If I could," Joslyn said softly. "Got a feeling that might not be real easy, though."

The old trail wound upward, away from the river, then crested where it turned back. Wilson was waiting there.

"That's the place." He pointed. "Not much there, but there is a crossing."

The settlement was only a quarter-mile away, near enough that they could see the dozen or so buildings, the horses at hitch rails in front of some of them, the ramshackle little raft ferry that plied from the Territory shore out to an obstruction midway across the river—it might have been an island, an old log jam, or both—and then on across to the Texas side. Joslyn gazed at the scene, thoughtfully.

"See what I mean?" Wilson asked.

"I see." Joslyn nodded.

Rudy's brow furrowed. "What do you see? What's wrong?"

"Little place like that," Joslyn said, "this time of day, how many men would you expect to see out and around?"

"I don't know. Two or three?"

"I see at least a dozen right now," Wilson pointed out. "Just out on the street. That's too many."

When the wagon came up to them, and the rest of the men, Joslyn pointed to the crossing. "Wilson thinks that might be a troublesome place yonder, Miss Justine," he said. "But it's a way across the river."

115

"Then we shall cross there," Justine decided.

Bodie—or Austin as he now insisted on being called—reined alongside. "What kind of troublesome?"

"Hard cases, looks like."

"What?"

Joslyn glanced at him, curious. "Toughs. Harness bulls."

"Oh." Austin nodded. "That all? Well, let's go." He drummed the horse with insistent heels and reined it toward the settlement, with Mason Fremont hurrying to overtake him.

"Ease up on the bit, Mr. Bo . . . I mean, Mr. Austin. Remember what I showed you. Let the horse do the horse thinking. That's what it's best at."

Behind them, Joslyn nodded at Rudy. "Like I thought. New York City. Harness bulls is street language."

The ferry was putting out from shore, men hauling at its cables. Aboard were a dozen or more men, with horses.

As they neared the little settlement, the ferry reached the island in midstream. Justine had been puzzled at how the craft could pass, with its cables anchored there. Now she saw.

Fifty yards from the island, the men aboard slipped the grapples from the taut cable and set them on a loose cable that she had not seen until they raised it from the water. Reconnected, the barge drifted downstream, looping toward clear water below the obstruction, Midway past, men aboard began turning a horizontal winch, hauling the contrivance upstream on the far side. There, they would reconnect and continue to the far bank.

116

The "island" was no island at all, it seemed. Just an old logjam, sandbanked over the years.

"Lot of effort been put into a ferry that's only needed when the river's high," Pete Joslyn commented, seeing her interest.

"Yes, it is," she said. "Why is that?"

He shrugged. "Real important to some folks to be able to cross borders in a hurry, no matter what the season."

Just outside the settlement, riders came out to meet them—armed men who spread across the trail, barring passage.

"Keep your eyes open and your mouths shut," Pete Joslyn told his party. "I'll see if I can sort this out."

A thick-set, whiskered man walked his horse toward them and raised his hand. "I don't know you people," he said. "What do you want?"

"No trouble," Joslyn said, keeping his voice mild and level. "The lady needs some supplies, and we want to cross the river."

"That's a private ferry," the man said. "Not open to the public."

"We'll pay a reasonable fee," Joslyn assured him.

The man grinned. "Yeah, maybe so. But you still ain't goin' over on that barge."

Joslyn hadn't noticed the New Yorker easing up beside him, but suddenly Bodie-Austin was there. "These the bulls?" he asked, quietly.

Joslyn glanced at him. "That's what they'd be called where you're from. Just let me handle this, all right?"

"No." Bodie's voice rose, harsh and challenging. "You gutter-trash are in the way," he demanded. "Back off or die."

Joslyn's mouth dropped open, and the whiskered

117

man went pale, staring in disbelief. "Wh . . . what did you say?"

"You heard me, jackass!" Bodie-Austin thundered. "Now move!"

"I'll be god damned . . ." the whiskered one rasped, his hand diving for the gun at his side.

It never made it. Beside Joslyn, the New Yorker's Colt was rolling thunder. Ahead, men fell while others fought their mounts and tried for their guns.

"Jesus Christ!" Joslyn muttered, then drew his own gun and joined in.

Chapter Ten

I never knew whether I saw that girl again . . . the one on McConnell's roof. Lord, I never was sure that I saw her the first time. There was somebody up there, all right, but I don't know whether the face that stayed in my memory was a face I really saw, or just a face I imagined. Maybe I saw her again. Maybe more than once. But it was the same thing. I just wasn't sure what I saw, those times. Except once.

There is a corner on Lower Broadway where artists show their work on good days. Painters, sculptors, scribblers, vase-makers, and like that. When the sun is out and people are on the streets you can see them there, hawking their crafts. I used to go and look sometimes. It could be a show — people with paint on their clothes and smudges on their faces, showing off pictures of plants or pictures of piles of fruit, or pictures of people. Pictures on planking, pictures on stretched cloth, pictures as big as walls and pictures as tiny as a thumb painted or carved on beads or little ovals of colored stone.

Sometimes there would be wood carvers there, sometimes glazers and tinsmiths, sometimes people who made shapes of stone. And jewelers with their baubles, cart-peddlers, tapesters, weavers and stitchers—anybody who knew how to make a representation and had hopes of selling the products. But mostly there were the picture-makers, of all kinds.

Once there was a man there—a scrawny little dark-skinned man who looked like a dodger and talked like a Frenchie—who made pictures from lines and blobs. For a bit of coin he would set up a sheet of paper and hand the buyer a chunk of charcoal, then stand back and bow. The buyer was supposed to make marks on the paper—a line or two, a circle, a smudge, just anything. Then the little dark man would take the charcoal and make a picture from what the buyer drew.

He was good. A few lines and smudges became a proud sailing ship cutting through the sea. An oval and a jot became a face—sometimes the very likeness of the person who made the marks. A series of straight lines became a street corner with people coming and going . . . you could even see stray pigs nosing around in the gutters. A rough square and a side-of-the-fist smudge became a fancy carriage drawn by two matched horses. A scrawl like tangled twine became a street clown juggling batons, or maybe a dogfight with bettors crowding around.

I had been watching for a while when the drawer squinted at me and offered the charcoal. I started to turn away and he tugged at my sleeve. I'd have flattened any regular native for that, but I guessed the little fellow didn't know any better. Finally I gave him a coin, took his charcoal and scribbled on his paper. I remember what it was—just a quick double curved line—like the S at one end of a saloon sign—and a smudge of charcoal where my thumb scuffed the sheet. Then I handed the charcoal back to him and dared him with a look to make something of it.

He squinted at the paper, then looked at me for a

moment, then began drawing and I swear I couldn't believe it. It didn't take half a minute, what he did. His hands fairly flew over that paper, and when he stepped back there was a face there — a girl's face. She was half turned away, but looking directly at me from the corner of her eye. She looked as though she were pleading. The picture said she wanted to say something . . . as though she *needed* to say something. To me. She looked like she was about to cry.

Her face was the same face I had seen — or imagined — that night on McConnell's roof. The night of the pretty fire. A pretty face, just like the one I thought I saw — but now frightened and pleading, asking me for help.

The artist took down the paper and looked at it, like he was confused. Or surprised. Then he looked at me. *"L'jeune fille, m'sieu . . . c'belle . . . c'la votre?"*

I didn't know what he meant, but when I reached for the drawing I had a funny feeling. I didn't want it. It was an imaginary face. There was no such face as that, and I knew it, and if I took the picture I'd be getting involved in something that had nothing to do with me. I felt disoriented, and irritated.

I drew back. "I don't want the stupid thing," I told him. I turned away and my elbow bumped somebody. There was a clatter of things falling on the pavement.

"Why don't you watch where you're . . ." somebody started to say, and I caught his eye. He was a vendor, and when I bumped him he'd dropped a handful of baubles. He glared, then dropped his eyes and knelt to pick up his wares. They were strings of stained-glass beads and ornaments. They lay scattered there on the gray stone, and the sunlight flashed on them . . . every color of the rainbow.

It was a while before I went back to that corner, and I never saw him again, the dark-skinned Frenchie. I saw the face again, though—that haunting, imaginary face of a pleading young woman. But that was later.

In the meantime, it gave me trouble. When I had the price in my pocket, I'd been as ready as the next man to go down to the brothels on Baxter or Worth for an evening's pleasure. But I couldn't get that damned face out of my mind. Seeing a drawing of it seemed to have frozen it in place. It spoiled the bawds for me. I couldn't even look at those women without seeing that face. She . . . it, the face . . . it stood between me and whoever I was looking at.

Wherever I looked, I could see that face. A heart-shaped face, wider across the cheeks than across the jaws, tapering to a chin that was small and subtly rounded, but seemed strong . . . the way the little tilted nose looked strong, and the small mouth with that full lower lip, it could have seemed pouty but it didn't. It seemed determined and strong.

And those eyes. Always those same eyes. Sad-seeming eyes, with a plea in them. Sometimes I felt like I had the Irish on me—like I was haunted or something.

I heard the whispers after a while. "What about Hands Bodie?" they wondered. "He acts like he's become a monk."

Nobody said anything like that to my face. Nobody I knew was ready for that kind of trouble, unless a smart fee went with it. But it was worrisome.

And now here I was . . . what, a thousand miles away from all of that? A thousand miles—at least that—from lower Broadway, from Five Points, from McConnell's Mercantile and the old tar roof. And still I saw that face in my mind.

When there was time to think about it.

The strange thing was, I used to see that face sort of like the Broadway artist drew it. Black and white. Lines and smudges on flat white paper. Somewhere along the way, though, that had changed. The face had come to life. It had blue eyes and dark red hair, and a few freckles across its nose, and I felt as though I knew how its lips would move if it spoke.

Ever since . . . when? It seemed like the image had been real ever since I crawled out of that shell crater on that silent battlefield. When I saw the rainbow.

I'd decided to give the Indian kid—Mason—a try at teaching me about horses, and about country ways. He had a good enough reason. He wanted some protection. That made it a fair trade, and I'd go with it as long as it served my purposes.

When among hayseeds, do as hayseeds do. There were things I'd need to learn, and I knew it. Unless I decided to go back to New York—which wasn't a very good idea for a while—it was hayseeds I'd have to deal with.

I thought I might start dealing the minute we got back to the wagon camp and found those five men there. Hayseeds, like everybody else west of the Hudson, but they were armed and crusty and they didn't know a thing about backing down. Especially the leader, Pete Joslyn. I thought seriously about killing him. He thought he was good with his gun, and he acted like it. Generally, it's best to settle matters with somebody like that. In the city, if you let a cocky dude walk away, he'll likely show up again and shoot you from behind, or have his chums waylay you in a dark alley.

Not settling a challenge is bad business.

Still, there was something about the fellow Joslyn—and the others with him—that I sensed, and wondered about. What made him think he might match me with a gun? That was just ignorance on his part. If he'd lived in the city, he'd have known a shooter on sight. In the city, anybody who lasts, does.

He'd have known what a shooter was. A man with a special knack, who has been trained to use the knack and knows every edge and how to get it. In the city, nobody tries to face down a shooter. Not even another shooter, if he can help it. Snipe him from a rooftop, net him into an alley and put steel in his guts, waylay him and shoot him in the back, if you can. But don't try to face him down.

If Pete Joslyn hadn't been a hayseed he'd have known that. But the puzzling thing was, I had the feeling that he didn't particularly want to shoot me, even though he thought he could.

He bore me no malice.

It is difficult to deal with someone who doesn't mean you harm. In the city, I hadn't encountered that very often. In the city, it's simple. A man faces you, he has one of two things in his head. Fear or anger.

But Pete Joslyn faced me, and I knew he didn't feel either of those things. It was puzzling.

I didn't know how to back down, but I watched him and he showed me. It was a new thing. Back off with honor—in the city only a fool would even think of such a thing. But out here, among the yokels, it was more complicated.

Maybe I'd ask Mason about that. He was just a kid, but he might know. He knew about horses.

Some things are simple wherever you find them, though. Bulls are bulls. Call them harness bulls or enforcers or just plain thugs, I couldn't see why the methods would be any different out here than they were back there. The rules are the same. Bulls travel in packs, and they will either bust you or block you. That's what bulls do.

I couldn't believe it when that Pete Joslyn tried to reason with bulls. You don't reason with bulls. Ever.

When the city man's Colt started talking, Pete Joslyn's mouth dropped open. Beside him, Bodie was firing steadily and methodically. Out in front, men were falling. But there were more of them there than there are loads in a Colt, and some of them were pulling guns.

Down in Texas, there were those who knew Pete Joslyn, and more that knew of him. A cool hand, they said. A man with sand in his craw. Steady as fieldstone, easy as old shoes but chain lightning with a six-gun if he had to be.

Now he had to be. The city man had dealt the hand, and it was in play. Joslyn drew and fired, picking his target, and heard other guns opening up around him.

It was over in seconds. Some of the toughs — a scant few — were scattering hell-for-leather, heading for the town. The rest of them were on the ground. Even as the echoes died, Joslyn realized that Bodie — or Austin, whoever he was — was calmly reloading his gun.

"Don't argue with bulls," the New Yorker said flatly. "Lose your edge that way."

Joslyn's bunch were putting away their guns, shaking their heads and shooting hard glances at Bodie. Wilson got down from his horse, walked across to look up at Joslyn, and said, "Hell of a note, Pete. That was plain murder."

Bodie turned to stare at him. "You think so? Then

125

go take a look behind those rocks right there."

Scowling, Wilson walked away. The "rocks" were a pair of claybanks thirty yards away, just flanking the area where the line of toughs had spread. Wilson went and looked, then walked back, slowly.

"He's right," he said, speaking to Joslyn. "Three snipers back there, with rifles. They're dead. One shot each, in the head."

"*Center* of the head," Bodie said, quietly.

"They'd have killed us," Wilson said.

"Well," Joslyn allowed, "now we know what this place is."

"Right." Wilson looked up at Bodie, his eyes curious. "And you're right about the shots. *Center* of the head, each one. You knew that, did you?"

"I put them there," Bodie said distantly. He wiped the cylinder of his gun, thumbed fresh caps into place and put it away. "That one with the big mouth"—he pointed casually toward the leader of the waylayers—"he has a bullet in the center of his chest. Same with that yellow-hair over there. The one in the bushes with his feet sticking up, his bullet's in the center of his neck." He looked across at Pete Joslyn, a look that was not a challenge, only a statement. You know me now, it said. Let's leave it at that.

Joslyn caught the look, but made no response. Six shots, he was thinking. Six men down, each dead instantly. Men who died not as men, but as targets. Casual targets, of interest only for the placement of the shot. What kind of man was this?

There was no time to think about it now. Just ahead, at the little settlement, men were swarming like ants on a bothered hill. Dozens of them. The escaped waylayers had arrived there, and the place looked—to most of them—like an armed camp getting ready for siege. To Bodie, it looked like the corner of Pearl Street and Park Row on any Thursday.

The wagon had come up, a white-faced and thin-lipped Justine at the reins. Wendell and Mason were gawking at the dead men.

"We've sure enough stirred the pot," Joslyn allowed. "Miss Justine, do you still want to go down there?"

"I still want to cross the river," she said, her voice tight with tension. "But I certainly . . ."

"Quicker the better, then," Bodie said. He drummed heels against his horse and set off at a high run, heading for the town. Mason was right behind him, waving his rifle and yelling. Rudy set off after them, then hesitated, glancing back, confused as to what he was supposed to do.

"Jesus Christ," Pete Joslyn breathed. Then, "Well, what are *we* waitin' for? Come on!"

Given a few minutes to fort up and get set, the outlaw element of Chase Landing might have put up a fight. Instead—faced with the fear-glazed eyes of the surviving ambushers, and a sudden assault by mounted madmen, they broke and ran in all directions.

By the time the wagon came down the hill, Pete Joslyn and his pards had the little settlement under tight rein and Hands Bodie—or David Austin or whoever, as Wilson had voiced it, was prowling around "like a damn snappin' badger that's spittin' mad an' fresh out of hound dogs."

There were people in the settlement—peering from shutters here and there—but the undesirable element seemed to have vanished into the brush. It had all been too sudden and too obviously lethal for any other reaction.

Wendell hauled up alongside the wagon team and

headed them in at a building with a store sign. "Let's get what we need and get out, fast," he urged his sister, "before that jasper gets us all killed."

On the river, the ferry raft had started its return trip and then had stopped. It hung in the flood tide just north of the island, suspended on its cable, while the four men aboard crouched and peered toward the settlement. Pete Joslyn's waves and hooraws had no effect. The operators weren't about to return to a shore that had sounded like a battlefield just minutes before.

Satisfied that there were no bulls left in the tiny town, Hands Bodie walked down to the ferry launch. Joslyn was there, trying to persuade the ferrymen to come on over.

"They're scared," he said. "I can't even get an answer out of them."

Bodie studied the situation for a moment. "Is that all? I saw a man freeze on a fire net one time. Building afire behind him, and he wouldn't go either way. I thought of a way to get him to move, though. Didn't really want him to fall. He owed money."

"How did you do it?"

"I'll show you." Bodie stepped to the little shed beside the dock and looked inside, then returned with an axe. Without hesitation, he raised it and began chopping at the cable-stays. Out on the river, the ferrymen stared in horror, then began to shout and wave frantically.

Bodie paused in his chopping and cupped a hand to his mouth. "Come over here!" he shouted.

The ferry began to move.

"Very effective," Joslyn admitted.

"Yeah." Bodie set the axe aside. "Better'n the other time."

"The man on the fire net? Why? What happened?"

"He waited too long. Blood and brains splattered all over Delancey Street."

Wilson came down from the settlement. "Talked to some folks," he said. "The rough bunch around here is Walshes and a bunch of drifters from wherever. They've took over around here. Old man Otie Walsh made a lease with th' Choctaw, so as long as they keep their hoorawin' local, nobody bothers 'em. Real nice little outlaw nest."

"Walsh the head man?" Joslyn asked.

"He died a year back. Fella named Carlile was runnin' things for a while, then he took off for Texas. Funny thing, he rode out with Federal troops. The boss since then has been one Jay Miller. Seems like he's been recruitin' hard cases from all over, then packin' 'em off to Texas. That's been the past month or so. That bunch we saw crossin' the river was some of 'em."

"Why Texas?" Joslyn wondered. "Where in Texas?"

"Best I can tell, Miller's still workin' for Carlile. He's sendin' him manpower, for whatever he's doin' yonder."

Joslyn looked thoughtful. "Might ought to look into that. If the man needs hands, maybe we'd do. Where is this Miller?"

"Right where we left him." Wilson shrugged. "That was his bunch that met us out there. He's the one what's-'is-name there did the heart-shot on."

"Huh. Nice bunch of folks, then."

"Not the best, I reckon. I did find out where that Carlile is, though."

"Where?"

Wilson grinned. "Rudy's old stompin' grounds. Hunt County."

Hands Bodie — or David Austin, as he had decided to call himself — had seemed to be ignoring them. He

129

stood at the end of the dock, watching the cable raft approach. But now he turned. "What's that about Hunt County?"

"Might be where we're goin'," Joslyn said. "Fellow there may be hirin', and we just busted up his employment agency. Maybe he'll hire us."

"Where I'm going, too," Bodie-Austin said, staring off into the distance. His frown looked puzzled. "Maybe I'm supposed to live there."

"What the hell does he mean by that?" Wilson muttered.

The city man had turned toward the river again, but his gaze was lifted above it, above and beyond. Joslyn and Wilson both peered in the same direction, then glanced at each other.

"You see something yonder, Mr., ah, Austin?" Joslyn asked.

"Yeah. Don't you see it?"

"I guess not. What is it?"

Bodie-Austin glanced around, looking irritated. Then he stared across the river again and pointed. "You blind, or what? There's a rainbow there. Way off, that way."

Chapter Eleven

Moss Jackson left Lone Oak with a short load and a mood as bleak as the low, gray sky. The intermittent rain soaked through his old coat at the seams, and made his bones ache and his bad leg feel numb. The talk he had heard in town had creased his weathered face into a scowl that deepened as the significance of it dawned on him.

Thad Carlile was back. That in itself was bad news. There wasn't a decent family in Hunt County but had suffered one sort of misery or another at the hands of the Carliles and their bunch around old Catsprings, back in the earlier years before a handful of good men banded together to run them out of Hunt County.

But now Thad was back — over in Greenville, they said, with a Federal commission in his pocket and Federal troops to back him up. Superintendent, he called himself. Provisional Authority. Deeds Reclamation, they said. Restoration and resettlement. The words were vague. They could mean almost anything. But Moss Jackson had a feeling he knew what they really meant. They meant that Thaddeus Carlile had found a devious way to settle some grudges.

A man like Thad Carlile would know about

grudges. Moss remembered him as a sneak and a back-shooter. The only one of old Ty Carlile's clan to have achieved some education, Thad was the one that had got into county politics and kept things quiet while his daddy and his brothers were robbing their neighbors. And when the robbing led to killing, there was no help from the law because — for a time there — the Carliles *were* the law.

Moss Jackson had reason to recollect the Sabine Bottoms feud. If the graves in the graveyards didn't remind him, his bad leg always would.

Where the twin-trace road veered around a stand of blackjack oak, water had pooled in the road, hiding the beat-down ruts. The buckboard veered, angling cross-track. Hard wheels fought the uneven ground, causing the wagon to jolt and sway, making his teeth rattle. "Easy, there, Sal!" he snapped at the plodding mule ahead of him. "Just go easy, will you?"

Mary Austin wasn't going to be pleased with the half load of supplies in the wagon bed. He wondered if she would understand the storekeeper's double-talk about tightening credit for "disputed" customers. He knew *he* didn't understand it, except that it seemed to apply to any place whose man had gone off to war, and it had something to do with the reason Thad Carlile was back in Hunt County. There was a list of questioned holdings posted at the courthouse over in Greenville, they said. Posted there by Carlile. Somebody from Lone Oak had gone over to see the list, and was supposed to bring back a copy of it. It hadn't come in yet, but rumor had it that places all over the county were on that list, including several spreads in the highlands above the Sabine.

Including, probably, both of the Austin places.

That would suit Thad Carlile — to get back at the

Austins now that the old man was dead and both boys gone off to war. Unless Thad Carlile had changed just a whole lot in the past . . . what, seven-eight years? Not likely a skunk could change his stripe anyhow . . . unless he had changed, it would pleasure him to make trouble for women and babies and old people. Old people like Moss himself, doing his best to keep a handle on Sam Austin's spread until the oldest son, Tom, came home.

And women and babies like Mary Austin and her little Davey. The baby Dave Austin hadn't even seen yet. Moss wondered if Dave Austin even knew about the baby. Mary certainly had written to him, but if there had been a response she hadn't mentioned it. The way things were now, the only way to be sure a letter got to a body was when the answer came back . . . if it ever did. Did the Austin boys even know about old Sam dying? Mary had written that, too. And Maude Carver wrote to Tom about it. Moss had taken both letters to the post office in Lone Oak.

So much had happened, so much had changed, since the day Tom and Dave left with their company.

Tom was the one. He had been rarin' to go, always talking about the Yankee threat and states' rights, always reading every newspaper he could find, and going off to Greenville or farther whenever there were speeches being made. Tom had been bit by the war bug, and had talked Dave into going, too. If Dave had known that Mary was in a family way, Moss knew the boy would have stayed. If they had known that old Sam didn't have but a few months left, probably both of them would have backed off and stayed home.

But who would have thought Sam Austin would ever die? The old man was like that big oak tree behind his house. He had always been there, it seemed.

133

Always had been, and always would be. But now his place was Tom's place, and Moss was doing his best to keep it up for when Tom came home.

And now there was a swaddling baby in Dave Austin's house across the creek, and trouble over all of them like the clouds in the rainy sky.

It would be like Thad Carlile, he thought darkly. Just like the polecat, to take revenge on innocent people. Especially so, since it was Sam Austin who led the raid on Catsprings. They ran the Carlile bunch out, then they burned the place. There wasn't even a settlement at Catsprings now. There wasn't anything there, not even a name, since there was another town by that name now, someplace 'way down south. Did Thad Carlile know Sam Austin had led that raid? Moss's scowl deepened. Of course he knew it. Everybody knew it. It was Sam Austin, mostly—along with the Peaveys and the Wallaces and some others—decent men pushed too far—who had put an end to the bad times in Hunt County.

He would have to tell Mary what he'd heard, but he hated to. The little thing had enough to fret about—the place falling down around her ears no matter how hard she worked, a new baby to feed and tend to, a spread to keep and not enough hands to keep it up, even when there was money to pay them. Like half the folks in the county, almost since the outset of the war, Mary Austin had too much to do and not enough to do with. Just hanging on, doing her best, waiting for things to get better . . . waiting for her man to come home.

It was months now, since there was any mail from back east. A year, nearly, since there was news of Dave or Tom . . . or of half a hundred other young'uns from these parts, out there somewhere fighting for the Confederacy.

The South had lost the war, they said. And that was obvious. More and more, there were Federals on the roads and in the towns, soldiers from other places, soldiers in blue like those bivouacked over by Greenville right now. Young men in blue uniforms, where the young men in gray had gone off to other places.

Why had they gone off, anyway? Moss had asked himself that a hundred times, in the time since the High Sabine Volunteers headed off for the Southern Pacific tracks, bound east to supplement General Hood's troops.

Why? There was still no good answer to that. Only that they were young men who had listened to the speeches, and it seemed like the thing to do at the time. What better reason did young bucks ever need?

What was Texas doing in that conflict at all? Moss had worried that question over in his mind, like a hound dog with a stew bone. It wasn't a thing a man talked about — not with the threat of Regulators and night riders always present — but he wondered.

The black slaves? That might have been the reasoning of a few. Some folks down in the Gulf plantations and over in East Texas had slaves. Maybe had a lot of money invested in them. But not around here. Why spend five thousand dollars for a slave when good hands could be hired on for fifty dollars a month?

Crossing the rock draw that led down to Cove Creek, Moss noticed that another section of rail fence was down. Nudged over by cattle, maybe. Or maybe pulled down by somebody, just for the hell of it. Either way, it was another job that would have to be tended to. There wasn't that much stock left on the Austin places, but those that were had to be contained or there would be none. Plenty of folks

135

wouldn't hesitate to drift off cattle that wandered outside their fences. Plenty of folks were hungry these days, and not too picky about how they got fed.

Stopping off at his own place—Tom Austin's place—to drag a sack of supplies into the shed, Moss Jackson limped over to the house and stuck his head inside, thinking about hot coffee on a wet day. But the house was empty. He wasn't surprised. Most days, as soon as the old woman finished her chores, she was off to Dave's house to look in on Mary and the baby. And if there were things there that needed doing, things she could help with, chances were she wouldn't be back until evening.

Jess and Willie had a pot going in the sleep shack, but Moss had no taste for the cowboys' brew. It reeked of chicory and was as thick as paste. "Some fence down, over yonder," he told Willie. "Best set it up before dark."

"Fence ain't worth gettin' shot for," the hand drawled.

"Nobody shootin', Willie. It's just down fence. Get to it."

With a sigh, Moss climbed back into the buckboard, snapped the reins, and headed from there across the creek toward Dave's place, to unload Mary's goods. And to tell Mary Austin what he had heard in town.

"I just thank the lord you're not a colicky baby," Mary Austin told her son as she changed his wrapping. "Sometimes I swear that's about the only good thing I can think of to say about you, Davey." She tied off the new cloth, with a three-way hitch in front the way her mother had taught her, tossed the soiled

136

cloth into the lidded pail, then smiled. Lifting the boy, she held him high and looked up at him. "Except that you're awful pretty, you little crawler," she added.

At the sound of her voice, Maude Carver looked in from the next room, then stepped through the door. "If ever I seen a child on its way to bein' spoiled," she said, "it's that'n there. Land, Mary, I never seen a mother so took with a child as you."

"Never was a child like this," Mary said. "Isn't he just the prettiest thing?"

"Every baby ever borned is the prettiest thing there ever was to somebody," Maude admitted. "But you ought to give yourself a rest now and again. A child can wear a body out, if you let it."

Mary glanced around, but held her tongue. Maude Carver had given birth to nine babies in her time, and raised seven of them to sturdy adulthood. Mary wondered if Maude had ever taken the advice she handed out now.

"Moss be here in a bit," the older woman said. "Seen the buckboard on the hill yonder. I expect some hot coffee would set well after that drive to Lone Oak and back."

"I'll put the pot on," Mary agreed, lowering Davey into his railed daybed—what Moss Jackson called his "holdin' pen."

"Already done it," Maude said. "Wet as it is, that old man's leg's prob'ly complainin', but he'd never think to have a pot ready over at the home place." The exasperation in her tone was old habit, nothing more. For as long as anybody around here could remember, Maude Carver and Moss Jackson had been landmarks around the Austin place. Jackson had been Sam Austin's foreman almost since the elder Austin had expanded his holdings to raise livestock.

137

And Maude had been housekeeper for Sam Austin's wife for years, then for Austin himself after she was gone. There were other hands on the Austin place — now the *two* Austin places, since the old man had given this spread to David on the day he and Mary were married — but they came and went. Maude Carver and Moss Jackson were fixtures, as near to being family as anyone not kin could be.

And they doted on each other, Mary knew, though it was hard to remember either of them ever saying a kindness to the other.

With Davey clean and dry again, and happy in his holding pen, Mary went to the front window and pulled back the curtain. Moss Jackson was just crossing the creek, starting up the slope. Old Sal in her traces plodded along as always — morning or evening, uphill or down, wet or dry, the big mule had one pace and never varied it. Sal didn't go anywhere fast, but Sal always got there in her own good time.

Moss Jackson sat hunched on the buckboard seat, white whiskers bright between his rain-soaked dark hat and his upturned dark coat collar. He didn't look happy, but then Moss Jackson rarely looked happy. He just looked like Moss.

She watched him approach, and wondered if the post office in Lone Oak had been open and if there had been any mail.

Maude seemed to be reading her mind. "Long time since you had word, child. Awful long time."

"I get to fretting sometimes," Mary admitted. "That awful war. If anything happened to David, I just don't know what I'd do, Maude. I just don't know."

"Best not to think on it too much," Maude said softly. "It's all in the Lord's hands. Not a blessed thing a body can do, and frettin' don't help."

138

"All in the Lord's hands." Mary nodded. "Still, I wish we'd hear something."

Moss Jackson pulled up out front and got down from the wagon, grimacing. He waved at the window, then hobbled around to the tail to unload. Mary frowned, seeing what was there. Three tote-sacks and a keg, along with two or three wrapped parcels. Not nearly enough to account for the things she needed, that Moss had gone to get.

He carried things to the shed porch, set them there, then led Sal to the cover of the open barn, where a couple of hired hands were waiting out the rain, and headed for the house. Maude met him at the door with a curt, "wipe your feet if you mean to come in here," then poured hot coffee in a mug and handed it to him.

"I'm nigh soaked," he grumped, then turned as Mary came from the next room. A smile tugged at his whiskered cheeks as he removed his hat. Mary Blaine Austin would pleasure any man to see, no matter what his age or condition. Even when she was just a little girl, she had been a pretty one. Old Judge Blaine's daughter had always made heads turn when she passed by. A heart-shaped face, Moss thought. Like the cherubs painted on the wall of the Spanish church over at Cato. Widest at the cheeks, where big, expressive eyes framed a small, uptilted nose with a few freckles scattered across. Auburn hair and a determined little chin beneath a mouth that made an old man remember the kisses he had caught in his time.

"No mail," he said, knowing her first question without her having to ask. "I reckon no news is good news."

"I suppose so." She nodded. "Are things in short supply in town, Moss? That looks like a small load."

"It is," he said. From a pocket he pulled a rumpled and rain-soaked piece of paper. Her shopping list. "Some things they didn't have . . . and some I couldn't get."

Maude glanced at him. "What does that mean?"

He sighed and slumped into a chair, easing his aching leg. "Only good news I come with was the no news," he said. "What news I do have ain't good. Colter and the rest, they're shortin' on credit, Mary. There's a fuss over land titles, and they're afraid they'll get stuck."

"Land titles?"

"Don't know much yet, but Thad Carlile is back. Right here in the county, an' he's fixin' to make trouble."

"But what does that have to do with us?" Mary hovered over him, worried. "This is all deeded land, Moss. Clear and tax-payed. David's daddy never let anything like that slide."

"Deeded, all right." Moss nodded, lowering his eyes. He hated to be saying this to Mary. "But this place—both these places, now—they're deeded to men in the service of the Confederate Army. I'm just afraid there's real trouble ahead."

Both of the women joined him, then, sitting around the plank table, and he told them everything he had heard in Lone Oak.

It was late afternoon when Moss Jackson and Maude Carver climbed into the buckboard for the short drive back to the other house, and Mary watched them go, feeling frightened and alone.

She didn't know what to make of Moss's news, but she trusted him and she knew he was concerned. It was the war, she knew. Everything was all upset by the war, and it might be a long time before anybody got over it . . . even after the young men—

her David, and Tom and the rest — came home.

They *would* come home, she told herself. Oh, men died in wars, she knew that. But it wasn't a thing she allowed herself to think about. Some of the young men might not come home, but David would. She *knew* he would. He just had to.

The sky was still low and gray, with sprinkles falling now and then, but as she turned and started into the house the setting sun peeked out from the distant edge of the clouds and she caught her breath. Off to the east, standing over the wet fields, was a rainbow.

It's an omen, she thought. David has always loved rainbows. Maybe the mail can't get through, but rainbows can. Maybe he's on his way home right now. Oh, dear God, let him be. Let him be coming home now. Let him be on his way this very minute, and traveling as fast as he can.

The plea was silent, but it caught at her throat and misted her eyes. She gazed at the bright rainbow, wishing it could answer her.

It gave no answer, only stood there, mute. But there was a feeling to it — a feeling in her — as she looked at it. As though David was indeed on his way to her, right at that instant. But there was something dark and troubling about the intuition. As though David was coming . . . but somehow David wasn't David anymore.

Chapter Twelve

Pete Joslyn and the other Texans went across first on the raft ferry, to scout and secure the far side of the river. Then the ferry was brought back and Justine's wagon was led aboard, followed by Wendell and Mason with the saddle stock.

Hands Bodie stood on the dock, supervising, his axe still in his hand. When everyone was aboard he stepped to the raft's deck and turned to scowl at the men who had come down from the settlement to watch. At his stare, some of them stared back and he bristled, then held his tongue. Yokels, he reminded himself. They don't know anything.

Drawing back his coat, he let them see the revolver at his belt. "I'm going to watch you people," he growled. "If anybody makes a wrong move before we get to that pile of sticks out there, I'll shoot him." He gazed at them one after another to be sure they understood. Most of them had begun to back away. As an afterthought, he gestured, indicating the four polemen who operated the raft. "Anybody does anything I don't like after we're past those sticks, I'll shoot *them*. Any questions?"

People on the bank scattered in all directions, wanting nothing to do with him.

Satisfied, he turned to the polemen. "Well, what are you waiting for? Cross the river!"

The crossing to the "sticks" — the little midstream island — was rough and bumpy. The raft was buffeted by floodwaters and strained against its cables. It was all Wendell and Mason could do to keep the stock tended. But after the raft was swung around the island and launched on the second leg of its journey, things were smoother. Past the main flood current here, the water was more shallow and placid. Justine used the time to stow her supplies in the wagon, sorting parcels into the places where she wanted them.

Pete Joslyn, Rudy, Jim, and Hank were waiting for them at the makeshift Texas dock. Wilson, they said, had gone ahead to scout trail.

The Texans helped them debark, flanking Justine's team to lead the wagon gently upslope to a clearing beyond which were woodlands fronting rolling hills that rose in the distance, away from the river. There was one trail, a makeshift track leading directly south. Joslyn led off, then the wagon and the other riders. Mason glanced back, and then hauled rein. The city man was still at the river, standing beside his horse, watching the ferry raft round the tip of the island.

Mason trotted his mount back, puzzled. "Aren't you coming?" he asked. "This is Texas. There's roads over there someplace."

Bodie glanced at him and turned his attention back to the river. The raft was beyond the island now, making for the Nations shore. Dropping the reins of his horse, Bodie stepped to the cable anchor, lifted the axe and began chopping. Half a dozen swings and the cable parted, splashing into

143

the water, disappearing there. Bodie tossed the axe away, then mounted his horse—more gracefully than he had a few days ago, Mason noted. Without a word he set off, following where the rest had gone.

Mason caught up and fell in beside him. "What did you do that for?"

"What?"

"Cut the cable. Why did you do that?"

"We didn't get all those bulls," Bodie rasped.

"The men back there? The ones that tried to stop us? They wouldn't come after us . . . would they?"

"I don't know," Bodie said. "But now they can't."

Cloudy dusk was on the land when Wilson met them, where the trail climbed away to forested slopes ahead. "Road forks ahead," he said. "One fork goes on south, the other turns east. Nobody around, but plenty of tracks. The same ones that came up from the river. They went ahead, south."

It was near dark when they reached the fork. Time to stop for the night. Scouting off the trails, Wendell found a clear-water seep with graze for the stock, and they made camp there. With new supplies, Justine made biscuits and cooked sliced bacon, then fried eggs in the grease. Watching the men put it away, she wondered how long it had been since any of them—including herself and her brothers—had a real meal.

When it was done, they sat around the camp, finishing off the coffee.

"We'd best head south from here," Pete Joslyn said. "The boys and me, we need to find work, and there's somebody down at Greenville that may be hirin'."

"We'll part company, then," Justine said. "We're

144

heading east, which should take us toward Pleasant Hill."

"Do you have someone there to go to?"

"I don't know," she admitted. "Our father knew some people around there. That was a long time ago, but maybe someone will remember. If not, well, I need to find a school where I can teach. I guess that's as good a place as any to start." She turned toward Bodie. "Mr. Austin?"

He sat with his back to the fire, scowling at the dark wilderness beyond its light. He might as well not have heard her. He seemed completely unaware of any of them there.

"He's going on with us, Big Sister," Mason said. "I made a deal with him. He'll go with us, and I'll teach him country ways."

"He can use a little of that," Wendell muttered. "Start out with manners, why don't you?"

Somewhere an owl hooted and Bodie seemed to come abruptly awake. "What was that?"

"An owl," Mason said. "It's a bird, comes out at night to hunt."

"Owl," Bodie repeated the word. "Sounded like Shirttails on the prowl. How do you know it's an owl?"

"Well, either it's an owl or it's a Cherokee," Mason said, seriously. "And except for Wendell and me, I don't suppose there are any other Cherokees around. What's shirttails?"

"Monk Riley's bunch." Bodie shrugged. "Night crawlers, mostly. They hole up along Bee Street, but they run from Stuyvesant to the Battery. Knifers and thieves. They sound like that when they spot a mark, to call the others in."

The answer meant nothing to most of them, but

Pete Joslyn chuckled. "You're from New York, sure enough," he allowed. "Hard to break away from it, isn't it?"

Bodie glanced at him, frowning. "Why would anybody want to?"

"Well, you're a long way from there now. I expect you had a reason to leave."

"Three hundred dollars," Bodie said. "Billy Bean owes me that, too."

"Heard about the draft." Joslyn nodded. "You could go back, though. Your side has won the war. Most of it, anyway. Even in Texas. There's Yankees in the state capitol, and the legislature's in hidin' or in jail or somethin'."

Bodie stared into darkness. "None of your business, why I don't go back," he said. "None of my business is any of yours."

"Problems back there, huh?"

Bodie seemed to tense, and looked around. "Don't push me," he snapped.

"I'd just as soon never have occasion to push you, mister," Joslyn drawled, completely at ease. "I've seen you shoot."

"You haven't seen anything, yokel," Bodie growled, still proddish.

"I wish you would stop that!" Justine said. "Land, I don't know what sets you off so, but there's no call for such behavior, Mr. Austin."

"Bodie," he corrected. "My name is Bodie."

"Bodie, then. I wish you'd make up your mind!"

"It doesn't matter." He was staring into the darkness again. "Those books you have . . . I want you to show me how to read them. And handwriting. That, too."

Then, as though none of them existed, he took

146

the best blanket out of the wagon, selected a bedding spot, lay down and went to sleep.

"I swear," Pete Joslyn said.

"Start with manners," Wendell told Mason again. "Either that, or let him get lost again and don't bother about findin' him."

By the time Justine and her brothers had packed and started in the early morning, after seeing Joslyn and the Texans off on the south road, Hands Bodie was already out of sight. He had awakened as surly and quarrelsome as he had been the evening before, swilled coffee, saddled his horse with only a modicum of assistance from Mason, and set off eastward.

"I don't know what winds that jasper's watch," Wendell grumped, swinging aboard his own mount, "but I'd just as soon he went on his way and we never saw him again."

"He isn't so bad," Mason allowed. "Weird, but I think he's all right . . . down deep, anyway."

"Hell, he . . ."

"Wendell!" Justine comforted herself on the wagon seat and picked up the reins. "You watch your language!"

"Sorry. What I meant to say was, I think that jasper is as crazy as a loon. He can't make up his mind who he is. First he calls himself one thing, then another. Times, he starts actin' all right and I think maybe he's got the hang of bein' civilized, then a minute later he's as touchy as a damn . . . pardon, Sis . . . darned badger. He acts like he's two different people, and neither one of them makes much sense."

Justine got the team started, and settled herself for the morning's drive. As Wendell fell in alongside, she said, "Be careful how you judge people, Wendell. I remember our pa saying that there is far more to a person than what seems on the surface. He said every one of us is many people, all the time."

"Yeah, but he was talkin' about special problems. I remember. He was tellin' some agency man about mixed breeds . . . like Mason and me. That was different."

"Are you sure it was different? Which do you feel like you are mostly, Wendell, white or Cherokee?"

"I'm neither one. I'm just me."

"Neither? Or both?"

"Well, it's the same thing. That's what Pa was telling that agency man . . . that all of us are a mix of breeds. The man didn't like hearing that, at all."

Mason was riding along on the other side, grinning. He didn't remember the incident, but he had heard the story many times. "He didn't like it because it turned out his father was English American and his mother was half German and half Jew."

"Hebrew," Justine corrected. "He never said she was Jewish."

The road wound eastward through a land of rolling hills and increasing forests. Pine trees were here and there, becoming more abundant by the mile.

"I remember land like this," Justine told her brothers when they stopped in late morning to rest the horses. "More pines than this, and it seems as though it was more hilly, but it still looks familiar." She had her old map out, and was studying it. "Pleasant Hill shouldn't be too far away now. We're going the right direction."

148

"Do you really think we'll find anybody there to help us?" Wendell frowned. "That was a long time ago, Big Sister. A long time before I was born. Will anybody remember our pa?"

"I don't know," she admitted. "Maybe, or maybe not. But it's a place to start. I remember what a pretty town it was, and everybody seemed so friendly. Besides, it's the only place in Texas that I know, really."

Near noon, where the road ran straight through rolling meadows bounded by woodlands on all sides, they saw a rider coming toward them from the east. At first, Justine thought it might be Bodie, but Mason's eyes were better. "It isn't him," the younger brother said. "Doesn't ride like him."

The man approaching was a stranger—a middle-aged man on a gaunt buckskin. As he neared, he stopped, looking them over. Then he came on. A few yards ahead, he stopped again, reining aside politely. At sight of Justine he removed his hat, but there was no friendliness in the scrutiny he turned on Wendell and Mason.

"Howdy," he said, curtly.

"Good day," Justine said. "Can you tell me if we are going toward Pleasant Hill?"

"You are," he said. "It's a ways on." He glared at the brothers again. "They's Injuns, ain't they?"

"They are my brothers," Justine said.

He frowned at her. "No offense, ma'am. But I know redskins when I see 'em, though we don't see none around here anymore. They know better than that."

"Better than what, sir?"

"Better'n to come around these parts. Injuns ain't wanted around here, ma'am. If they're with you, I'd

149

sure have a care about where I went if I was you."

"I don't understand," she said.

"You said Pleasant Hill, ma'am? If I had squaw get with me, I'd stay mighty clear of that town. That's a Regulator town."

"Squaw get? That is a very impolite term, sir."

The man seemed honestly surprised. "Then I'll apologize to you, ma'am, that you heard it from me." Again he glared at the brothers, letting them know that the apology was to the white lady in the wagon, not to the likes of them.

Wendell's eyes were narrowed, his teeth clenched. "I don't think I'm goin' to stand for . . ."

"Wendell! There's no harm done. Let's just go on." She flicked the reins, gazing coolly at the man beside the road. "I thank you for your time, sir. Good day."

He watched them pass, then called, "I sure would have a care, ma'am, if I was you. But if you're bound for it, there's a fork yonder. Take the right-hand road, to get to Pleasant Hill."

Mason glanced back, then turned his horse and trotted it back to where the man sat his saddle. "You don't mean us harm, do you?" he asked.

"Well, no, I reckon not," the man said, surprised to find himself actually having words with a red-skin. "I got nothin' for your kind, but nothin' against, either." As he looked more closely at the youth's features, his eyes widened. "She meant that, didn't she? About y'all bein' her brothers."

"We all had the same father," Mason explained. "Did you see a man pass this way ahead of us? Tall, brown-haired man up on a . . .?"

"Saw him, all right," the man frowned. "Son of a

bitch ordered me off the road so he could pass. What is he, a Federal or somethin'?"

"No. Just a fellow I'm trying to look out for until he learns his way."

"Why?"

"I don't know," Mason admitted. With a nod, he turned and followed after the wagon. Behind him, the man shook his head, replaced his hat and went on his way, pausing two or three times to look back.

They nooned beside a pretty little creek where a narrow wooden bridge crossed. Mason decided that it must have been here that Mr. Bodie ordered the man off the road. The bridge was wide enough for riders to pass—it was wide enough for a fair-sized wagon—but the city man was funny about a lot of things. Maybe he just didn't want to get that close to strangers. He kept the story to himself, though. Telling it would just have set Wendell off again.

It was late afternoon when they found Callahan Bodie. He sat beneath a tree at a place where the road forked. His horse was nowhere in sight. When they approached, he got to his feet, looking sullen. "This is the wrong way," he said.

Justine pulled up to him and reined in. "What do you mean, it's the wrong way? This is a fork in the road. We need to go to the right."

"They're both the wrong way," he said. "I need to go that way." He pointed back the way they had come.

"What on earth are you talking about?"

"There's somebody I have to look for," he said, slowly.

"Who?"

"I don't know. But we're going the wrong way."

"You're not going anywhere very fast without your horse," Mason said. "Where is it?"

"Over there, somewhere," Bodie said, vaguely, "It wandered off."

"Mercy," Mason muttered. "All right, I'll go find it."

Justine squinted at the man standing beside her wagon. "Mr. Bodie . . . or is it Austin now . . .?"

"Bodie." He shrugged. "I guess. I don't know. Everything is kind of mixed up. It seems like I'm . . . hell, I don't know what it seems like! Leave me alone."

"Are you all right?"

"Of course I'm all right. I'm Hands Bodie!"

"Well, are you going to Pleasant Hill with us, or not? It's up to you, but you *did* tell Mason that . . ."

"A deal's a deal," he snapped. "But you show me how to read. And handwriting, too. I want to know what this letter says."

He pulled out a wadded and dirty scrap of paper. It was the same letter the boys had found on him, the evening they found him unconscious.

"I told you what it says," she reminded him. "But I can read it to you again if you want me to."

"No! I have to read it. *He* has to. Austin, I mean. Damn him, why won't he just die?"

She stared at him, not understanding a word of what he said, but suddenly feeling a deep concern for him. Behind the strange patchwork of the man — one moment silent and aloof, the next as jumpy as a wild animal — she had just glimpsed something else. He was terribly . . . terribly confused. He was so confused that he seemed lost.

"I'll show you how to read it," she said, quietly. "We'll work on it this evening."

"Good." He turned away, his shoulders setting into that familiar, slightly threatening posture that seemed to say, "I'm Hands Bodie. Stay out of my way." She could almost hear the words in his head. But what he said was. "I'll read it. *He'll* read it. Then maybe he'll go away. Him and his damned rainbow."

Chapter Thirteen

From the fork it would have been two days' travel to the town of Pleasant Hill, if they had pressed on. Bodie, though, insisted on frequent stops and the stops sometimes lasted for an hour or two, depending upon how the lessons went.

He seemed obsessed now with the letter—with reading it, for himself, by himself. Hour by hour he puzzled over the mysteries of characters and words, sometimes making real progress, sometimes lapsing into fits of frustration and storming off along the road, leaving the rest to follow him as they would.

Justine decided that, whoever he was, he was the most unusual person she had ever encountered. Sometimes he frightened her, when a sullen period of silence would erupt suddenly into aggressive, bullyish behavior or tight-lipped rage, or when he seemed as though he were in some other place entirely, seeing things, hearing things that were not there for her or her brothers. But then the silences or the rages would vanish, and he would be back, insisting that she teach him more.

"These are all separate letters," she told him. "All these little shapes, each one is a letter and

154

part of a word. And each one looks something like the alphabet that you're accustomed to, except they have been changed to script. That makes it easier for people to write them."

"They aren't all the same," he complained. "Even the ones that are the same are different. This thing here," he pointed, "you say that's an 'S'."

"That's right. The letter S."

"Then why is it different from the other letter S right next to it? That one looks like that other one over there—that F."

"It's the way it's done sometimes," she sighed. "It's a style of writing."

"Why?"

"I suppose it's to emphasize that there are two of them there, together. Maybe somebody decided a long time ago that it was more important to learn to spell than to learn to write. I don't know."

Between lessons, when they were on the move, Mason did his best to stay close to the city man, giving him a constant barrage of lessons of his own. "Both hands on the reins," he would say, "but let just the forward hand do the work. The other hand is for taking up slack." And, "If you'll sit straighter in the saddle, you won't cramp up after a long day. Yeah, like that. Roll your butt right up underneath you. Now quit kickin' the stirrups out front that way. Bring 'em back in line with your body, so you can raise up on them if you want to."

A dozen times, when he'd heard enough, Bodie told the kid to shut up and leave him alone. Still, he seemed to be picking it up. Sometimes he didn't seem to be listening, then Mason would notice him later, practicing what he had told him.

By lantern light at evening camp, Bodie pored over his letter—David Allen Austin's letter from his wife—with a scowl on his face, as though by sheer concentration he could make the scribbles speak to him. Then, abruptly, he looked up. "Pa's dead," he said, a stricken look on his face. "The old man . . ."

Justine nodded, thinking that he had deciphered that part of the letter. He knew what it said, but it seemed it had new meaning to him when he could read it directly. Justine was pleased. He was getting there.

But then he said, "He was only sixty-eight years old."

"That isn't in the letter." She frowned.

He seemed not to hear her. "I don't see how that could be," he muttered. "Sam Austin never had a sick day in his life."

She stared at him. The letter said that David Allen Austin's father had died. But it said nothing about his age, and it did not say his name.

He stared off into darkness. "I guess the home place is Tom's now," he said. Then he shook his head, frowning. "That doesn't make any sense! Tom's dead. He said so. *Somebody* said so!" With abrupt, angry motions he got to his feet, put the letter away and stalked off into the darkness.

They watched him go, then exchanged puzzled looks.

"That jasper is crazy," Wendell said. "I mean it, Big Sister. He's nothin' but a lunatic."

Justine sighed, wanting to respond but not knowing what to say. Wendell could very well be right, of course. Every evidence—the man's actions, his attitudes, his very confusions—said that he was. And she knew—she had seen—that he could be extremely dangerous. He was deadly. Yet a deep intuition said that he was not a danger to *them*. In spite of everything, a part of her agreed with Mason, that the man called Bodie—or whatever—could be important to them. He had already put an abrupt end to one situation, back at the river crossing, that could have been nasty.

It *had* been nasty, she reminded herself. Sudden and brutal and murderously nasty. But they had crossed the river then, with no further trouble.

Could the other men with them—Mr. Joslyn and his friends—have handled that situation back there? Certainly they would have gone about it differently, but what would have happened? There was no way to know. Hands Bodie had simply opened fire.

She was still trying to think of how to answer Wendell when Bodie came back into the firelight. The angry look was gone from his face, replaced by an expression that might have been sadness, or maybe of longing. He paused at the light's edge, then came on toward the camp fire. "This is like the burned-out section on Delancey," he said. "Nothin' but ashes and brush and trash, but with Baker's Street still paved on through, just like there was some reason for a street to be there."

They stared at him. Wendell said, "What?"

"This." He waved a casual hand. "In the dark it looks like it, except that the walls around don't have any lighted windows."

Justine eased back toward the wagon. "What walls?"

"Those." He shrugged, waving his hand again.

She saw it, then. In the dark of night, with only starlight and the fire's reflections, the clearing where they were camped *could* have been a leveled area in a city, and the ranked pine trees beyond might have been facing walls.

"Just over there," he pointed, "that would be Five Points, the back section with the slaughterhouses beyond, and down the other way would be the Battery, and over there where there's a gap, that could be Broad Street coming down from City Hall. One thing, though. If this was there, you'd all be robbed or dead by now, sitting out here like this."

"And you?" Justine ventured. "If this were there, I mean . . . and we were robbed or dead, where would you be?"

The question seemed to startle him. He didn't answer for a moment, then said, hesitantly, "If this were there, I'd be as likely as anybody to be the one doing it. But this isn't there, is it?"

"No, this isn't there. This is here."

"So it's all different," he said. "No, it wouldn't be me. Not here. And not anybody else, either, I guess. Not if I can help it."

"Thank you, Mr. Bodie." She smiled. "We are glad to have your protection."

"A deal's a deal." He nodded. Then, "Those men, the ones that crossed the river with us. They went to Hunt County, didn't they?"

"Well, yes, I think that's where they were going. They were looking for work."

"That's too bad," he said. "Yeah, that's a real shame."

"What do you mean by that?"

158

"I don't know what I mean," he said. He scuffed a boot at the rocky soil and frowned. "I wish I'd never found that shell crater, you know. I could have just died. For a while I thought I would. It wouldn't have mattered if I had, either. I didn't care. Maybe I was supposed to die there. Maybe if I had, he'd leave me alone."

"What . . . wouldn't have mattered?" She tried to choose a thread to follow, something that might make sense.

"If I had died. It never mattered if I lived or died. I don't guess I ever cared much, and nobody else cared at all. That's how it is, don't you see? Nothing matters, not really. Except that things mattered to him. Not to me, to *him*, damn him!"

"Who?"

"David Allen Austin. Him and his rainbow! It's all his problem, not mine. Can't you understand that?"

"You've never said what happened to you, Mr. Bodie."

"I don't know what happened." He squatted on his heels by the camp fire, looking lost. "I thought I knew. It was artillery shells, and most everybody died. Something hit me, then I was in a shell crater and it was raining, and there was somebody else there, too. Him. David Allen Austin. A Johnny Reb in the mud." He looked up, away from the fire, into the high distance. "One of us died in that crater. I thought it was him, but sometimes I wonder. Sometimes it seems like maybe it was me that died, instead."

"But, Mr. Bodie, that isn't logical. You *are* here, and you *are* alive . . ."

"Logical?" He stared at her. "What's logical,

anyway? Faces that aren't there? Remembering things that only another man would know? That Johnny Reb and me, we saw a rainbow, there on that battlefield. Are rainbows logical? Is it logical that Pete Joslyn and me . . . that we're liable to be looking down gun barrels at each other, because of somebody neither one of us ever heard of, in a place I've never been?"

"You're imagining things, Mr. Bodie."

"Am I? I don't know. But I can see her face."

"Whose?"

"Mary's. She's the one who wrote the letter. I know it's her. I've seen her for a long time."

Justine sensed that Wendell was trying to catch her eye. She refused to look his way. She could imagine the wolfish smirk playing at his cheeks, and she didn't want to give him the satisfaction of being obviously right.

He was right, though. Mr. Callahan "Hands" Bodie was a long way from being a normal person, and maybe from being a sane one.

On a rain-speckled afternoon they crested a piney hill and reached the town of Pleasant Hill. It was both larger and smaller than Justine remembered—larger in overall size, but with the look of a place with far fewer people than it might once have had. There were more buildings on more streets than her old memories held, but many of them were deserted.

The war, she thought, noticing that most of the people on the streets were women, children, and old people. It's the war. So many of the young men are gone. Still, there *were* men around. Mak-

160

ing the turn toward the main square, they saw men gathered on the rock-walk in front of a pair of boxy slab-wood buildings. Sullen-looking, hard-faced men, they gathered in small groups and clusters, talking among themselves. Several of them turned as they passed, watching them closely. For a moment she was afraid Mr. Bodie might take violent exception to being stared at, but she realized that it wasn't him their eyes were on. He wasn't even in sight. He had gone on ahead, somewhere. The men were staring at her brothers, mostly.

A Regulator town, the man on the road had said. She didn't know what that meant — Regulator town — but she was sure it couldn't be too bad. The word had a sound of civilization about it, of law and order. Certainly Wendell and Mason were part Indian, and it was in their appearance, but that meant nothing. These were civilized people in a civilized town, not savages.

They went on by, Justine staring around, looking for landmarks. It had been so long, and so much had changed.

Past the square she hauled up, gaping. Beside her, Wendell and Mason both gasped. Just a few yards away, in a cleared lot facing the street, was a freshly constructed gallows. Three men hung from its wide beam, dangling in the breeze.

Several men stood casually around the gallows. Eight, she counted. Unlike those they had passed before, all of these were armed. One glanced their way and — at sight of Justine's horrified expression, grinned and touched his hat brim. "Quite a sight, ain't it, ma'am . . ." he started, then looked more closely at Wendell and Mason. The grin fell into a sneer. He turned to a man nearby. "Hey, Joey! Take a look at them two. What do they look like, to you?"

Justine glanced around, trying to locate Hands Bodie. He was nowhere in sight. He had gone on ahead, even before they had reached the square.

The second man was looking at them, now. All of them were.

"Look kind of like red Injuns, don't they?" the first man said, his sneer carrying to his voice. Stepping away from the gallows, he pointed a finger at Mason, who was nearest. "You, boy! You talk English?"

"Better than you, mister." Mason was backing his horse away, his eyes on the man.

"Don't you back talk me, boy!" the man snapped. "You got a name?"

"My name is Mason Fremont."

Wendell had edged his own mount closer, flanking his brother. "If my brother's name is any of your business," he said, "then your name is our business. What is it?"

The man's sneer didn't relax. "Feisty, ain't they?" he said over his shoulder. Then to Justine, "Ma'am, these with you?"

Justine's mouth snapped shut and her eyes narrowed. She didn't like this man, or the others, either. She didn't like them at all. "My brother asked your name, sir," she said. "You owe him the courtesy of an answer."

"Well, my, my, listen to that, Joey! The lady claims that there redskin is her brother. Ain't that the beatin'est?"

The second one, Joey, stepped forward, hard eyes on the two boys. "Long ways from where your kind is s'posed to be, ain't you, 'skins? You!" He faced Wendell. "You better not let that rifle come level. I ain't scalped me a Injun in a coon's age, but I reckon I can."

"Let's hang 'em, Joey," another of the group said. "Plenty of room on that beam."

"I don't hold with hangin' women," another said.

"Then hang the 'skins, at least." Someone laughed. "Give 'em to me. I'll do it."

Without realizing that she had picked it up, Justine found a revolver in her hand. One of those Bodie had collected back in the Nations. She didn't even know if it was loaded, but she raised it and pointed it in the general direction of the men before her. "Leave us alone!" she demanded.

They were still staring at her in disbelief when a new voice spoke, behind them. Hands Bodie, afoot, had come from beyond the laden gallows. "Who's boss in this town?" he asked, his words harsh and clipped.

The first man turned to face him. "Who wants to . . ."

The fist that smashed into his face might have been an anvil, or a striking snake. Straight from the shoulder it came, and its recipient flew a yard backward and sprawled on his back, not moving. His face was a mess of blood and flattened cartilage.

"I don't want conversation," Bodie snapped. "Just an answer. Who's boss in this hayseed town?"

In stunned silence, they all turned to face him. He waited a second, then doubled the nearest one over with a gut-crushing blow to the pit of his stomach and straightened him out with an uppercut. The man fell as though poleaxed.

"Hayseeds," Bodie growled, and went straight for the one named Joey. That one had a gun half drawn from a side holster, and one of Bodie's hands closed over his gun hand while the other gripped his throat. With a quick motion, Bodie wrenched the gun hand upward, turned it, and squeezed. The gun's discharge was muffled, but blood sprayed from a sudden hole in Joey's side.

With a quick clench of the fist on Joey's throat, Bodie dropped him. The man crumpled to the ground, writhing in silent agony, his throat crushed.

"Shot himself in the gut," Bodie said. "Just like a third-rate street thug." Even as he said it, he had two others by the ears, bouncing their skulls off each other. He spun, delivered a crushing kick to another man's kneecap, and ducked as a fist went past his ear. When he came up, the man screamed. Bodie had a fistful of crotch and was lifting him off his feet by it.

The remaining two had gawked and started to run, then stopped when they found themselves staring into the muzzles of rifles held by Mason and Wendell.

The man whose private parts were at the mercy of Bodie's big fist was still screaming — a high, burbling scream that resounded off walls all around. He was on tiptoe, his arms flailing.

"Shut up," Bodie said.

The scream went on and on. With a growl, Bodie lifted the tough a foot off the ground, flipped him over, and dropped him on his head. Then, as though nothing of note had happened, he went about collecting guns. He gathered them up and tossed them into the back of Justine's wagon. His own gun, she noticed, was still in its holster at his hip.

Looking down his rifle barrel into the terrified eyes of his captive, Mason Fremont grinned as wolfish a grin as a sixteen-year-old face could manage. "You all heard the man," he said. "He wants to know who the boss is in this hayseed town."

Chapter Fourteen

It wasn't much of a town. The whole thing would have fit into the Lower East Side south of Wall Street, with room left over, and there wasn't a building that I could see that was more than three stories high. But it was a town, and it had the smell of trouble about it. The kind of smell— or feel—that a neighborhood has when a new gang has moved in and is putting down its rivals.

There was trouble here . . . and buildings. In a slight way, it felt like I'd come home. Me, myself. Not that nagging part of me that used to be somebody else. This didn't mean anything to him. But it did to me. To Hands Bodie. It was the kind of place I could survive in. The kind they trained me for, Billy Bean and the Dutchman and the rest.

I knew what to do. When you go where there's trouble, you go looking for trouble. You find it as fast as you can, and you get in the first thump, and keep on thumping until you're in charge. You attack, before they even know you're there, and you don't stop. Difference between New York City and a hayseed town is, in the city everybody knows how that works. Back when the Devil Dogs moved into Five Points, that was how they did it.

166

Up to that time, everybody knew that Five Points belonged to the Tappers. But the Devil Dogs didn't see it that way. There was good action in Five Points and they wanted it. They probably scouted the lay of the place for a month, but when they moved in it was all over in one night.

They knew where every Tapper hangout was, and all their runners' routes, and who made what moves when.

I heard that more than thirty Tappers died that night. Nobody ever knew for sure. It's the city, and who keeps count? But by the time the Devil Dog leaders walked in on the Tapper bosses—Cap Duval and Lonnie Cole—there wasn't any Tapper gang left.

They took Duval and Cole up to the roof of the ropeworks—the highest place in Five Points back then—and threw them off. It was symbolic. It let everybody around know that there was a new gang in charge now, and a new boss to say how things went.

A lot of us gave a lot of thought to how the Devil Dogs pulled that off, and it was worth it. When *we* took Five Points from them, a few months later, we did it just the way they'd taught us—except for throwing their leaders off the ropeworks. It was Sully who came up with the idea for a new symbolism. He and some others took the last three Devil Dogs down to the school sink and stuffed them into refuse pipes.

Sully was always like that. If he could make an enemy take all day to die, he would.

Nobody ever took Five Points from the Battery Boys. No other gang, anyway. Bigger things were afoot by then, and before long the gangs were all organized. We were the street arm of bigger out-fits, like Billy Bean's business, or the Immigrant League, or the Tweeds. And there were opportunities for advancement, for those with special skills.

Like me.

I thought I'd have to go hunting, to find the current gang in that hayseed town, but I didn't need to. By the time I'd found a place to tie my horse, the gang had found the schoolteacher and her brothers. It worked out just fine. They made good bait, and I took it from there.

There were six down. One was dying from a belly shot—from his own gun—and another two might not get up again. But none of them was going to be a problem for anybody, any time soon. I made sure Justine Fremont noticed that I hadn't used my gun. The fact is, I hadn't needed it. In New York I'd never have jumped a bunch like that. Gang types in New York react quickly to an attack, because they always expect an attack. But these were yokels. Slow-talking, slow-thinking woods-bunnies. They just couldn't get hold of what was happening to them, until it already had.

So I put on a show for the schoolteacher. Hands Bodie isn't a cold-blooded killer, I wanted her to believe. Hands Bodie doesn't do more than is necessary to keep the peace. Hands Bodie is a man you can trust.

I wanted her and her brothers to believe that, as long as it was convenient for me. Something kept telling me I needed them for a while, and if I would tag along with them—help them get whatever they wanted—then they would be useful. Except for them, I wouldn't have even been in that hayseed town. But since I was, and it was where the teacher thought she wanted to be, I'd pacify it for her. That was simple enough.

And if they got the idea that I was looking after them because I cared about them, so much the better.

I didn't care about them, of course. Only a fool starts caring about people. Where I'm from, caring gets you killed. What you do, you do, for what's in it for you. Nothing else matters. Justine Fremont was teaching me to read handwriting, and I wanted that. Odd, that I'd care about that. I wasn't sure why I wanted that, but I did and you go after what you want.

She would teach me to read script, and her brothers — one of them, anyway — was teaching me how to get by out here in the sticks. That much made sense to me, and if they thought I cared about them, so much the better.

There had been enough ruckus in that few seconds to draw a lot of attention, and people were coming from all over, craning their necks to see what had happened. I didn't see any more enforcer types among them, or even anyone carrying a gun, so they didn't mean anything to me. The two that still mattered were the two toughs still on their feet, and the Fremont boys had them covered.

Covered, and talking.

Like I thought, the town had a new gang. They called themselves Regulators, and they hadn't been there very long. Only since word came that the war was maybe over, and the Johnnies had lost, and there was new law in Texas. Yankee law. Martial law, they said, but this bunch wasn't soldiers. They'd just seen a chance to grab off something good — a town — in all the confusion. So they rode in and took over.

The three hanged men on the gallows were a sheriff, a town marshal, and a grocer. They were there as an example to the rest of the town.

The gang was bigger than just these eight here. There were a dozen or so more, and they had a leader. A fellow named Hayes. A shooter, they said.

"Keep an eye on the local yokels," I told the boys. "And help your sister down out of that wagon, so she can wait in the shade. I'll be back in a little while."

I took the two Regulators with me. Those good people wouldn't have known what to do with them, but I did. I hauled them along by twisted arms until we were out of sight, then I used "Tony's tag-along" on them.

It's a method of taking people where you want them to go, without trouble. I heard a fellow named Anthony Culhane thought it up. He was a Tweed captain. Whether or not it came from Big Tony, it's effective. I shoved those two up against a wall, grabbed one hand each and broke their thumbs, and stuffed their mouths full of cloth when they opened them to scream. Then I tied the two broken thumbs together with a strip of cloth, leaving enough loose for me to grab.

It only took a second or two, and after that those gentlemen would go anywhere I wanted them to go. All I had to do was tug on their lead strap.

I didn't want to waste any time with them. It was important to behead the gang before anybody knew what was happening. Only a fool stands around and waits for the enemy to realize he's at war.

170

They led me to a stone-walled building just the other side of a little spire-topped church. The stone building had a sign on it, that I couldn't read, but whatever it had been it wasn't anymore. It was Regulator headquarters now, and I could see why. Two stories high, its roof would offer a good view of the streets around, and its walls were like a fort. It was the place I would have chosen for headquarters, if I'd been bossing a gang.

There were a couple of armed toughs out front, looking curious and jumpy. Probably wondering what the ruckus was over by the square. In a minute or so they would go see, or somebody would come and tell them, but all I needed was that minute or so. I led my thumb-tagged pair right straight across and right up to them, like I had something to say.

Maybe it looked to them like the two Regulators were bringing me to them. It didn't matter. They weren't sure what they were seeing until I got there, and that was all I'd needed. I dropped the thumb-lead and rushed them. Fingers in their eyes, heels of my hands under their chins, and their skulls against the stone wall behind them. It was the kind of work I was best at back home, until I got to be a shooter.

The lower floor might have been a store at one time. Maybe it was that hanged grocer's place. There was a stairway, and voices above. I went up.

There were three of them, in a big room with whiskey bottles on the tables and piles of stuff all around – loot from the town, I guessed.

They all looked up, and I spotted the boss right off. He acted like a boss. I stopped in the doorway and said, "You must be Hayes."

He came to his feet, flipping his coattail back from a polished gun in a low-slung holster. A real yokel. Maybe a shooter, but he was acting like a boss — wasting time, glaring and posturing, sweeping that coat back so I could see his gun and be impressed.

I shot him first, then the other two. It was like the Dutchman always said, if you are going to shoot, shoot. Don't threaten, don't talk about it, don't waste time. Shoot.

That Regulator bunch wouldn't have lasted past breakfast where I came from.

It was a nice gun that Hayes had. Army Model, .44 caliber, smooth and hand-stocked and with the barrel slicked off by a gunsmith. I kept it.

They had some pickings in that upstairs room. China dishes and silver services like the ornate stuff Mrs. Jessup — the do-gooder lady from uptown, back in New York — kept in her house. There was whiskey, and tobacco, and bags of loot from people's houses. Stacks of all kinds of guns, bits of furniture, ornate thingamajigs that came from wherever the marauders had found them, pieces of jewelry, some watches, a gold-banded darkwood gavel, some lawman badges — just all kinds of things. And money. There was money in a box. I was looking at the loot when something raised my hackles and I turned. On the wall next to the door was a rainbow — a real, honest-to-God rainbow, just like in the sky, but this one was in the room with me.

And like the rainbow had called it up, there was the face again. The one in my mind — that pretty, pleading face, looking at me, trying to say something . . . and I heard myself whisper, "Don't

172

worry, Mary. Don't fret yourself. I'm on my way home to you."

It was my voice, but the words weren't mine. I didn't mean to say them, and they didn't sound like me. They were slow and drawn-out, the way Southerners talk. Just like the Johnny in the shell crater. Like it was him talking, and not me.

"Let me alone!" I said. Maybe I yelled it, because the walls echoed and the rainbow on the wall seemed to dance. "Go away and let me alone!"

The rainbow was still there, and I grabbed something to throw at it—some stuff from the nearest loot table, by the window. But something hit the floor and the rainbow was gone. The thing on the floor was a crystal-shade lamp, that I had brushed aside. I picked it up, held it by the window and there were rainbows again on the far wall. Bits and fragments of rainbows that darted here and there. One of the baubles came loose in my hand, a glass crystal the size of a pigeon egg. I held it up by itself, and when the sun came through the window to strike it, it made a rainbow on the wall.

I dropped it on the floor and hurried out. I felt confused, and dizzy. Like I had felt for a while after coming off that battlefield. Like when the hick doctor said I might have a head wound.

All I could think of was to get out of there, to get away from the rainbows . . . to get away from a dead Reb who got inside my head and wouldn't go away.

Outside, on the street, I took some deep breaths to clear my head. Then I went back inside. The job wasn't done until the symbolism was complete.

I didn't have a ropeworks to use in this hick town, and if there was a school sink I didn't know where it was . . . and anyway, that was Sully's kind of thing to do, not mine.

With the confusion faded away, I went back inside to get what I had left there.

For a few minutes, Justine had the weird feeling that she and her brothers were alone on an island with dead men and injured men. The gallows was there, with its dangling bodies, and the ground was littered with fallen toughs, and there they were in the middle of it, while other people gawked at them from safe distances.

Some of them approached, then—cautiously—and the odd picture dispersed. But even when there were people all around, staring at the Regulators strewn here and there, nobody said anything. It abruptly occurred to her that nobody could figure out what to say or even what questions to ask.

The silence was awkward, and when it had stretched to its limit Justine turned to some of the nearer townspeople and said, "Good afternoon, can someone direct me to the church?"

Mason grinned, and Wendell shook his head. "I can't believe she said that," he muttered.

It broke the ice, though. A man in the crowd stepped forward, frowned cautiously at the two "injuns," then pulled off his hat awkwardly. "How do, ma'am. I wonder if ye can tell us . . . ah . . . what happened here?"

"I'm not really sure," she admitted. "The gentleman traveling with us asked these gentlemen a question, and they didn't give him as prompt a response as he is accustomed to, so he . . . ah . . ."

"He surely did," Mason agreed. "Somebody ought to do something about these jaspers layin' around here. Some of 'em are still alive."

"But they have friends!" someone in the crowd blurted. "What will the others do when they see this?"

"Burn the town, prob'ly," another said.

"Oh, here he comes," Mason pointed. Fifty yards away, Hands Bodie appeared, coming around the corner of a building, dragging a man behind him. In silence, he approached. The man behind him was obviously dead. Blood was beginning to darken around a small hole in the center of his chest. Bodie had him by the coat collar, dragging him. The man's boot heels left little twin ruts where there was loose dirt.

"Another one," Wendell muttered.

Then someone in the crowd gasped. "It's Hayes," someone said. "That's Hayes himself he's got yonder."

Mason noticed that Bodie was wearing two guns now, each in its own rig, both holstered on the right, the new gun riding behind and below his other one.

Without more than a glance at anyone, Bodie strode to the gallows and up its steps, the dead man's heels bouncing on each riser. Atop it, he dropped the man, pulled out a knife, knelt, and cut the ropes of the three men hanged there. Their bodies crumpled to the ground beneath. Bodie chose the dangling end of the center rope, tied a loop, and picked up Hayes's body, supporting it in sitting position while he put the loop around its neck.

175

He stood, then, and kicked the Regulator leader's corpse off the platform, through the trap. The body hung high, head and shoulders above the level of the platform, but the effect was enough. Bodie turned, looked down at the townspeople, and said, "You need a new gang. This one's through."

By nightfall, the town had recovered from its shock and confusion. A committee had charge of Hall's Grocery Store and its upstairs quarters, people were lined up at the door to claim the things that had been stolen from them, and angry armed men carried torches through the streets in search of remaining Regulators. They found none.

Justine Fremont leaned on her crutch by last light, looking at the weathered little church and the overgrown lot beyond where once had stood a cozy house.

She hadn't realized until now how long it really was since she had lived here, as a child, and her father had spoken the Gospel to Sunday congregations in a church that, to her memory, had been tall, whitewashed, and tidy. Now it looked small and ill kept, though there was lamplight in its windows. People were inside—mostly women, children, and old men—thanking God for their deliverance from the Regulators.

"It isn't at all as I remember it," she said, sadly. "So much time has passed . . . so much has changed."

The man who stood beside her, hat in hand, was hunched and white-bearded. His name was Paxton, and he remembered her father. "Times change." He nodded. "Nobody much left around here from them days. Few of us, I reckon, but not

176

many. All the young ones, they been gone for years. Better times, better places. I can show you where most of Pastor Fremont's congregation is. It's yonder on that hill."

"Yes, I want to go there when there's light. My mother is buried there."

"We tried askin' around some," Wendell said, from aside where he waited, a dark shadow in the dusk. "Mostly, people won't even talk to Mason or me. They don't like us."

"Don't expect they do," Paxton said. "Some things changes with time, some don't. Not that long ago that this was all Indian land hereabouts. Now none of it is, and there's folks still remember how it came to change hands. Not happy memories. Most folks just as soon forget things like that, but it's hard to forget with Indians around."

"What do they expect?" Wendell bristled. "Do they think my brother and I are going to massacre them, like they did to the people here before?"

"That's enough, Wendell," Justine said. "It isn't Mr. Paxton's fault. He's just trying to help."

Wendell subsided. Big Sister was right, as usual. Nobody could now be blamed for what other people did, thirty years before. He wondered, though, if the old feelings in this place had something to do with their father's decision, back when Justine was a child, to take his daughter and go where the Indians were—to spend the rest of his life serving their needs in the only way he knew. Atonement? Pastor Fremont had nothing to do with driving the Indians out of East Texas. He hadn't even been here then.

But could a person feel guilt for something others did? Maybe so. These people in this town, their guilt was not their own, but it was enough to fuel a silent hatred that Wendell sensed each time they looked at him, or at his kid brother.

They turned away, Mason coming from somewhere to join them as they walked back toward the old barn where they had left their wagon and their stock.

"Will y'all stay on?" Paxton asked. "No school here right now, but there's a few young'uns could stand some teachin'."

Justine didn't answer. She felt confused and tired. For such a long time, all the way south from the Cherokee Nation, she had expected . . . what? A half-remembered dream that no longer existed?

Hands Bodie was waiting by the barn, crouched beneath a tree. "Seen enough?" he asked when Justine limped in on her crutch.

"I haven't seen very much," she said, tiredly.

"You won't, either," he said. "You can't stay here, you know."

"Can't stay? What do you mean?"

He stood, and spread long arms in a languid stretch . . . a big man, harsh and brutal in so many ways, yet with eyes that seemed to see what other eyes did not. "I give this bunch about a day and a half to get their mess here sorted out, then they'll need somebody to blame for their miseries."

"Us?" She stared at him. "Why? We . . . well, *you* . . . you gave them back their town."

"Not for long," he drawled, practicing a Texas sound in a voice whose words still came out clipped, harsh, and alien. "There'll be another gang come along. Or maybe some of these folks will form their own gang and take over. Either

178

way, *somebody's* got to get stepped on. It's how things work. Clears the air to place the blame. Won't be me, 'cause I'm leaving. So it'll be you . . . no, *y'all*. You're the only strangers around."

She glanced at Paxton, who was standing aside, looking embarrassed.

"The man's right," he said. "Be best if you was to go someplace else. Things are mighty unsettled hereabouts."

Justine shook her head, feeling as though she wanted to cry. "But I don't know any other place. Where could we go?"

"If you plan to teach me to read and write, like you promised," Hands Bodie said, losing his drawl, "then you'll have to be where I am."

"And where will that be?"

"I already told you that, lady. Hunt County. That's where I'm going."

Chapter Fifteen

On the day that Thad Carlile received his appointment as provisional superintendent of Hunt County—provisional meaning that he would serve until the occupation government was set up and permanent county jurisdictions were worked out—he walked across to the courthouse in Greenville and took charge.

There would be a time of martial law now, in Texas, and Carlile had spent nearly two years preparing for it. Only one company of Federal troops was put at his disposal, but it was enough. Without ceremony, he posted blue-clad soldiers at every entrance and had the flag of the United States of America lofted on the flagpole. Then with a squad of soldiers at his back he toured the courthouse, closed and sealed every county office except the sheriff's office and the office of tax assessor-collector.

The notice he posted on the public board just inside the rotunda was brief and to the point. The established government of Hunt County, being an instrument of the now-outlawed jurisdiction of a state recently involved in illegal rebellion, was hereby revoked. All matters affecting the conduct of county business would be under the direction of Thaddeus Carlile, Superintendent, until further notice. Done by order of the Commanding General, the Army of Occupation, Texas Theater.

Without ceremony, Carlile appointed Vince Terrell as provisional high sheriff of the county, with powers of arrest, detention, search and seizure, and various other authorities as directed by the superintendent. Terrell's first act was to seal all assets of the county's three banks as bond against expenses of the new order, following which Carlile issued vouchers for the employment of deputies.

The deputies would be chosen by Terrell. A deputy himself for nearly two years, back when old Ty Carlile had run the county, Terrell had later spent some time on the other side of the jail bars, thanks to certain citizens.

Vince Terrell knew where to find the kind of deputies he would need.

The job of tax assessor-collector, Carlile gave to Reuben Blaes, a former crony of the Carliles in the old days. Blaes had been the "banker" for Ty Carlile and Uncle Jim Carlile, and had worked with Thad Carlile in the courthouse. He had a knowledge of deed records and tax rolls, and had kept records for the local militia units at the time the war broke out. Blaes knew who had gone to war, and who had not come back. And Blaes had reasons of his own to hate certain of the county's upstanding citizens.

With law, order, and finance thus accounted for, Carlile sent a message off to Jay Miller, up in the Choctaw Nation. The Nations were full of white renegades willing to use their fists and their guns for pay, and Carlile was going to need men.

181

He spent several days, then, driving around the county in a shiny buggy — with a squad of soldiers following him — looking at the properties subject to his administration. In a leather-bound folio, he carried Reuben Blaes's roster of Confederate volunteers, matched to deed records from the tax collector's office. As he toured the county he made notes to himself. It had been a long time coming, but now it was time to settle some scores. He had a list of those who had opposed the Carlile regime years before, and now he matched that list against property and residence rolls and old militia rosters, and licked his lips.

There were just a lot of people who were going to regret that they had ever offended the Carliles.

Moss Jackson was mending fence above Cove Creek. Maybe Willie had set up the broken section a few days earlier — he said he did — but it was down again now and Moss had decided to do it himself. It was easier than fussing with Willie and Jess.

Split-rail fence it was, the same fence that he had helped Sam Austin and the boys to build, all those years before. It seemed such a long time ago. Tom was just starting to get his growth, and David was still a gawky kid with legs longer than his britches. Both of them would be big men, like their father. Moss remembered thinking that, and he remembered the quiet pride that Sam took in watching his sons do a man's work. That was back when they were still stumping and clearing, still building the spread that was Sam Austin's dream.

So long ago. Yet, as he tugged at rails and reassembled them on the cross-beam uprights, Moss was pleased at the weight of the timbers. Silver-gray with age and weather, still they were sturdy rails, down only because their supports had been knocked over— pushed, roped down? He couldn't tell. There were seeps here above Cove Creek, and maybe the ground just gave way beneath them.

But the posts were reset now, done right, and should stand. And the rails were strong and sturdy. Weathered and gray and honest and still plenty tough, he thought. Just like old Sam had been, right up to the last few days of his life. Just like Moss, himself, he realized. The land here made trees that could be split into lasting rails. Maybe it made men the same way. Sam was gone, but there was still Tom, and there was still David.

He *hoped* the boys were all right. There still was no word of them. Defeated soldiers had been making their way home to Texas for months now, and some dispatches had come listing men dead or wounded, and those taken prisoner. But still there was no word of the Austin boys. No word, for that matter, of any of their company.

Mary Austin was worried. She tried not to show it, but Moss saw clearly that she was. And he knew that Maude Carver saw it, too. Mary tried not to let on, busying herself with the constant chores of a shorthanded spread, and with the constant tending of little Davey. But in her eyes, sometimes, there was a deep, silent fear . . . the fear that something might have happened to David. The fear that where her young husband had gone off to war, maybe nobody would come back.

War and feuds, Moss thought, shaking his head. Whatever kind of fightin' it is, fightin' is always hardest on the women.

The heaviest rail was a top span trimmed from an entire ash bole. Nearly twenty feet long, it had spanned the deep of the draw. Now it lay aslant, just below the uprights that had supported it. Moss studied it, tried to lift it, then set about laying poles at angle against the uprights on both sides. When he had them in place, he tied ropes to the big span, halfway between the middle and each end, then led his old mule around above the gap and secured both ropes to her saddle horn. "Come along, Sal," he said. "Your turn to do some liftin'."

With the angled poles as skids, he worked the big span upward, Sal leaning into the pull. The slender end reached the top first, and Moss used a pry bar to drop it into its cradle. He puffed with exertion, pausing to catch his breath, eased down to the bottom of the gully, then turned to complete the task. Just a few feet away, above him on the lip of the draw, three horsemen sat their saddles, gazing down at him.

The foremost of them, a big-bellied man with a wolfish grin, said, "Will you just look at this, boys? An old man and an old mule, tryin' to raise a timber."

Moss bristled. "What do you want here, Kale?"

"That ain't any way to be talkin' to an officer of the law, old man," the grinning one said. With a languid hand he opened his vest, letting Moss see the stamped badge on his shirt. "I'm the one that asks the questions. Not you."

Moss frowned at the badge. On Kale White, it

184

looked absurd. White and his buddies were good-for-nothing lowlifes, not lawmen. Moss shook his head. "I don't know what kind of game you're at, Kale, but there ain't a man in this state that would give you a badge."

"There is now." Kale's grin widened. "The new High Sheriff of Hunt County, Vince Terrell. I reckon y'all over here in the uplands don't keep track of things too well."

"Terrell?" Moss felt the blood drain from his weathered cheeks. "Vince Terrell is sheriff? I don't believe it."

"Don't matter what you believe, old man. He is, and we're his deputies. Now, what do you think you're doin' out here? You think that fence belongs to you?"

"It's Austin fence," Moss said. "I'm tendin' the Austin place 'til Tom gets home."

"Are you, now?" Kale's grin disappeared. "You know this is questioned property, old man?"

"I heard about Thad Carlile's list. I don't know what the hell it means."

"Well, it means that this might belong to Tom Austin, or it might not. Deeds has got to be verified, by superintendent's order, and no Tom Austin has showed up at the courthouse to swear a statement. This property here might belong to just most anybody, you see, and I don't believe you've got call to go tamperin' with fences here."

"I'm not tampering! I'm fixing!"

Kale eased his horse forward, leaning to put a large finger on the loop of rope holding the top rail. "Is this your rope here?"

"Damn right it's my rope!"

"Is that your mule?"

185

"It sure enough is."

"Well, you see the problem, then, don't you? Your rope, on your mule, tied to a fence rail that sure isn't yours. Old man, we wouldn't be doin' our jobs as deputies if we let a thing like that go by." With a vicious grin, Kale grasped the loop of the snag and tugged on it. The rope slipped, then came loose and Moss tried to dodge aside as the rail swung down toward him. His foot slipped, and the heavy timber knocked him against the far wall of the cut and pinned him there. He felt a bone break in his leg, and pain washed over him. Pain and blackness.

Suddenly released from the weight of the rail, Sal staggered a step. Rope sliding off her saddle horn snapped against her side, and she jumped aside and bolted. Behind her a gunshot sounded, then another. Empty stirrups flailing, the mule dug in her hooves and headed for shelter.

At the gully, Kale White put away his pistol, irritated at having missed two shots at a running mule. The boys might rag him about that, about missing a target that size. He didn't think they would, though. He might not be good with a handgun, but there weren't many men who would stand up to his fists.

The others were looking down at the old man pinned under the timber below. "He might be dead," one said. "Vince didn't say to kill anybody."

"Accidents happen." Kale shrugged. "Old fool got hisself caught by a slipped post, that's all. Ain't it a shame?"

Without further words, he wheeled his mount and rode away, the others following him.

When Sal showed up alone, Jess and Willie went to look. It was sundown when they found Moss Jackson, and a half hour past when they got the buckboard to the draw and loaded him aboard. The nearest house was David Austin's, so Jess took him there while Willie went for Maude Carver.

By lantern light the old woman set his leg and bound his ribs, while the others watched. Moss drifted in and out of consciousness, mumbling and groaning. Only once did he speak. "Kale White," he said. "That varmint did it. Says Vince Terrell is sheriff now. They had badges." He closed his eyes and drifted off again.

Maude wiped sweat from his brow with a cool cloth, then turned away. "He'll be all right," she said. "Take more than that to kill this old fool, but he'll need tendin'." She squinted at the bandages she had applied, then shook her head. With the moist cloth covering her hand, she removed the soot-darkened globe from the nearest lamp, set it aside, and took down a clean one to replace it. It made the room brighter.

"We shouldn't move him," Mary Austin decided. "Leave him here for a while. I can look after him."

"You got your hands full with that baby," Maude said. "Lay me out a pallet on the floor yonder. I'll stay. You all"—she turned to Willie and Jess—"you get on over to the main house and look after things."

Jess and Willie glanced at each other. "Moss said it was Kale White done that," Willie said.

"Said Vince Terrell is sheriff an' they're law."

"So?"

Willie scuffed the floor with a boot toe. "Well, it's just . . ."

"It's just that we hired on as hands," Jess filled in. "That's all."

"So go and do what you're paid to do," Maude snapped. "Nobody's askin' more."

"Yes, ma'am." They turned and filed out.

"Come trouble, they'll run." Maude sighed. "I expect your hands will, too, Mary. Wish I knew how to keep 'em, but what's happenin' here in this county—Thad Carlile's doin', most likely—well, honey, men generally ain't any better'n they have to be, 'specially skittish ones like ranch hands. They'll dig a well if they have to, or nail up a roof patch or mind the critters, but the only way they face up to trouble is if there's a lead bull in the herd to show 'em what gumption looks like. Without that, men are no more than dust on the wind. An' we're real short on lead bulls around here, seems to me."

"David will be home soon," Mary said. "I just know he will. And Tom, too."

Maude turned away, not answering. The girl was right to hope, but Maude knew better. Instinctively, she knew that if the Austin men were coming home, there would have been word by now. They weren't coming home. It had to be faced. Mary had to face it. With a sigh of deep regret, she turned. "Mary, honey, I . . ."

But Mary wasn't listening. The girl stood rapt, her sleeping baby at her shoulder. She stared wide-eyed at the closed door. Maude turned to look. The lantern's flame sparkled on a ripple in its

188

clean glass globe. On the front wall, across the door, were bands of colored light. Like a rainbow.

"He's coming," Mary said, as though only to herself. "Oh, Maude, see . . . David is coming home."

Chapter Sixteen

"How do you spell 'Sully'?"

Justine blinked, eased the draft reins, and looked around. Behind the wagon seat, Hands Bodie was sprawled on a pile of blankets, resting on his elbows and frowning at a piece of paper half covered with careful scrawls. In his right hand, seeming wholly out of place there, was a graphite pencil.

Hills and woodlands crept by as they rolled along an overgrown westward road where little, blue-gray rain showers strode upon the lowering hills and the morning meadows. Somewhere ahead, out of sight beyond a curve, Mason and Wendell rode, scouting the trail.

Justine looked back again. "Sully? Do you mean, like to soil or spoil something?"

"No. I mean a name. His name is Sullivan, but everybody calls him Sully."

"Oh. Well, I suppose it would be the same spelling. S-U-L-L-Y."

Behind her he scribbled on his paper, his tongue peeking from the side of his mouth in concentration. "Two L's, huh? Why not just one?"

"It's a phonetic rule," she said. "Remember, I told you how some letters determine the sounds of the letters next to them? If it only had one L, then the letter U just ahead of it would sound like double-O. Sooly."

"No, they call him Sully. So it's a double-L, then." He bent to his writing again.

Justine noticed that he was keeping his lines straight, and was no longer having trouble with the connective script. He was learning remarkably fast, as though he were obsessed with the learning. "What are you writing?" she asked.

"I'm writing about where I come from and how I came to be here. You said to write what I know, so that's what I'm doing."

"You're writing about yourself? That's called autobiography."

"Whatever," he muttered, absorbed in his work. Since leaving Pleasant Hill, he had concentrated on writing. The first few pages of script had been rough and ill formed, but he had improved and now page after filled page went into the leather valise that he had picked up somewhere, and he no longer asked her to read them, to correct them. He wrote, and what he wrote he put away without showing it to anyone.

Mason and Wendell were in sight again, just topping a hill ahead. The wagon rolled along comfortably on the grassed-over road.

"You think I'm crazy, don't you?"

The abrupt question startled Justine and she looked around again. Bodie was putting another finished page into his valise.

"It's all right," he said. "You won't be the first

one to think I'm crazy. Maybe I am, I don't know. But everything is changing so fast . . ."

"*You're* changing," she admitted. "Sometimes you're . . . well, like when we first met you . . ."

"A wild animal, you said."

"Well, yes. Some ways. But more often now, it's as though you were some other person entirely. Your speech changes, your mannerisms . . ."

"I *am* some other person," he said, sounding sad. "I told you, sometimes . . . somehow . . . I'm that reb. David Allen Austin. I know that's crazy, too, but he's here. He's here with me and I can't get rid of him. I'm not even sure I want to, anymore." He paused, frowning in thought. "I like him better than me," he muttered.

"You like yourself when you feel like him," Justine tried to rationalize. "Maybe you have put an idea together in your mind, of how you would like to be, and maybe that man just . . . well, kind of came to represent all that."

"Sure," he growled, the harsh, urban Yankee clip suddenly returning to his words. "Sure, and I dreamed up his wife's hair color, too, and . . ."

"You might have," she pointed out. "You have a picture in your mind of how you think she might appear, but imagination is like that, Mr. Bodie."

". . . and dreamed up this road we're on, that I never saw before, but I know there's a fork just ahead with a signpost that points to Greenville to the right and Lone Oak to the left."

"You couldn't possibly know something like that," she reasoned.

"We'll see," he said. "The post is horse high

192

and the two signs are crosscut lumber, with the names burned into it. Maybe there's no such thing, but *he* thinks there is. And the fork to Lone Oak is the one that takes him home."

He got out a fresh sheet of paper and started writing again. Justine sighed, wondering for the thousandth time what sort of strange processes went on in the big man's head. "Well, at least you're enjoying learning to write," she said, finally.

"No, I'm not," he snapped. "I'm writing about home. Mine, not his. And it's ugly. How do you spell Dutchman?"

She spelled out the word for him. "Is the Dutchman a friend of yours?"

"No."

"If you don't like writing all that, you could practice writing something else," she suggested.

"No, I need to write this," he said, sounding puzzled. "I *need* to."

"Why?"

For a long time, he didn't respond. Then he said, "Because he matters. The reb, he *matters*. And because I don't matter. I never did. But he does, and it feels good to matter. He doesn't even know how it would be, not to. People know about him. People care where he is . . ."

"You said he was dead."

"He is. But people don't know that, and they care about him and when they know he died they'll care about that, too. Don't you understand? *He matters*. Maybe if I write down about Callahan Bodie, maybe someday somebody will care about *him*, too."

193

"I care, Mr. Bodie," she said softly. "And Mason cares, and even Wendell . . ."

"No, you don't. You don't know enough to care, and if you knew more you'd care even less."

"Then why are you writing it down?" she snapped, irritated at the man's everlasting rudeness, his callous verbal slaps.

"Because I feel like it," he said. "Shut up."

Two people. Justine shook her head and concentrated on the road. Sometimes he spoke softly, with a comfortable drawl that became more natural each time he used it, and at those times she sensed a young man with an eye for beauty, an ear for music, an easygoing toughness cloaked in real gentleness. Then, abruptly, he would change, and it was difficult in the extreme to find anything at all likable about the side of him that called itself Hands Bodie. That side of him—that person—was cynical and barbaric, a murderer, a casual, ruthless killer to whom no one and nothing seemed to matter in the slightest. Not even himself.

Like two people. For all the world, like two entirely different, separate people.

Clouds drifted above the brushy trees, flowing their shadows over the contours of the land. In the near distance ahead a little shower crossed a hilltop and crept on, a soft cloud-hand wielding a misty whisk broom in exquisite slow motion.

"This is mine," Bodie said.

"What?"

"Nothing. I just said, 'this is mine.' The land, I mean. But it isn't. Saying so doesn't make it mine. I tried before. Who'd want it, anyway?

194

Bunch of yokels." Behind her, Justine heard paper rustle. "I better write that, too," he said.

"I expect you had better," she murmured, wondering where Mason and Wendell were now. Somewhere not far ahead, she knew, but the old road wound here and there and they were seldom in sight.

"How do you spell Joslyn?"

"Pete Joslyn? Ah . . . J-O-S-L-Y-N, I think. You're writing about him, too?"

"I will. He thinks he's good with a gun. He thinks he can kill me."

"Mr. Joslyn? Really, Mr. Bodie, I'm sure Mr. Joslyn wouldn't want to kill you. He seems like a decent enough man."

"I didn't say he wants to. But he thinks he can. Poor, dumb yokel. Best for him if he never has reason to try. He wouldn't have a chance. And he doesn't even know it. What's a drifter?"

"Drifter? It means a footloose person. Someone who just . . . drifts around."

"That sounds right. He said him and those others are just like dust on the wind, now they're out of the war. Drifters. That other one, Wilson, he said drifters are dust on the wind."

Ahead, Mason appeared atop a rise, waiting for them. When they approached, he waved and came to ride beside the wagon. "The road forks yonder," he said. "Which way, Big Sister? Right or left?"

"Left," Bodie said. "To Lone Oak, like the sign says."

"There isn't any sign. Just a place where the road forks."

195

Bodie didn't answer. Justine snapped reins to urge her team up the rise, Mason trailing along. Just beyond the crest was a fork, where the old road became two, one continuing west, the other angling southwest. Wendell's horse stood ground-reined beside the trail, and something moved in the brush beyond. Wendell emerged from shadows there, carrying a broken post with slabs nailed to it.

"This must have been a sign," Wendell said, holding it up. "It was off there in the weeds."

The wood was old, splintered, and weathered, but the burned-in messages were still clear. GREENVILLE, the upper plank read. And the one below it, at an angle, said LONE OAK.

"I told you," Hands Bodie said. "Now do you believe me? That left fork leads to home."

"What's he talkin' about . . . home?" Wendell squinted at him, then at Justine. "Whose home?"

"David Allen Austin's . . . he says," Justine said.

"Mine," Bodie said.

"My lord." Wendell turned toward Mason. "He's back on *that* nonsense again."

Bodie clambered from the wagon's covered bed and unhitched his horse from the tailgate. As nimbly as one raised to the saddle, he swung aboard and necked-reined the animal aside, staring off into the distance. Then he touched heels to the mount, reined full circle, and set off at a controlled trot, down the right-hand trail.

"He said left," Wendell snapped. "Didn't he just this minute say left?"

Mason was already in motion, following after

the New Yorker. Thoroughly confused, Justine stared after them. The old road wound away, westward, and beyond — where the rains had passed — was a spire of color, pointing like a beacon. It was not a complete arc, only a portion of one side of a rainbow, but it pointed downward, past distant hills, and Bodie was following it.

"That jasper is crazy as a loon," Wendell said. "Now where's he goin'?"

"I don't know," Justine admitted. "But I guess we had best follow along."

Two hundred yards down the hill, Mason caught up to Bodie and reined alongside. "I thought you wanted to take the left-hand trail, to Lone Oak," he said. "This is the right-hand trail. This goes to Greenville."

"That's right," the big man said, his easy drawl as Texas-sounding as any Mason had heard. "Six-seven miles yonder. County seat of Hunt County. Got business at the court . . ." He paused, and looked around. His scarred face creased in bewilderment. "I don't know where I'm going," he muttered. "Courthouse? Why the courthouse?"

"I don't know." Mason shrugged. "I'm just followin' . . ."

But Bodie seemed not to hear. "Trouble?" He frowned. "Trouble for her . . . for Mary? What?" He paused, seeming awkward in the saddle, seeming lost and confused. Then, "You'll get me killed, is what you'll do."

Mason pressed close, staring at him. "Mr. Bodie, I don't . . ."

"Leave me alone," the man said.

Mason started to back away, but Bodie didn't

197

seem to be speaking to him at all.

"You're dead!" Bodie's cry was a roar. "Can't you just . . . be dead and leave me alone? I know it was a mistake, it should have been me, not you, but that isn't how it went! But you . . . yes, damn it, you matter. She needs you, so you matter. But if I let go, you'll get me killed. You don't know anything about . . . you don't know shit!" He squeezed his eyes closed and shook his head as though trying to shake ghosts away. "You need me, too," he whispered. "You'll need what I know how to do, because you don't."

Perplexed, Mason Fremont rode alongside. He wanted to help. Whatever the big man's problem, he wanted to help him with it, but he didn't know how. Too Indian not to sense that something very real and very critical was happening, Mason was too white to grasp what it was.

Bodie rode in ashen-faced silence for several minutes, seeming completely unaware of the world around him. Then he took a deep breath and nodded. "Maybe it will work," he said, to no one but himself. "Maybe we . . . maybe I can handle it that way."

On a rainy morning near midday, Mary Austin wheeled Moss Jackson's old wagon along the street called Highland Road, and reined in at a hitch rail in the lot next to the courthouse. It seemed a long time since she had been in Greenville. A year or more, she thought. No, it was more than two years. She hadn't been up the road from Lone Oak since the day David rode off with his militia company. On that day the little town had seemed lively and boisterous. There had been banners flying, and a drum and bugle band playing, and people everywhere on the streets.

It was different now. The town seemed sullen and wary. Few people were about, and their faces were as bleak as the clouds overhead. Some of them. There were others, too. Men here and there, gathered under awnings and in doorways — languid men who wore guns and seemed out of place in a quiet little town like Greenville.

Carrying her old leather-bound case — David's case — under her arm, Mary walked the short distance to the courthouse entrance. There were men there, just standing around out of the weather, and she lowered her eyes and started past them. A large arm blocked her way, and she looked up. One of the men had thrust out his arm and was leaning against the door wall, grinning at her. "Well, now," he said. "Pretty little thing out on a day like this? I'll just bet you're all cold an' wet, missy. I'll bet you could use a little . . ."

"That's enough of that, Frank," a voice behind her said. "Leave the lady alone."

The man blocking her way looked up, over her head, and his eyes went ugly. "You say somethin' to me, Joslyn?"

"You heard me," the quiet voice behind her said. "Get out of her way."

"And what if I don't?"

Mary glanced around as the man behind eased up beside her. Strong, gentle fingers took her shoulder and eased her aside. The man was middle-aged, slender, and tough-looking, and his gaze didn't waver from the eyes of Frank. "Oh, you

199

will," he said, quietly, "One way or another. It's your choice, Frank."

For a moment Frank just stared at him, then he averted his eyes and backed away from the door. "You're gonna push it too far, Joslyn," he muttered. "I'm warnin' you."

"Any time you're ready, Frank," the older one said. Then he turned his back on Frank, removed his hat, and smiled down at Mary. "You go on about your business, miss," he said. "Nobody here will bother you."

"Thank you," she whispered, and hurried past, into the courthouse.

The place seemed mostly deserted, but she heard voices coming from upstairs and followed them to the second floor. A man at a desk behind a rail glanced up. "Can I help you, ma'am?"

"I . . . I've come about the deed registration," she said. "The notice we got, it said our land has to be rerecorded."

"Talk to Reuben Blaes." The man pointed. "Right through that door."

Mary entered a large room. A portly man sat at a big, wooden desk, his feet propped up between stacks of paper. Several other men stood or sat around the room, most of them the out-of-place-seeming types like those downstairs. A term she had heard somewhere came to mind, and seemed to fit. Gunmen. Hired gunmen.

The man at the desk looked up, his eyes lingering on her face. "Yes?"

"I've come for the deed registration," she said again. "Our land . . . the paper said to come here."

"The notice was to owners of record, Miss . . ."

"Mrs. Mrs. David Austin."

"*Missus*, then." The man shrugged. "Are you the owner of record?"

"My husband is," she said. "And his brother. The two places are side by side, down near Lone Oak. I have the papers here . . ."

"Then your husband and his brother need to come in," the man said, shaking his head. "I can't deal with . . . Austin?" his eyes came up again, narrowed now. "You said, David Austin?"

"Yes, sir. And his brother, Tom. I have the papers."

"Well, my, my. I recollect those names, sure enough I do. Old Sam's boys, right? Way I hear it, missy, they ain't neither one of them around. What I hear is, they might have gone off to participate in an illegal revolution against their gover'ment. I hear they just never made it back, so I don't see how they can claim to own real property in this county. Especially not if they ain't even here to claim anything."

Loud noises echoed through the building, raised voices and sudden slamming, crashing sounds. All the men in the room looked toward the door. After a moment, the man from the outside desk looked in. "Something going on downstairs, Reuben. I don't know what."

Blaes waved a hand. "You men, go take a look," he ordered.

Most of the other men in the room hurried out. Mary waited a moment, then when it was obvious that Blaes was ignoring her, she stepped to the rail and slapped the leather-bound case

201

down on it. "Sir, I insist on registering the deeds," she said.

He looked up, frowning. "You don't understand, I guess. The properties here are in question. That means the superintendent has given strict orders that they can't be registered unless the owner of record or his next of kin signs the register, personal."

"And if they are not registered?"

"Why, then, the superintendent will decide what to do with 'em. An' you know, Mr. Carlile has got a right special interest in the Austin places. Personal interest, you might say."

Mary bit her tongue, trying to hold her temper. It was obvious the man was intentionally blocking her compliance with county orders. "And what does 'in question' mean, exactly?"

"It means the land belongs to a Johnny Reb that had the misfortune not to make it home, where all might be forgiven. Can't forgive a dead man, now, can we?"

The voice from the doorway behind Mary was deep and slow, with a well-remembered drawl that made her breath catch in her throat. "Get out your register," it said, "or get out your gun."

Blaes's startled eyes stared past her, and Mary turned. Her eyes went wide. "D . . . David? Are you . . . ?"

"It's all right, Mary," the big man said, with a voice that might — almost — have been David's voice, hard eyes reassuring in a scarred face that might — almost — have been David's face.

"Who . . . ?"

"We'll talk later," he said, stepping to her side.

"We have business, first." He reached across the rail and engulfed Reuben Blaes's cravat and shirt-front in a big fist, hauling the portly man to his feet with ease. "The register," he said quietly.

Two of the armed men had remained, and those were on their feet now, but not moving. Mary saw that there was another man in the room, just inside the door. A youngster with a grinning Indian face and a rifle held ready. "Don't interrupt the gentleman," he warned the gun-toters.

Reuben Blaes's face had gone dark purple, and his mouth opened and closed like a fish out of water. The newcomer held him, strangling, for a moment, then shoved him back down into his chair. "The David Allen Austin property," he said. "And the Tom Austin property. Mary, show him the deed papers."

Stunned and silent, she took out the instruments and started to hand them across.

"No," he said. "Just show them." To Blaes, "You can see these just fine, can't you? Good. Fill in the register."

Blaes hesitated, bug-eyed, and abruptly found himself staring into the muzzle of a large pistol. Aside, one of the gunmen gasped and the other muttered, "Lord a 'mercy." Neither had seen the gun drawn. It was just there.

At the doorway, the Indian-looking kid glanced out and said, "Better get a move on, mister. The gentleman is in a hurry."

Blaes wrote in the register, and Mary noticed the big man beside her was watching carefully, his lips moving as he interpreted the script. David had never done that, and yet . . .

"That's fine," the man said. "Both properties."

"But you . . ." Blaes started, then winced as the gun's hammer went back. "I mean, which one are you, David or Tom?"

"Well, now, maybe I'm both," the man drawled. "Always room for one more, I guess. *Do it!*"

"Y . . . yes, sir."

He scribbled, then handed the register across. The man put away his gun, took the pen, and slowly, painstakingly, signed both registrations. *David A. Austin,* and *Thomas Austin.*

"You'll want receipts," the Indian youth said.

"Right. Receipts." The gun appeared again, as if by magic, and Blaes wrote hurried receipts.

The big man took them, handed them to Mary, put away his gun again, and stepped to where the two gunmen stood, frozen in place. Without hesitation or warning he drove a hard fist into the face of the nearest one. The man crumpled and sprawled on the floor.

"Clumsy," the big man said.

The second gunman was staring at him. "It's you," he whispered. "It *is* you."

"Yeah, I know," the stranger said. "You need the same, Rudy?"

The red-haired one shook his head, pulled out his gun, and tossed it aside.

"You boys are in bad company," the man said. "Tell Joslyn I said so." Turning away, he took Mary's arm and led her out of the room. The Indian youth closed the door and followed, grinning.

Reuben Blaes still sat at his desk, shaking,

when some of the other men came back in. "Hell of a mess downstairs," one said. "Somebody kicked down the service door, broke up some furniture . . . what's the matter with you? You look like you seen a ghost."

Reuben Blaes didn't answer. He didn't know exactly what he had seen.

Chapter Seventeen

"But who *is* he? I mean, who is he *really?*"

Mary Austin felt as though the world had just gone crazy. From the moment the man—the one who looked like David, but not quite—had appeared at the courthouse, nothing had made sense. She had her registered deeds, and the registrar's receipts. She had been whisked from the courthouse through a side door, across a rainy lot, and into the back of an unfamiliar wagon with a pleasant-faced, middle-aged woman at the reins. Now the wagon was rolling southward on the Lone Oak road, with her own wagon—Moss Jackson's wagon—coming along behind. The Indian-looking youth, whose name was Mason, was driving it, and there was another Indian-looking youth—Wendell—riding guard ahead.

"His name is Callahan Bodie," the woman—Justine Fremont was her name, and the Indians were her half brothers—told her. "That's who he *really* is. But I believe he *thinks* he is your husband, David. Or he thinks part of him is. It is very strange, but it makes sense in a way. He was with your husband when he died."

And that was another part of the shock. Mary

had suspected for a long time that David would not come home. In a way, she had known it, and the grief she masked behind a facade of optimism—mostly for the sake of those around her—was real. Still, there had been the rainbows. Rainbows at the oddest times and places, like omens.

But now to hear—from strangers—that David was, indeed, dead . . . it hurt with a numbness that would last until it was set free to hurt and heal.

Justine Fremont had seen the pain in her eyes, and as they rolled along the road Justine had talked to her. Mile after mile, the woman had talked, letting Mary take shelter in the sound of a caring voice, letting her grasp the parts of it that she wanted to, or save it all for later.

It was a kindness, and after a time it took her mind off her grief. And into puzzlement.

"I have some notions about what might really have happened," Justine said "When we first found Mr. Bodie he was in a bad way, and had come a long way without attention. I don't know what all happened to him back there, but I know he had a head injury, and that can do strange things sometimes. He was with your husband the night your husband died, and I think he may not have been sure which one of them died, for a while. He said he heard your . . . heard David . . . talk. About you, about home, about rainbows. He said he didn't pay any attention, but he was hurt, too, and maybe he doesn't know how much he heard . . . or how it affected him. Maybe

207

everything he knows about David Allen Austin, is from your letter and from things your husband said when he was dying."

Mary felt tears in her eyes again, and Justine handed her a cloth. "Here," she said. "I'll shut up and let you alone if you want."

"No." Mary sniffed, wiping her eyes. "No, please. Talk to me. It does help."

"Some things I can't explain." Justine shrugged. "He didn't know how to write, and wanted to learn. I showed him how. But I can't believe a person could learn so fast, and so well. He says the . . . other part of him, the part he thinks is your husband . . . knows how to write, so he just picked it up. I don't know . . ."

"Maybe . . ." Mary sniffed again, gaining control of her emotions. "Maybe he knew how to write, before, and just forgot."

"Maybe." Justine shrugged again. "Anyway, he has been writing. About himself, and about his experiences. He doesn't show me what he writes, but I've looked at parts of it. I can't imagine the sort of life he must have had, before going off to war. It's, well, it's very ugly. But there is beauty in it, too. He is convinced that he has seen your face before—like in dreams or something—for years."

"Can that be?"

"Who knows? The better I get to know Hands Bodie the less certain I am about anything. It could be, I suppose, that he *has* had a dream face in his mind. Possibly since he was a child. And maybe it—the image—was vague enough that when he saw you, your face became that face."

"He'd know that, though, wouldn't he? I mean, if it became clear only when he saw me? I mean, he couldn't have ever seen me before, yet he recognized me at the courthouse. As quickly as . . . as David would have."

"Your hair?" Justine suggested. "He knew you had auburn hair. He told me. He said that proved he was David Allen Austin, for how else could he have known the color of your hair?"

"How could he?"

"Who knows what your husband might have told him, that night on the battlefield? Who knows what he might have heard and remembered, even if he didn't remember hearing it? He's a strange man, Mrs. Austin . . ."

"Mary, please."

"Mary, then. Hands Bodie is a strange man, and I know he has been badly hurt. What baffles me just now is, how did he know you would be in that town back there, and at the courthouse. How did he know exactly where you were?"

Mary shook her head. "It was strange, back there. For a moment, I thought . . . well, I almost thought he *was* David. He seemed so like him, sounded so like him, and with his face scarred that way, it seemed he might have been . . . but there was something more. Something cold and belligerent and . . . and *brutal* about him. Something frightening."

"Hands Bodie." Justine nodded. "That part of him is nobody else. Like an animal, crouched and ready to spring."

"Yes. Exactly like that. I had the feeling that he

209

was very dangerous."

"He is," Justine said. "Yes, he is dangerous. But I don't think he is a danger to us."

"He got my deeds recorded. I couldn't get the man to do that, but he did." Mary looked around, "Where is he now? I haven't seen him since he put me in your wagon."

"Oh, he's around somewhere. He'll show up. If he doesn't, Mason will go and find him."

"Mason likes him, doesn't he."

"Like a mother hen likes a stray chick," Justine agreed. "Wendell doesn't care for him, or says he doesn't. But that's how Wendell is."

"Your brothers look like Indians."

"They are. Half Cherokee. Their mother was Cherokee."

"I haven't seen many Indians. I don't think there are very many in Texas, except the wild ones out west. There." She pointed. "That's our road yonder. That's our place. Tom's place is just beyond it." She paused, and again the world was a hazy blur of sudden tears. *Our* place? *My* place, I guess, now. Mine and Little Davey's. And Tom's dead, too?"

"So it seems. I am truly sorry, Mary. That awful war."

Justine turned her team into the winding lane toward the house, and Mary glanced back. Behind them, Mason was following with the buckboard. As he turned, he also looked back, into the misty distance. Looking for Hands Bodie.

* * *

210

After Bodie led Mary Austin out of the court-house and saw the two wagons safely on their way, he pulled his hat down lower in front and muttered, "All right, you happy now? Then back off. It's my turn."

He turned full around, sizing up the town in a long glance. Eyes accustomed to buildings and people, to reading the subtleties of streets and alleys, fences and walls, and to reading the nuances of expression, position, and posture of the people among the structures, took it all in. "Hick town," he muttered. "Yokels."

But there was something different here, from the other little Texas town. Here the gang in charge was different, and the townspeople—the herd—were different. Cowed and silent, like people always were when a gang took territory, but here there was a deep resentment, a barely contained anger that waited just below the fear.

Like the old Third Ward, he thought. Like when the Blood Gang came back, after the people there ran them out. The Blood Gang had been gone for more than a year from the streets of Third Ward, but people on those streets remembered. And when the Blood Gang came back in force, to retake their territory, the people on the streets were outraged. There wasn't much they could do, of course. The Tweeds were backing the Bloods by then, and nobody wanted to buck Tammany Hall. But there was an alert, watchful atmosphere and the Bloods were smart enough to recognize it. They held the Third Ward, but carefully. No rampaging, no rape-and-burn stuff.

The Bloods knew that the people they were squeezing would stand for only so much, and beyond that it was anybody's guess what might happen. Always, just below the surface, the Bloods—and even the Tweeds and their trained bulls—knew that the people of the Third Ward would only stand for so much.

"Like that here, now," Bodie told himself. Making up his mind, he started for the front of the building. He had almost reached the corner when a man came around it, frowned at him, and stopped. A big man, barrel-chested and big-bellied, he wore a shiny badge. He stared at Bodie for a moment, noticing the big .44 at his hip, and said, "I ain't seen you. You one of Mr. Carlile's boys?"

"No," Bodie said, starting past him.

The man stepped into his path. "Civilians ain't allowed to carry . . ." A fist like an anvil collided with his face, and he rocked backward on folding legs and dropped, out cold.

Bodie went on, as though nothing had happened. Around the corner, he came to the main entryway of the courthouse. There were men there, some just lounging around, some peering inside with idle curiosity. As Bodie approached, several of them looked him over, and one—Pete Joslyn—grinned.

"You," the Texan said. "You have anything to do with the rumpus in there, by any chance?"

"I'm not in there, am I? What rumpus?"

"Not sure. Somebody just recorded some deeds at gunpoint, is what I hear." He raised a knowing

212

brow, still grinning. "Somebody named Austin. Seems to me that's a familiar name."

A heavy-shouldered man near Joslyn glared at Bodie. "Who's this? Somebody you know?"

"We crossed the Red together," Joslyn said.

"That don't mean anything. You." The man pinned Bodie with a threatening glare. "Who are you?"

Bodie ignored him. "Who's the boss in this place?" he asked Joslyn.

"Fella named Thad Carlile. He's hirin' men, if you want a job."

"I don't want a job. You just tell him I said to stay away from Mary Austin."

The other man's frown became a snarl. "I asked you a question, stranger!"

Pete Joslyn glanced around. "Might not want to push it, Frank."

"I push as I please," the man rumbled, stepping down from the porch. Swaggering, he planted himself in front of Bodie. "I said, who . . . ?"

The thick finger he aimed at Bodie's chest never arrived there. The hand that intercepted it was like a wrench—bending and twisting. A bone snapped and Frank's mouth dropped open. Then a fist from nowhere closed it.

Bodie didn't even look down at the man falling at his feet. His eyes had never left Pete Joslyn's. "You tell him," he said.

Without looking back, Bodie turned and walked away, heading for the hitch rail down the street, where his horse waited. Behind him there were excited voices, then a voice raised above the others,

213

"That's him! That's David Austin! He made me record his deeds!"

In front of the courthouse, men started to draw their guns, then hesitated. A crowd had gathered, townspeople standing on the street in the misting rain. People standing in hard-eyed silence, just watching . . . waiting.

One by one, the armed men reholstered their guns and averted their eyes. No law had been broken here, that they could see. A man lay unconscious in the mud, his face a bloody mess and his right hand ruined, but he had brought it on himself.

"Stop him!" the portly man on the steps shouted. "He invaded my office! He roughed me up! Get him!"

"I don't see any bruises on you, Blaes," someone said. "Did you record his deed?"

"Yes, but that . . . don't let him get away. That's Austin!"

Among them were some who might have acted— who might have gone after Bodie—and even more who might have drawn and fired as he rode leisurely past them, heading south. They might have, but they didn't. There was something about that crowd of people in the street. Silent people. Local, Hunt County people. Watching.

Reuben Blaes cursed and implored, then subsided. "Somebody go find Sheriff Terrell," he said. "And find Thad Carlile. He's gonna hear about this."

In the crowd on the street, old men looked at one another. David Austin? Was it true? Old

Sam's boy, back from the war . . . back to do something about the mess here, about the provisional government? To do something about Thad Carlile and his cronies?

"Did sort of look like the boy," someone said.

"That wa'nt no boy," another allowed. "That's a growed-up man, yonder. An' a right hard one."

"Sam was, too, when it was needed."

Rain was falling again, and people withdrew into the shelter of doorways. It was some time before someone chanced to go around to the side of the courthouse, where Kale White lay unconscious in the mud of the hitch lot.

Some miles south of Greenville on the Lone Oak road, brush parted beside the track and Mason Fremont urged his horse into the open, nodding his approval at the approaching rider. "Now that's the way to sit a horse," the youngster said. "Loose and easy. You look like Texas cavalry, sure enough."

"Obliged for the compliment," Bodie drawled, sounding the way he had sounded in the courthouse—like Texas. Then he frowned, and it seemed to Mason that the change of expression changed every part of him. In an instant, his posture in the saddle became awkward, his presence intense and domineering. "How do you do that?" he demanded, his words fast and clipped.

Mason blinked. He felt he would never get used to these sudden changes. "Do what?"

"I want to know how you manage to hide, like

215

you just did . . . out here where there's nothin' but trees an' weeds."

"I don't know." Mason shrugged. "I don't hide. I was just waiting. It's more comfortable to wait in cover than out in the open, I guess."

"I didn't see you there." The man glared. "I should have, but I didn't. How do you do it?"

"You know the land," the youth said, slowly, remembering something an Indian at Tahlequah had said, "then just be part of it. You told me you know how to hide in the city."

"That's different."

"I doubt it. It's probably the very same thing."

"You don't know anything about it." Bodie looked around, at the land. Where they were, the trail wound through trees. Beyond were brushy meadows. "Know the land, huh? Why? There's nothing here."

Mason arched a brow at him. "You really got somebody else inside you, like you said?"

"Yeah. When it suits me . . . or him."

"Well, then, *he* knows about the land. It may not matter to you, but it does to him. Otherwise why would you have gone to the courthouse and straightened up his deeds? That's all registering a deed does, is protect a piece of land."

Bodie frowned in thought. "That's what that is? Owning land?"

"I don't know what else it would be. If you're David Allen Austin, like you said, then you own land up ahead there, and you just registered it so those people back there can't take it away from you legally."

216

Bodie . . . or Austin . . . straightened in his saddle and looked ahead, at the rolling fields opening before them. "It's mine," he muttered. "That land. It's mine."

"If you really are him, then I guess it is," Mason agreed.

Minutes passed in silence, then Mason glanced at the man riding beside him. Glanced, and saw in that scarred, brutal face what seemed to him to be a deep sadness. "What's wrong, Mr. Bodie?"

"It doesn't look any different," the man said. "Not to me, anyway. If it's mine, that should make it look different. But it doesn't. It's just the same, and it doesn't look like anything at all to him, because he's dead."

Thoroughly confused, Mason gave up. "Big Sister took the lady home," he said. "The house is past that rise."

Chapter Eighteen

The face . . . it was Mary Austin's face. It always had been, I suppose, but I never knew it because I had never seen Mary Austin. The half-seen face on McConnell's roof, that wasn't her. That was someone else whose face I only glimpsed and never really saw. But the impression in my mind from that face—bits of light and shadow seen, with the voids filled by my own fancies—was of the same face that Mary Austin wore. And it was the face the little Frenchie street artist drew, because it came to him when he saw me.

I knew she would be there in that hick town courthouse, and I knew she was in trouble, and I knew I had to help. *He* had to help, the Johnny Reb she had loved. But he was dead, and that only left me.

But to help, I had to know the lay of the land, as the yokels would say. That, after I thought about it, was probably why I went to that other town first, with the crippled woman and her kid brothers. It was to find out how things stacked, on the streets of places where a street was only a dirt road with some ramshackle little buildings along it.

It's a thing you learn early, where I come from. There is always a way to do what you want and get what you want, no matter where you are. But what works along Bowery Street doesn't always work on Delancey, and what stacks up on Water Street won't stack at all on Baker. Different neighborhoods have different ways, and the wisdom of the streets in Five Points is not smart down in the Battery.

The thing they all have in common is their gangs, but a gang boss stays boss because he knows the beat of his streets, the tune of his neighborhood, and he knows how to dance to that tune.

Practice. It was one of the Dutchman's favorite words, and he drilled it into me. And when I didn't please him by practicing, Club would show up and beat it into me. I was big for my age even back in the Battery Boy days, and I never took a scar or a bruise that I didn't learn from. Even before Billy Bean turned me over to the Dutchman, there weren't many men in New York that I'd have backed away from. But Club—he was something else. Club was huge and hard as a rock and nothing short of killing him was ever going to hurt him. I wondered sometimes if Club was even human, or if maybe he was something that climbed up out of the old shafts over on the Lower West Side, and learned to walk on his hind legs so that the Dutchman could keep bulls away.

Whatever he was—and whatever the Dutchman was—I practiced. I practiced with the Beals revolver, and with other weapons, too. I practiced using my fists and using my feet, and using my eyes to see what was around me and my head to figure how to get the advantage and keep it.

I practiced and I learned. And while I was learning skills, I was learning more and more about how things work ... how power is won, and how it is held. How deals are made, and how they're enforced. How the daily take in any neighborhood gets spread around, from street gang to neighborhood boss to other bosses on up the line, everybody taking a cut to lay off somebody else's territory. Right up the line to Billy Bean on the East Side, or to Silver Tooth Jack Meriwether on Broadway, or to some Tweed lieutenant in the Tammany crowd.

Back there, I learned how things shake out. Out here, all I had to learn was how those same patterns look when it's a bunch of hicks and yokels operating in the sticks.

The gang at Pleasant Hill was nothing much. A bunch of looters with the guns and the guts to take a neighborhood ... a town, out here ... but without the brains to keep things stacked neatly while they bled the herd for whatever they wanted. They wouldn't have lasted very long, even in that town. All I did was just speed up the process. Where I come from, they wouldn't have lasted even that long.

In busting that gang, I learned what I needed to know. I had dealt with a looter bunch in Five Points, back when I was with Billy Bean, and now I had dealt with a looter bunch out here. The differences were the same differences I would find between a *sanctioned* gang back there — sanctioned was what they called a gang that knew how to dance to its tune, and that shared its rake with the bigger mobs that held the territories — and a sanctioned bunch out here.

That was what I had found in Greenville. A sanctioned gang. It had a boss, Thad Carlile, and he had connections higher up. Sanctioned.

And Mary Austin. And the face that had haunted me for all those years.

The house was a neat little four-square with a narrow porch on the front and a wide one on the back, and beyond it were a barn and some sheds, and a windmill. There were chickens and goats around, some pigs penned beyond the barn, and out in the pasture there were cattle being watched over by a man on a horse. Another man was over by the barn, working on something. Justine Fremont's wagon and Mary Austin's wagon stood side by side near the house, and Wendell Fremont was unhitching the teams.

As we stepped down, Wendell came over and shot me that suspicious glance of his, then asked Mason, "Is there going to be trouble?"

Mason just shrugged. "Ask him," he said.

"There already is trouble," I told the older one.

"You started it, then, I guess? Like at Pleasant Hill?"

"I didn't start that," I said. "I ended it. I was practicing."

"Practicing? For what?"

"For what's going to happen here."

"I told Big Sister we should stay away from

you," he bristled. "I told her you're crazy."

"Could be," I admitted. "Now shut up and get out of my way."

Inside the house, it went silent when I walked in. Mary Austin was there, holding a baby and looking at me with those eyes I had thought about so much—eyes that seemed to look right into me, looking for someone else. Looking for a dead man who should have been there instead of me. Eyes that couldn't seem to understand why I had lived and he had died, any more than I did. Eyes that had other questions, too, like was that really what happened or was I mistaken some way. I couldn't look at her, though *he* wanted to. I had to look away.

Justine Fremont was there, leaning on her crutch, and another woman—an old woman who looked me up and down and didn't care much for what she saw. Beyond an open inner door, a white-haired old man lay on a bed.

"Mr. Bodie," Justine said, "You've met Mary Austin. This is Maude Carver, and the gentleman in there is Moss Jackson. I'm sure everyone has questions about . . ."

"I'm hungry," I told them. "Get me some food."

Maude Carver glared at me. "You can just mind your manners or get out of Mary's house," she said.

Mary Austin raised a hand to hush her. "Mr. . . . Bodie, is it? I owe you thanks for helping me at the courthouse. I couldn't have recorded our deeds, but for you. Thank goodness it's over."

"It isn't over, Mary," I told her, and it was him

222

talking, not me. The words were slow and gentle. "It can't be over until it begins. All we did was begin it."

From the next room came the old man's voice, "Dang right you begun it. But Thad Carlile's not goin' to stand for what you did, Davey. You know that."

"Hush up, Moss," the old woman said. "This here isn't Davey. You can see that plain enough, if you look."

I was still looking at Mary Austin, not wanting to, but I couldn't help it. *He* wouldn't let me stop, now. "There were two of us there, Mary," his voice said through my mouth. "Only one could come back. It was the only way. Accept what you see, angel."

Her eyes were as big as dollars. "You . . . nobody ever called me that, except . . ." Then the dollars were full of tears and she turned away.

"Hush, Mary," the old woman hurried to her, comforting her.

"Remember what I told you, Mary," Justine Fremont said. "Who knows what really happened there? Or how?"

I was still looking at Mary, and I didn't want to look at her anymore. Looking at that face hurt, the way seeing a rainbow hurts because you know that what you see isn't really there for you, never was and never will be. None of the rainbows ever had been mine. They were his. The reb's. So was Mary, and him being dead didn't change that. I pushed him aside in my mind, and turned away.

223

"I told you I'm hungry," I said. "Get me something to eat."

It was evening when Thad Carlile returned from his tour of the bottoms—that portion of the county cut off by the Sabine. In Greenville he dismissed his military escort and watched them ride off northward, toward the abandoned farm that Captain Brooks had taken over as his headquarters, and turned his team toward the Longmont house. It had been a long day, and he was ready for supper and a night's rest.

He had gone less than a block, though, when one of Vince Terrell's deputies flagged him down. "Sheriff an' them, they need you at the courthouse, Mr. Carlile," the man said. "There's been trouble."

An hour later, by lamplight, Carlile glanced again at the deed records for the Austin properties, and swore under his breath. Raising his head, he stared at the tax assessor-collector across from him. "I ought to have you horsewhipped, Blaes," he gritted. "One man. And you let him get away with this."

"Nothin' else I could do, Mr. Carlile," Reuben Blaes said for the dozenth time. "You weren't here. You didn't see. That Austin . . . he's a madman. He'd have killed me."

Beyond, in shadows, Vince Terrell added, "That may be right, Mr. Carlile. I saw what the jasper done to Kale White. White never knew what hit him, is my guess. But he may be laid up for weeks. And one of your . . . ah, hired men . . . that Frank Chadwick? He's got a busted hand that might never work right, and a busted jaw full of busted teeth."

"Yeah," Carlile sneered. "And a dozen armed men stood and watched, then let Austin just ride away. What's the matter with you people?"

"I questioned everybody," Terrell said. "They said there wasn't much they could do. Too many witnesses. I can send some of my boys out there, though . . ."

"And have those same witnesses start sending messages to Austin? My boys were right, you know, not to gun him down in the street. There's way too much at stake here, to find ourselves up to our ears in citizen protests—or worse. But why didn't they detain him? Lock him up for questioning?"

"I didn't see the man, Mr. Carlile. But those who did, they backed off. Your own men, too, I might add."

"The man's a killer," Blaes piped up. "I've seen the kind before. A crazy killer."

Carlile gazed at them, first one and then the other, with eyes that were glowing slits in the lamplight. "David Austin," he said slowly. "You're talking about the Austin boy, right? The younger one?"

"David Allen Austin." Blaes nodded. "He had a kid with him, too. An Injun kid, looked like."

"You're absolutely sure it was Austin?"

"You see the signature there." Blaes pointed. "That's his, all right."

"Signatures can be faked. You knew the Austins, back then. You remember them, and you saw this man face to face today. Are you positive it was him?"

"He's changed some," Blaes said. "Changed a hell of a lot, in fact. Scarred, like he's been burned. But it was him, all right. Couldn't be anybody else. Ask your own men. At least two of them recognized him. That gunny Pete Joslyn, and Rudy. I don't see anything we can do, Mr. Carlile. He's got his record receipts. It's his property."

"Not if he winds up dead," Terrell suggested. "Easiest thing might be to . . ."

"It won't be his property if he doesn't pay his taxes," Carlile cut him off, coming to a decision. "Blaes, I want a tax inventory on the Austin property. Every kind of tax you can think of, and if you need to make up some new ones, do it."

"But tax deadlines are . . ."

"Tax deadlines are when I say they are, Blaes. I'm superintendent here. I want that tax statement, as soon as you can draw it up. Get up some tax bills on a few other places, too, so nobody gets wind that this one is special. And you, Sheriff, you can deliver the bill when it's ready. I want those properties, and by God, I'll have them. The Austins humiliated my family, and the Austins are going to pay for that. Now get busy."

Terrell left them there, Blaes dreaming up taxes to levy against the Austin properties and Carlile fuming and plotting.

A lawyer and a bookkeeper, the sheriff was thinking. Words and numbers. Carlile had a score

226

to settle with the Austins, and he intended to wind up owning their places. The superintendent intended to own just a lot of this county, by the time real provisional government was established. But the thing with the Austins was personal.

Personal, and maybe clouding his judgment. Terrell had spent time in the state prison, and he knew how to deal with tough nuts that got in a man's way. He had seen what this Austin did to his deputy, Kale White. And he had heard what he did in the courthouse.

A real tough nut, that one. The kind you don't deal with by words and numbers. The kind that needs bullets.

Carlile would play it his way. He was the superintendent, and Terrell owed his job to him. But he had his own notions about getting things done. Delivering the "tax bill" would give him a chance to size up David Austin, but he questioned whether such a maneuver would put him down. A man like Austin, a man who could step up and poleax Kale White, wouldn't likely be impressed by legal warrants. It would be interesting to see what he would do, when Reuben Blaes sent him a bill for taxes that undoubtedly would call for more money than anyone in this county had.

But would he let himself be evicted?

A slight, cold smile played across Terrell's face. Hell, no. Not without a fight.

Words and numbers, he thought. The superintendent and the tax man would try it their way, but then it would be his turn.

Vince Terrell had scores of his own to settle with

the good citizens of Hunt County, and his ideas didn't stop at stealing property. He wanted payment in blood, and the sooner the shooting started the better he would like it.

Things needed a little stirring up, he decided.

Carlile had turned thumbs down on simply going out and finding David Allen Austin and shooting him down. But he hadn't said a word about anybody else who might be with him. A kid, Blaes said. An Indian kid.

This was still Texas, and who the hell would care if some Indian kid got shot?"

Far to the east, at the Bossier Docks on the Red River, a man stepped off the deck of a New Orleans Shuttle cargo boat, walked down the rough gangway, and faded into the dockside crowds.

A young man, an observer might have said, had anyone noticed him. Fairly young, but with features aged beyond his years. Not a large man, but not small, either. Slim and quick-eyed, dressed in clothing that seemed to blend into the dockside environment as easily as it had blended into the motley garbs aboard the shuttle boat. Not a memorable man, at all. Not even a noticeable one, an observer might have thought, had anyone had reason to observe him at all.

But none did, and he knew none would. It was one of his better skills, this blending into the surroundings. When necessary, he could become virtually invisible. The talent had kept him alive often, and was part of his stock in trade. Better than anyone he knew, even in places where many practiced surreption, he could come and go as he pleased and never be noticed . . . until he chose to be.

Where he was from, it was a valuable skill. Where he was from, it could be the difference between success and sudden death.

Unnoticed, he strolled up Haven Way, then turned in at a doorway. "I need transportation," he told the man at the counter. "The fastest I can find."

"Depends on where ye aim to go," the man said, not even glancing up. The past few months, it seemed like every voice he heard was terse and clipped, just as this voice was. The war was over, and there were Yankees everywhere.

"Texas," the customer said. "Lone Oak, Texas. As fast as possible."

The counter agent did look up then, and promptly wished he hadn't. There was nothing remarkable at all in the appearance of the man facing him . . . not until he looked into his eyes. There was something there that sent cold chills up his spine. Something furtive, and deadly.

"Yes, sir," he said. "There's coaches runnin' now. I reckon that's best."

Texas, he thought. Somebody in Texas just might be about to die.

Chapter Nineteen

There were more people on the roads now, an ever-increasing traffic of the dispossessed. It was the aftermath of war, in a land where the articles of peace were not yet in place. Years would pass in the grueling transitions of Reconstruction and Restoration, and the scars of peace for many would be worse than the scars of war.

Right now, though, people in many parts of Texas were discovering that the worst of the carpetbaggers were the first of the carpetbaggers. Into the vacuums that had been organized counties and civilized towns came the scavengers—sometimes gangs of looters to rob, burn, and run, sometimes imported bullies to swagger and terrorize and take what they wanted. And in many ways the worst of all were the "locals," men who planned for just this kind of opportunity and now had plots to hatch and scores to settle, who stood ready to do whatever was needed, in this time of chaos and confusion, for their moment of profit or revenge.

More than one Texas county had its home-grown Thad Carlile to contend with, and the roads were full of homeless people. Farm wagons, pack animals, even carts and wheelbarrows were common, as families gathered what they could carry and evacuated their homes, often at gunpoint.

In Hunt County, much of the traffic had been people from other places, evicted and homeless and on the move. But now, some of the movers were not strangers. They were neighbors, moving on as—one by one—Thad Carlile's provisional authority took over their homes and their lands. The first evicted were the weakest—tenants on lands whose owners were no longer present to record deeds or whose taxes were in delinquency. Then, here and there, the defenseless families of Southern soldiers killed or missing. And in some cases, squatters who might have thought the properties were theirs but had no proof.

In each case it was the same. Men with badges came to serve papers, followed by "civilians" with guns to evict and occupy, establishing possession in their own names—possession which would establish ownership, which then would be transferred to Thad Carlile, Vince Terrell, or Reuben Blaes.

Little by little, the story made its way around the county, and people shook their heads and muttered among themselves. Plainly, Thad Carlile was out to steal as much of Hunt County as he could get his hands on. And plainly, he had the ability to do it. With war's end, the South was a conquered land, and Texas along with it. Whether or not Texas had ever had any business joining the Confederacy of States didn't matter now. Texas had joined, the Confederacy had failed, and Texas must pay the price.

Still, among those who understood, there was a

231

smoldering outrage at what Thad Carlile was doing. It was a revenge, pure and simple. Those who had rid the county of old Ty Carlile and his bunch, years ago, were going to suffer for it now. Thad Carlile and his cronies had the power and the will, and there was little anyone could do unless the takers so overstepped themselves that the new Provisional Government in Austin—the Government of Occupation—was forced to step in.

Some of those evicted were "old families" in the county, and some had relatives to stay with until they could decide where to go. And a bastion of "old family" stock was the little town of Lone Oak. The Harrison Chadwicks, Tyler Chadwicks, and the widow and children of Jefferson Chadwick found refuge there with other Chadwicks. The families of Sim and Alex Reynolds were taken in by Tobe Reynolds and his clan. The Sutters made room for Sutters and for cousins of Sutters, and Lone Oak suddenly was full of people.

"It's them children yonder that I worry about," Maude Carver said one afternoon, watching out the window of Mary's house as more refugees passed on the road beyond the gate. She had come to the second house to collect Moss Jackson and take him home to rest in his own bed. Now she turned to Justine Fremont. "You bein' a schoolteacher an' all, an' bein' footloose like y'all are, you might want to have a look at the old schoolhouse down there. Could be there's need of a teacher."

Justine glanced up from the stack of papers on the table before her. "This is unbelievable," she

232

said.

Mary Austin stepped in from the next room, where Moss was sitting upright, his hat on his head, waiting to be carried out to the wagon. "What is, Justine?" she asked.

"This." Justine indicated the stack of scrawled papers. "Mr. Bodie's . . . well, his *writings*. My Lord, what sort of place does he come from? It must be like something right out of hell."

"That what you're readin'?" Maude came to look over her shoulder. "Why, he writes a fair hand for a man that only just learned. Spellin' ain't much, though. What's a 'runer'?"

"I think it's 'runner'. I'm not sure what it means. Where is he today? I haven't seen him since we set his breakfast out for him."

"Still takin' shy, I reckon," Maude shrugged. "He's a strange one, sure enough. Takes all his meals out yonder, an' the way he prowls around . . ."

"I don't think he's been in the house since the day you all arrived," Mary said. "It is so odd . . . sometimes, just for a moment, he looks just like David. Little things, like how he'll turn his head when birds sing, and the way he bends down sometimes, to look at the ground. David used to do that. He did love the land so much. It's as though I really do see . . . my husband . . . there. If I didn't know better I would swear he is David. Then a minute later he's like someone else entirely. And when he sees me watching him, out in the yard, he turns away. It makes me feel funny, as though he's afraid of me."

233

"Whatever he's afraid of, it's in his own head," Justine said. She stood, needing to work the kinks out of her bad leg. From the window she looked out on the yard, the corner of the west pasture beyond, and the Lone Oak road beyond that. There was no traffic there just now, but in the pasture Wendell was working with Mary's two hired men, pushing a few animals back eastward, away from the road. Just visible was the mound of fresh-turned dirt where they had buried the remains of a cow shot by someone in the evening hours two days before. Shot from the road.

She started to turn away, then looked again. On the road beyond, just coming into sight, were riders. Three large men, with shiny badges.

"May be company coming." she said.

From the next room came Moss Jackson's voice, thin with outrage. "If that ain't the most pitiful sight . . . yonder's that snake Vince Terrell, with a *badge* on his coat. Land, I never would'a thought I'd see such a thing. Y'all best tell Davey trouble's comin'!"

Maude Carver muttered, "That old fool. Can't get it through his head that Eastern jasper ain't David." But she hurried away, then, through the house toward the back door. The jasper might not be David Austin, but the jasper was the most man around just now, to handle trouble.

Out by the barn, Mason Fremont spotted the riders at the same time and called, "Mr. Bodie, if you're still being Mr. Austin, you better have a look."

Bodie was crouched inside the covered bed of

234

Justine Fremont's wagon, where he kept the things he considered his—a few pieces of clothing, a collection of weapons picked up along the trail, a closed box . . . odds and ends. He had been looking for his folder of papers, wondering if the crippled woman had them. He hadn't said she couldn't look at them, but he had not invited, either, and somehow he found it intensely irritating that she might be reading what he had written about himself. It was none of her business. It was none of anybody's business, what was written on those pages.

At Mason's shout he scuttled to the rear of the wagon, stooping to avoid the rounded canvas cover and its supporting bows. In the distance, beyond the house, riders were approaching the gate.

Maude Carver appeared at the back door of the house, saw him, and called, "Badges yonder on the road!"

Ignoring her, he dropped to the ground and stood, straightening his hat and gun belt. A few yards away, Mason Fremont was applying grease to the axles of Moss Jackson's old buckboard. The mule was already in harness, waiting. "You want your horse?" the boy asked.

"What for?" Bodie snapped, and started for the front yard. When he heard Mason following him, he turned and waved him back. "You stay here," he said. "Stay out of the way."

He was just passing the front porch, his eyes on the men approaching the gate, when the front door opened and closed, and Mary Austin came tagging after him, wrapping a shawl around her

235

shoulders.

He started to wave her back, but she came on. "If it's business, it's my business," she said quietly.

"Those bulls don't come to see you, lady," the man who was Bodie rasped.

"No, probably not. They'll be looking for my husband." She stepped past him, turned, and looked up into his eyes. "Is he here, Mr. Bodie? Is . . . is David here?"

Bodie stared at her, cold and hard-eyed, then something changed in his eyes. Something she couldn't understand. When he spoke now, it was a different man speaking. The words, the manner, the soft drawl, they were like David's. "I'm here, angel," he said. "Don't fret."

She felt short of breath, hearing those words, so like David's words. And so like David's voice. For a moment she couldn't speak, then she lowered her eyes, not really understanding but accepting. "That's Vince Terrell," she said. "You . . . David would know him. David despised him for a thief and a murderer. But now he is sheriff of the county. David would be outraged. He would resent it. But he wouldn't make trouble. David would hold his temper and hear the man out, then think for a while about what to do."

As she was speaking, she glanced at him again. He was listening intently, as though memorizing what she said.

He nodded, then, "Vince Terrell," he said. "Well, I reckon we'd best see what *Sheriff* Terrell has on his mind."

Again she was stunned. It was exactly what

236

David might have said, and exactly the way he might have said it. He started for the gate again and she trailed along.

The three riders were at the gate, and the nearest one was leaning to lift the bar when Bodie came up to them. "This is private land," he said, quietly. "And that gate is a private gate."

The man stopped in surprise, withdrawing his hand. The voice had been cordial, but there was a hint of steel behind it.

Vince Terrell stared at him, then stifled his anger and smiled a hard smile. "Well, well, if it ain't Mr. David Allen Austin, fresh home from the war. I just couldn't hardly believe it when I heard you'd come back, Davey boy."

"And I just couldn't hardly believe it when I heard what was passin' for law in this county," Bodie-Austin drawled. "What do you want here, Terrell?"

Terrell's fake smile had faded. "That's *Sheriff* Terrell, sonny," he growled.

"Is it? I asked you what you want here." The hint of steel was more than a hint now.

Behind him, he heard Mary's whisper, "Don't push too hard. You . . . David wouldn't."

"I saw what happened to Kale White," Terrell rasped. "No witnesses, of course, but I know it was you, Austin. What did you do, jump him from behind? Maybe used a gun butt on him? You won't have that kind of luck again."

"Kale White's a deputy," Mary whispered. "What . . . ?"

"Your *deputy* is a dunce, Terrell," Bodie-Austin

237

said evenly. "Prob'ly knocked himself out tryin' to pick his nose. You got anything else to say?"

Terrell stared at him with real hatred, and for a moment his hand lingered near the butt of his gun. But he hesitated, then dropped his hand away. Thad Carlile had said not to kill Austin. Not yet, anyway. Besides, there was something in the way the younger man held his eyes . . . and in the way he made no move toward his own gun. Something about him was frightening. "Well, you've got to be a real tough nut, ain't you, boy? Well, we'll see about that. When I'm ready, we'll see. Here's what I come about." He pulled a folded document from his coat and held it out, over the gate. For a moment, the mean grin returned. "First things first. I hereby serve you with this notice of taxes due. And since you 'registered' both these places, why, the county just added up what's owed on both of 'em. Due date is one week from today, tough nut."

Bodie made no move to take the document. After a moment Terrell let it fall to the ground, just inside the gate. "You been served," he said.

"Then go away," Bodie said, the drawl falling away from his words. "And don't come back."

A look of disbelief widened Terrell's eyes. "What? What did you say?"

"Don't come back," the clipped, deep voice repeated. "I won't warn you again."

Mary stood behind him, wide-eyed, as the riders turned and left. Bodie made no move until they were out of sight past the near bend in the road. Then, as though nothing had happened, he

238

turned, looking beyond her at the house. "My papers are none of that woman's business," he said, and walked away.

Mary stared after him, then picked up the tax notice and opened it. For a moment she didn't believe what it said, then a dread like a cold hand touched her. So much! Stunned and shaken, she barely heard the sound of a gunshot that came from the north, muffled by distance.

More than three thousand dollars! Mary stared at the tax statement, barely seeing it. Was there that much money anywhere?

Bodie had stopped, halfway to the house. He stood there, looking northward, a frown on his scarred face. Then he glanced back at Mary, and something in him shifted. She was still by the gate, looking pale, stricken, and very small. Deep within the cold depths of him, something responded and he hurried back to her.

Beside her, he put a big, gentle hand on her shoulder. "Mary? Angel, what's wrong?"

Behind him, Mason Fremont had come from beyond the house, and Maude Carver was at the door, both peering northward.

With trembling fingers, Mary handed the tax statement to Bodie. "It's this. Oh, Lord, I don't know what to do."

He looked at it with David's eyes, then something shifted again and it was Bodie—brusque and brutish—who crumpled the paper and handed it back. "That's easy," he snapped. "Pay it."

"But I don't have that much money. I can't . . ."

"Don't you know how things work?" He

sneered. "A bill's a bill. You get a bill from a boss, you pay it. Then . . ." his voice grew thin and icy, "then you make sure you got your money's worth."

"But we don't have the money."

"Sure you do." He cocked his head, seeming confused. "David has that much . . . or somebody. Come on, I'll show you." He took her hand and led her up the path, angling to go around the house.

In the dooryard, Mason said, "Did you hear that shot?"

"I heard it." Bodie went on past, leading Mary by the hand. Beside the house, Moss Jackson's buckboard waited. They went past, and stopped at Justine Fremont's covered wagon beside the barn. Bodie stepped up, into the wagon, and lifted Mary up after him as casually as one might lift a cotton doll. Inside he ducked past the bows and knelt beside a small pile of things. Guns, a roll of blankets . . . he lifted out a closed wooden box and set it on the floorboards, and opened the lid. Inside was money—more money than Mary had ever seen. There was a small stack of bills in the now-worthless Confederate scrip, and another stack of Federal certificates of various denominations, but most of the space was taken up by coin. Gold and silver.

Mary stared at the treasure, then at the man. "Where did you get this?"

"Took it off a boss," he said, casually.

"You stole it?"

His glance was like a slap. "I didn't steal it! I

240

took it. Gang money, from that other town. The gang didn't need it anymore."

"But I can't use that . . ."

"I can," he rasped. Shoving her aside, he climbed out of the wagon, carrying the box. "It's mine. I can do what I want. I'll get that teacher to count it, then maybe I'll watch that tax man eat it."

At the corner of the house he stopped. Maude Carver, Mason, and Justine were on the porch, and Moss Jackson was peering out the window. A half mile northward, people were on the rise, coming down. Mary's two hired hands, riding their mounts and leading another horse—a horse with a motionless form draped over its saddle.

As they approached, those at the house watched in silence, then Justine gasped and staggered against a porch upright as her bad leg buckled. Her hands went to her mouth.

Beside her, Mason Fremont stood like one lightning-struck—motionless and staring. "Wendell," he whispered. "Big Sister, that's . . . that's Wendell."

Chapter Twenty

Wendell had seen the man who shot him, but Wendell would never tell his name. The bullet hole in his chest was a close-range wound, and said he had been looking at his killer when he fired. It also said that Wendell had not expected to be shot. He had done nothing to escape or to defend himself.

The tracks in the far pasture told Mason the same thing. The three horsemen were on the road, northbound. One had stopped at the pasture's edge while the others went ahead. Wendell had been out in the pasture—alone at the moment, away from the two hired hands. He had gone to the roadside fence, to meet the rider there.

Obviously, his assailant had called to him. And Wendell, unsuspecting, had simply approached the man . . . and died. Then the rider went on, following where his companions had gone.

The tracks told Mason one thing more. The killer was the same man who had sat his horse at the gate and handed a tax statement across. Vince Terrell.

The only thing the tracks did not say was why. But Bodie had an answer to that. "You went in the courthouse with me," he said. "Terrell wasn't there, but he heard. Indian kid, that's what he heard. So he didn't know there were two of you."

"But . . . but *why?* Why kill him?"

Bodie shook his head, wishing he could explain, but not knowing how. How to explain that a criminal in a killing mood is plain going to kill somebody? How to explain the kind of man who'll press for a showdown by killing innocents? How to explain what, in the dark streets of the city, everyone would understand? How could a yokel kid in the sticks ever understand that?

"I'm going after him," Mason said, wiping his eyes. "I'll kill that . . ."

"You won't do anything," Bodie said harshly. "You wouldn't last a minute against that bull. Even out here, you wouldn't."

He stepped back, looking around at the walls of the house. It was the first time he had been inside since his arrival here, the first time he had let himself look at the familiar, comfortable surroundings of a home of which he knew every little detail but had no right knowing.

Looking at this place was like looking at Mary Austin. The memories came flooding in, and they hurt. Memories belonging to another man . . . memories that no Hands Bodie could ever have had, on his own.

They had laid Wendell out on the main bed — Mary's bed . . . and *his* — and covered him with a quilt.

The same quilt he and Mary had . . . no, *David* and Mary had . . . With a snort, he turned away and strode to the table. On its cloth-covered surface rested the money box. Moss Jackson sat in a chair beside it, looking wild and bewildered. Justine, Mason, and Mary were beside the bed where Wendell lay under his quilt. Maude Carver was in the next room, crooning to the baby.

The baby—David Austin's baby son—that Hands Bodie had carefully ignored, because he felt that something inside him would change if he looked at that baby too closely. Something inside, that must not change. Something as delicately balanced and as vulnerable as the mechanisms inside a fine watch. He didn't know what it was, but it was there and if it changed—if it shifted beyond his control—something would die.

Bodie opened the box and looked at the old man. "Can you count money?"

"I'll count it, Davey," Moss said. "What you fixin' to do?"

"Pay some debts," Bodie said. He picked up the tax statement that Mary had dropped. "Count out this much, then count how much is left over."

Mason got to his feet and turned away from the bed where his brother lay. "I've got to do something," he said. "I can't just let this go."

Justine reached up to grasp his arm. "Mason . . . Mason, let it alone. At least for now. Please." Then she began to sob. "I thought I could take care of you boys. I really thought I could. But . . . oh, Wendell . . ." Her voice broke and she slumped forward, over the body of her dead brother.

Mary Austin put an arm around the older woman's shoulders and held her close, comforting. After a moment, she looked around at Bodie. There were tears in her eyes, too. "David wouldn't let a thing like this go by," she whispered. "It isn't . . . wasn't

244

his way. He was like his father. He believed in justice."

Bodie looked away. He felt as though other voices were calling to him, voices of dead men, echoing what the girl said.

The Indian kid, he thought. What did Wendell Fremont—or any of them—have to do with David Allen Austin? For that matter, what did he—or any of them—have to do with Hands Bodie?

Still, the voices called and their echoes went on and on, inside his head. Echoes that seemed to come from the very walls of David Austin's house, that went around and around like the little spinning wheels in a fine watch, amplifying with each thing they touched in this house—each of the cherished things that David Austin had held dear . . . and that Hands Bodie remembered now more clearly than any memories of his own.

Moss Jackson was staring at him. "Davey? Boy, what's wrong? You're white as a sheet!"

He turned away. On a shelf was his leather folder, with its paper and writing tools. Beside it was a stack of papers covered with handwriting . . . whose? His? It didn't matter. Hurry, the voices inside him said. We have things to do, and nothing else matters.

"I matter," Bodie whispered, to the voices inside him. "Damn it, I *matter!*"

"Davey?" the old man pressed.

"Mine," he whispered, his eyes closed but still seeing every detail around him. Then he grimaced, and whispered, "His, not mine." And his whisper echoed in agreement. "Mine," it said. "Mine . . . mine . . . mine . . ." It was a chorus of echoes, ringing like a rainbow in his mind.

Like a rainbow arching across a dark blue sky, singing a chorus of colors. The colors had always been there, he realized. For *him,* but not for Callahan Bodie.

Mary was looking at him, too, with eyes that were huge. "Mr. Bodie? . . . David?"

Bodie squared his shoulders and shook his head. With an angry growl he grabbed the leather folder and writing tools. "Count the money like I said," he hissed. "Let me alone and count the damn money!" Like a tormented animal, he strode through the front door and out, letting it slam behind him, and turned toward Justine Fremont's wagon.

Behind him, Moss Jackson's voice said, "What's the matter with Davey? Where'd he go?"

More than an hour passed before Bodie returned to the house. When he did, he looked as bleak as winter winds. "We . . . I dug a hole for the boy," he said. "He'll need burying."

He strode to the table, where Moss Jackson still sat, looking old and pale. The old man had counted the looter money, as he was told. There was a bag of coin equaling the tax statement, and another, smaller pile beside it. The currency was in two stacks—Confederate bills and Federal silver and gold certificates. He picked up the tax money—the sack was heavy with coin—and thrust it into his coat pocket, then turned around. Justine Fremont sat in a rocker by the fireplace, her tears dry now but the mourning still strong on her face. Mason sat on the floor beside her, staring at nothing.

Bodie squatted in front of the rocker, and took Justine's hands in his. In a voice like David Austin's voice, he said, "Justine, listen to me now. There's money there, on that table, and it's yours. Yours and Mason's. Do you understand?"

"I suppose," she said distantly, not caring.

"Good. Because you have to decide something now."

She sighed, and gave him her attention.

"Tom Austin died without any family of his own," he said. "So his place—the other place, across the gully—that belongs to David Austin now."

"David Austin is . . ."

"Hush. Just listen. I want you to buy that place. Buy it for cash, fair and square, from David Austin. Deed recorded and tax paid. Take out a little money to see you and Mason—and Moss Jackson and Maude Carver—through the season, then pay the rest to David Austin for that land. Do you understand?"

"No," she admitted. "How can I buy something from a man who died . . ."

"He didn't." Bodie shook his head. "Ask anybody. David Austin is back, and he's alive."

"But that was . . . that was you."

"It doesn't matter. What's legal is what *seems* legal."

"But it wouldn't be right." She looked past him at Mary Austin. "It's yours, not his. What . . .?"

Mary was staring at the kneeling man, her eyes wide and thoughtful, as one who has—almost—unraveled a mystery. For a moment she didn't respond. Then she said, "If he wants to sell it to you, he can sell it."

"You sellin' Tom's place, Davey?" Moss Jackson asked.

247

"I'm sellin' Tom's place." He nodded. "But you and Maude stay on. That's part of the deal." He turned to Justine again. "Well?"

"Mason?"

The Indian youth had stopped pacing. "I think Wendell was right," he said. "This jasper's crazy as a loon. But it was you who told us we could trust him. So, trust him."

"Well?"

Justine nodded. "What have we to lose? You took the money . . ."

"Found the money," he corrected.

"Found the money, then. If you say take it, and pay it back to you for a place, then I guess that's what we do."

"Good." He stood, wrote out a bill of sale in a hand that looked very much like David Austin's writing, signed it David Allen Austin, and handed it to Justine, along with some of the coin in the second stack. The rest he pushed aside. "This is yours, Mary. It belongs to your husband, by rightful sale of property duly registered and tax-paid." For a moment, something like a smile tugged at his scarred cheeks—a smile that made Mary's heart jump because it was so like David. Then the bleakness returned, as suddenly as clouds rolling in on a spring wind.

In a voice that belonged to no one but Hands Bodie, he said, "Hitch up the team, Mason. There are people to take home now . . . and one to bury."

Mason glanced at the covered body of his brother, then looked away. "Where . . . where will we bury him?"

"I already dug a hole," Bodie said. "Over there,

248

on the other place. He'll be buried on his own land."

There were older graves on the hillside behind the "Old Austin Place," graves that held the mortal remains of Sam Austin, his wife, and three of their five children. And aside from them were other graves—some marked and some not—where various other people associated with the Austin family were laid to rest. The grave Hands Bodie had dug for Wendell Fremont was apart from those, as well.

"New owners, new plot." Moss Jackson nodded, removing his hat as Maude Carver climbed down from the buckboard and took Little Davey from Mary. "It's fittin'."

Bodie brought the wrapped body from Justine's wagon and lowered it gently into the hole. Then they stood around, all except Moss in the buckboard, and looked down, each thinking private thoughts.

Jess and Willie stood aside, their hats in their hands, each holding a shovel. "That jasper wouldn't let us dig," Willie whispered to Moss, indicating Bodie. "Said 'back off or else,' is what he said. Said it was his to do. But we'll do the coverin' if he don't mind. Who is that, anyhow, that's bein' planted?"

"Name's Wendell. Them's his sister an' brother, there."

"I mean the big jasper that dug the hole."

Moss turned surprised eyes on him. "Y'all don't recollect Davey Austin? Ever' body knows him."

Willie and Jess exchanged puzzled glances. "That's Davey?" Jess muttered. "Well, Lord, but ain't he changed some!"

By the grave, Justine tried to speak, and choked as fresh tears welled from her eyes. "Our pa was a preacher," she managed, "but I surely don't know what to say."

"He was my brother," Mason said.

Justine hesitated, then nodded. "He was my brother."

"He was my brother," Hands Bodie said, in a voice that might have been David's but wasn't . . . that might have been the voice of a back-east hoodlum, but wasn't that, either. "My . . . my brother."

"He was my brother," Mary Austin echoed, slipping her hand into the crook of Bodie's arm.

Then Moss Jackson and Maude Carver said it, almost in unison. "He was my brother." And behind them, Willie and Jess muttered, "Amen."

They took Moss Jackson to his own bed, and Maude handed Little Davey back to Mary and said, "I'll get these folks settled in, Mary. You and . . . David go on home. I'll look in on you tomorrow."

In silence, they walked across the fields, across the gully and the back pasture, Mary carrying her baby, the big man with the burn-scarred face tagging after, as bleak and alone as though no one but himself were there.

At the house, Mary went in, nestled Little Davey into his "cage," and lit a lamp. Bodie had stopped at the door, and now she went to him, holding the lamp to look up at his face, her eyes searching. "David? You are, aren't you? Somehow, I mean . . . you really *are* David."

He gazed down at her for a long moment, then took a deep breath and let it out in a shuddering sigh. "Let it alone, Mary," he said, gently. "It's best, for now, just to let it alone."

Stepping past her, he gathered up the blanket roll that had been in Justine's wagon, then turned and stalked out without a word.

Mary held the door open behind him. "You don't have to leave, you know . . . David. You could stay."

For an instant he hesitated, but only for an instant. Without answering, he stepped off the porch and into the deepening dusk. A minute later she heard the barn door open and close, and knew she would not see him again this night.

"Let it alone," she whispered, lingering over the words. They had been words in David's voice, but the eyes above them were not . . . not exactly David's eyes. They were someone else.

"It's best," she whispered, "for now, just to let it alone."

In the barn, Hands Bodie spread blankets for a place to sleep for the night. When the bedroll was made, he squatted beside it and spent a half hour cleaning guns, checking their actions, putting in fresh loads.

"She's right," he told himself. "David wouldn't let a thing like that go by. It isn't his way."

Chapter Twenty-one

Hurry, the voices told me. The voices in my mind. Hurry, they said. There isn't much time, and there are things to do, so hurry. Nothing else matters.

But the voices were wrong about that. Things had changed since nothing mattered. It's all different now, I tried to tell them. Things *do* matter. I matter. Me, Callahan Bodie. *I matter!* Because of what I remember, because of what I have seen and where I have been, because people I didn't know have trusted me, the way Mrs. Jessup once trusted me, for all these reasons. I matter. Because I have seen rainbows . . . and because when I don't matter anymore, I'll never see a rainbow again. Not through these eyes or any eyes.

Dust on the wind. That's all I'll be when I don't matter anymore. Just what Pete Joslyn said. Dust on the wind.

The voices were wrong. I matter.

But why were they urging me to hurry? Why did they say that time is running out? Is it because things are changing so?

It's the memories that are changing, mostly. But there are other changes, too. Puzzling changes — things that might make sense except that I don't really want to know what they mean. Things that are frightening.

Like that deputy in town, the one that got in my way. He was a big man. Big and strong, but I put him on the ground with my fist. Sure, I know how to use my fists. Where I come from, you learn to use everything you have. You learn, or you don't last long. I've hit men before, put men down before. But this was different, and it was the tin-star bull, Vince Terrell, who made me realize it. He said I must have jumped Kale White from behind, or used a gun butt on him.

I didn't think about it just then. It was later, looking around David Austin's house at David Austin's things and remembering them, that it hit me. Vince Terrell was right. That's what Hands Bodie would have done—jumped the bull from behind, never given him a chance, never let him see who or what hit him.

That's what Hands Bodie would do. But not David Allen Austin. David Austin would do what I did. Face to face, man to man. It would be his way.

And that's where the confusion came from, and where the memories began to shift.

Hands Bodie wouldn't have taken on a harness bull face to face, because Hands Bodie wasn't strong enough to put a man like that on the ground, and he knew it. It's why I worked so hard to be a shooter, back in the city. Because the gun was my best tool, not my fists.

What I did to Kale White, I really wasn't capable of doing.

But then, David Allen Austin might have, if he had known how. David Allen Austin was never a half-starved kid on the streets, and as a man he had the

253

strength of muscle and bone that comes of growing up healthy and never going hungry. David Allen Austin was big enough — and strong enough — to poleax a harness bull, if he knew how.

But he didn't know how. It takes more than hard fists and muscles. It takes skill. Street skill, back-alley skill. City skill. Austin didn't have that, facing that big man out there in the courthouse lot. He didn't have the skill. But Hands Bodie did.

And now the voices in my head said hurry, and the memories were changing, and the two things meant the same thing. Hurry, before things change too much. Hurry, do what must be done — for Mary and the baby — because when the memories stop dancing around and become clear, then it will be too late.

Too late for what?

Don't think about it, the voices said. Just hurry, and do what you know has to be done.

Destroy another gang. This time, a sanctioned one.

Hurry. Time is running out.

On a winding little road below a cleared-over hill, a creaking old wagon crept along behind a gaunt horse. In the wagon were two women, several children, and a pitiful collection of hastily assembled belongings. A milk cow on a lead plodded along behind, and farther back two young boys and a flop-eared dog drove a dozen or so sheep.

The procession went along the dusty road, and only the youngest children looked back at the now-deserted little farmstead that had been their home.

The new law in the county seat had come with a bill for taxes, and there was no money to pay it.

254

Three horsemen sat their mounts on the hillside, watching quietly as the little procession crept past and away. All three wore guns at their belts, and pulled-down hat brims shaded their eyes from the morning sun.

When the wagon and flock were no more than settling dust in the distance, two more riders came from the deserted farm. At the road they paused, then headed on up the hill to join the three waiting there.

"Well, they're cleared out," Rudy said, "I guess the place is ours."

"Ours?" Wilson sneered. "All we do is set on it 'til the papers are drawn up, then turn it over to Carlile." He pushed back his hat, troubled eyes looking at the place below. Not much of a spread. A hundred acres or so, but only fifteen or twenty cleared for use. A slanting old pole barn and a sag-roofed dog-run house. Not much of a spread at all, yet it had been home to those women and their children. With men gone off to war and not come back, it was all they'd had left. Wilson shook his head. "Can't say as I like this kind of work, Pete. Not the least bit."

Pete Joslyn stared off into the distance, where the procession had gone. Lone Oak was over there, a few miles away. The movers would find shelter there for a time, he supposed. After that, who knew? It wasn't Thad Carlile's concern what happened to the people who lost their land in this county. His concern was simply to take what he wanted.

"It's work," Joslyn said. "It's what we came for, and the pay's fair enough."

"Sure." Wilson nodded. "Two hundred when we sign the place over, another couple hundred for the next claim. Easy work an' good money. All I said was, I don't much like what we're doin'."

"We don't, somebody else will."

Jim and Hank sat their mounts, just listening. The youngest of the five, they would go along with the rest, whatever. But they didn't fully understand it. Now Hank asked, "Why us, though? That Carlile's got a sheriff in his pocket, an' all the deputies he wants. How come he hires private guns for his land swindles?"

"Politician," Wilson muttered. He leaned over to spit, as though the word had a foul taste.

"Trappings of law," Joslyn explained. "If a law officer takes land for resale, that doesn't look right and folks get upset. But us and the others, we're just legal squatters. Not likely anybody will get too righteous about us occupying this or that abandoned place. Then, if anybody ever even notices that the head law winds up with it, the deal is foggy enough that nothing can be made to stick."

"Lawyer finaglin'," Wilson muttered, curling his lip.

"That sheriff looked me up yesterday, Pete," Rudy said. "Wanted to know about that crazy jaybird we traveled with, the one that done the ruckus over at the courthouse. Sheriff wanted to know if his name was Austin."

"Asked me the same thing." Joslyn nodded. "What did you say?"

"Not much. I don't like that sheriff. I just said I'd heard the name Austin when we met up, and never asked any more about it."

"About what I told him, too." Joslyn's cheeks crinkled above his whiskers. "Don't know what the feller's game is, but if he wants to call himself Austin and rough up tax collectors, I don't see how it's up to us to disabuse anybody about it."

Wilson looked again at the dismal little farmstead below, then raised his eyes to look at distances, gazing southward. "I keep hearin' about all the Spanish cattle down yonder," he mused. "Just there for the takin', the way I hear it. You ever thought about the cow business, Pete?"

Joslyn gazed at the tracker, thoughtfully. Wilson was rarely a talkative man, but when he did have something to say it usually made sense. "Speak your piece, Wilson," he said finally. "What's in your craw?"

"This." Wilson shrugged. "What we're doin'. It ain't right, Pete. I never minded goin' off an' shootin' at Yankee soldiers, with them shootin' back. An' I don't mind hirin' out for gun wages, most ways. But we ain't fightin' anybody here, Pete. All we're doin' is help a sidewindin' politician kick widows an' orphans out of their homes. It makes me sick, tell the truth."

"I get the same feelin', Pete," Rudy said. "Nobody around here's makin' a fight of it . . . an' if they was to, what chance would they have? I feel like a damn robber."

"From what you told me, that Bodie did all right for himself at the courthouse. And from what I saw, he might give Carlile a run for his money if Carlile doesn't back off."

"Well, he won't back off. He's pullin' a tax dodge on the Austin place, just like he done here. I heard 'em settin' it out."

"That might get interestin'," Joslyn said.

"The schoolteacher an' the Injuns are out there with them," Hank offered. "I heard that over on the road."

Joslyn's eyes widened. "Miz Fremont? She's here? I hadn't heard that."

257

"What a feller said. That Bodie . . . or whatever he calls hisself here, he's still got them with him."

"She's gonna get herself killed, hangin' with that jasper," Wilson noted.

Joslyn came to a decision. "Hank, you and Jim get on down there and 'legally occupy' this place, like Carlile said. I think the rest of us ought to go have a look around."

"Just two of us?" Jim asked. "Is two enough here?"

"You see anybody else makin' claim on this place, Jim? Yeah, you two. It doesn't take five men to squat on a two-hole spread. Go on, now. We'll be back directly."

Miles to the east, a westbound coach was loading in the town of Nacogdoches. There were only a handful of passengers, though two of the men boarding wore the braided blue uniforms of field officers with the United States Army, and a company of Union cavalry was assembled to escort the coach.

Among the civilian passengers, one was a nondescript, quiet young man who seemed to blend into the background of the stage depot as surely as the hitch rails alongside did. So well did he blend that the two army officers looked up in surprise when he boarded the stage, and one of them glanced at a passenger list that the agent had provided for him. He looked, and then shrugged. There were, in fact, five civilian passengers booked on the coach. Somehow, he had only been aware of four of them as the loading was done. But there were five.

Turning his hand, he showed the list to the colonel sitting beside him and pointed at a name.

The colonel glanced at it, then at the newcomer just taking a seat opposite. As the nondescript young man settled himself, the officer extended a hand. "I believe I've met everyone else traveling with us. I am Colonel Travers, Army of Occupation. And you are . . . ?"

"Sullivan," the man said quietly, taking his hand for a quick shake. His voice was clipped, the syllables foreshortened in the manner of lower Manhattan. "The name is Sullivan."

Travers relaxed, leaning back. Coaches were in short supply and long demand in Texas these days, and mixed military-civilian travel was common. But there was always the worry of trouble, should some ticket agent breach security and assign a Southerner to a stage carrying blue-coat officers.

There was no doubt of this one, though. Mr. Sullivan was no Southerner. His New York City dialect was real. For the rest of the bouncing, gruelling trip westward by stage, Colonel Travers would not give "Mr. Sullivan" another thought. Even within the confines of a jostling coach, Sullivan seemed to just disappear among the other passengers, to blend into the woodwork.

Overnight, the word spread across southern Hunt County, from Lone Oak to Greenville. There had been a killing. A young man, shot down from the road someplace above Lone Oak. An Indian, some said, although most of those who heard the story rejected that. There were no Indians in north Texas. Not in this part, anyway. To the west, it was said, Tonkawa still were seen occasionally camping in the isolated bottoms. But not here.

Still, there had been a shooting, and word spread in whispers, from neighbor to neighbor. The killing had been on the Austin place, they said, and that sparked further speculation. Many had seen David Austin ride away unscathed after confronting the "provisionals" in the courthouse. Some had even recognized him, though he was much changed from the strapping, bright-eyed young man who went off with the volunteers to take part in the war. Much changed, but still in his size, his bearing, and beneath the scars on his face, there was recognition.

It had been thought that both the Austin boys were dead. But now young Davey was back, and had made it clear that Thad Carlile would not easily take revenge on the Austins.

The killing out there now . . . was it the next move in the game? Some thought so, others not, but there was that strange story that Davey had had an Indian kid with him when he went to the courthouse to find his wife and register his land. Maybe it was that Indian who was dead now, if there had ever been such a one at all.

Whatever, there was a sense among the watching citizens that something was happening. And a readiness began to grow. Just in case Davey Austin did manage to stand up to Thad Carlile and the provisionals—if he showed that it could be done—there were others who might join in.

Thad Carlile heard the rumors over breakfast, from some of his backers. He heard the words, and sensed the simmering unrest of the people. From his apartment he went directly to the courthouse to find Sheriff Vince Terrell.

"You did it, didn't you!" he demanded. "You just had to shoot somebody."

"Nobody but an Indian kid," Terrell rumbled, holding his gaze. "You said back off on David Austin, and I did. You didn't say anything about anyone else."

"But why? What good did it do?"

"You gave Austin a week to pay his taxes, Thad," Terrell said. "There's just no tellin' what trouble a tough nut like Austin can cause in a week. Maybe I lit his fuse, though. Maybe he'll try somethin' to get back, and maybe I'll eliminate your problem for you when he does."

Carlile's hard eyes blazed at the larger man. "I do the thinking around here, Terrell! I thought I made that clear."

"You do the thinkin' all you want, Thad," Terrell's voice carried contempt. "But when you think wrong, I'll set matters straight for you."

"You'll do what I say," Carlile snapped.

Terrell leaned back in his chair, lazily. "When it's best, I will. Look, Thad, I know you're the superintendent an' all, but there's just a hell of a lot you might not know about dealin' with tough nuts. That's what this Austin is. I've seen the kind." He grinned, his gaze boring into Carlile. "And while we're about it, Thad, I wouldn't push my weight around too much if I was you. Not with me, anyhow."

"I put that badge on you," Carlile hissed. "I can take it off just as easy."

"Can you, now? When you made me sheriff you made me a piece of this pie, Thad. You want the 'good citizens' around here to see you losin' pieces of your pie, right when you're startin' to cut into it?"

"I'm the law," Carlile said. "If I have to, Terrell, I'll bring in troops to put you out."

"My." Terrell shook his head. "What troops?"

261

"You know what troops. Captain Brooks's company."

"Oh, them. They'll be on their way to Austin in a day or two. There's a Colonel Travers on his way to collect them, right now. Meanwhile, they don't answer to you, you know. Oh, they'll follow you around if you say to, but they take their orders from me as long as they're here."

Carlile stared at the man, stunned.

"Read your own orders, Thad," Terrell said mildly. "You set up this 'provisional' scheme yourself, you know. Real good lawyer work, too. Got your tailfeathers covered ever' which way, even left yourself some outs in case Reuben Blaes or me got too much crossways of your 'constituents.' If the taxes are falsified, that's ol' Reuben's fault, ain't it? Not yours. An' just in case folks got too upset about bluebellies followin' you around, you covered yourself there, too. They don't rightly answer to the superintendent. They answer to the sheriff, just like you set it up."

Before Carlile could think of a response, the door of Terrell's office slammed open. A scar-faced deputy stood there. "You best come have a look, Vince. That Austin feller, he's just rode in. Looks like he's comin' here."

Chapter Twenty-two

Morning sun was high over the streets of Greenville when the man most people knew as David Austin rode into town. There were people on the streets, and he took his time, letting them look at him. Letting them wonder about why he had come back into town.

It was a thing that Callahan Bodie had learned, coming of age in the reeking streets of lower Manhattan. The greatest threat to a ruling gang in any neighborhood, even more than rival gangs, is a population outraged and up in arms. Any gang boss knew that the herd could bolt, given the right conditions. And every gang boss knew that when the herd bolted, it took more than a gang of thugs to stop them. Even the Tweeds and Tammany Hall knew that. More than one another, the bosses feared an outraged public.

But it rarely happened on its own. People were afraid, and lethargic. People would rather look away than take a chance — up to a point.

Hands Bodie knew the streets, and knowing them he knew about people in ways that David Austin could never have known. And he knew, from practice, that the games of the streets were the games of any place where a gang is in control. Even yokels were people — in that sense not much different from the people of his youth, the bakers and cobblers and tinsmiths and street artists, the butchers and tanners, the crafters and swampers, the hawkers and vendors, sign painters and glaziers, and all the rest who filled the streets by day, working at their trades to make the pennies they needed to live — the pennies the gangs sought by night, and took by fear and force.

The gangs and the politicians. The smart ones, though, didn't take it all. They only took a portion.

Taxes. The taxes of the streets. Faced with a demand for "taxes," the first thing to do was pay the taxes. But there were ways of doing that, that could cut to the quick of the gang's hold on the neighborhood. A man could cut the foundations right out from under a street gang.

If he was man enough, and if he lasted long enough.

He rode slowly into town, taking his time, letting the townspeople see him and wonder what he was doing.

Within sight of the courthouse he reined in and sat for long minutes in midstreet, just looking at the county edifice. Letting people see him look. Then, when he felt the weight of eyes upon him, he touched heels to his mount and reined into an easy trot along the street, past the courthouse, around the next turn and the next, making a full circle around the county's lots, hard eyes surveying the area and missing nothing.

He saw a few men with badges — Vince Terrell's

men—watching him cautiously. Don't you fellows wish we were alone here right now? he thought. Just you all, and me, and no witnesses? Frustrating, isn't it, that there are all these good people around?

And another inner voice with something like a sneer thought, look at them! Dummies think they could take me out if they had the chance. Yokels! They wouldn't last an hour where I come from.

Part of him said to ignore them, but another part rebelled. Each badge that he passed, he stared at—a cold, challenging stare that lasted until the other dropped his eyes.

When he was satisfied, he walked his mount to a hitch rail diagonally across from the main steps of the courthouse and stepped down. Looping his reins, he stepped up onto the walk, paused long enough for anyone interested to see him, then turned and went through a doorway. The sign on the windows said, BANK.

Inside, an elderly man behind a wrought-iron window looked up, blinked, and said, "Good morning," then took a closer look. "Ah, Davey? Davey Austin, is that you? Why, I couldn't hardly believe it when I heard you were back."

Bodie-Austin just looked at him.

"It's me, Davey," the teller reminded him. "Ralph Boswell. Remember? I did business with your daddy, boy. Land, but you've changed some. The war, I reckon."

"Mr. Boswell." He nodded. "Yes, I came home. Is this bank open for business?"

"Well, I reckon you could say so," Boswell shrugged. "Not that there's much business to be

265

had." He squinted. "You sound a mite peculiar, Davey. Is something . . .?"

"No, I'm all right." Subtly, the voice changed. Slower now, with an easy drawl. "Been a long time, that's all. Mr. Boswell, I received a statement for taxes on our property . . ."

"Well, I'm right sorry about that," the man said, real sincerity in his words. "Lot of folks havin' that kind of troubles these days. Some manages to pay off, but most can't. But we can't lend money for taxes, Davey. Superintendent's orders. Even if you was to put up the place, I couldn't . . ."

"I'm not here to borrow," he snapped, the drawl disappearing momentarily, then returning. "I came in to town to pay the taxes I owe. I don't need a loan."

"Oh." Boswell blinked. "Well, in that case you need to see Reuben Blaes, over at the courthouse."

"I know." Bodie-Austin pulled a heavy sack from the pocket of his coat. "But the money I have is all in coin, you see, and as I recollect, where Reuben Blaes is concerned, hard money has ways of getting lost. I want a bank draft. You can still do that, can't you? Accept hard money and issue a draft on it?"

"Why, I suppose . . ." Boswell took a deep breath and squared his shoulders. "I sure don't see any reason why I can't do that, Davey. No orders against currency transactions, that I've heard."

"Good." Still holding his money sack, he strode to the front door, opened it, stepped out, and waved an invitation at the sizable crowd of people standing around on the street outside. "You folks come in here, will you? Come on . . . that's right,

266

all of you, come on in. We need some witnesses."

Curiosity being what it is, the bank lobby was full of people within minutes, and more crowding near the door to listen.

Bodie-Austin stood beside the teller's cage and raised his sack of coin. "Some of you know me," he said. "David Allen Austin. I have a place down by Lone Oak, that my pa had before me, and I reckon some of y'all knew him. His name was Sam Austin, and he took a hand in clearin' out that thievin' Catsprings bunch back before the war. But that was a long time ago, and he's dead now, and I come back to find out that the varmints have come back, and are runnin' things in this county. Varmints like Reuben Blaes, and that gunslick Vince Terrell, all workin' for a weasel named Carlile."

He paused, letting his words soak in. Whispers flew like bees through the crowd, and here and there a grin formed itself upon a face. Near the door, a man with a badge edged away, eased himself out and ran, his boot heels thudding into distance. "Yonder went one of them," the easy voice of David Austin said, and there were more grins.

"Well, it's tax time," he continued. "I got a bill for property taxes on my place and my brother Tom's . . . for about three times what the places are worth . . . and I come to pay my taxes. But I won't hand good money over to any Reuben Blaes, for him to steal. Mr. Boswell here"—he indicated the teller—"is going to take my money and give me a bank draft on it, and I'll pay taxes with that. Then if Reuben Blaes or Thad Carlile want to use the money for anything sneaky—like maybe put it in their pockets to buy up forfeited properties — they'll have to explain about that to somebody in Austin. Y'all understand?"

A man nearby raised a hand. "How come you're tellin' us all this, Davey?"

"Witnesses," he said. "Every one of you is a witness that I'm legally paying my taxes. An' maybe some of y'all might want to pay yours the same way. It'd take a Lord's miracle to make Reuben Blaes and Thad Carlile honest, but the more attention folks give to that, the closer they might come."

Turning, he emptied the bag of coin onto Boswell's counter and said, "Count that out, Mr. Boswell, and make out my draft."

The bank was full of voices now, not just whispers but spirited conversation.

"Is that what they're doin', Mr. Austin?" a man asked. "You think they're usin' tax money to buy up forfeited places for themselves?"

"I know that's what they're doing," a voice not quite the same as Austin's easy drawl said. "It's an old game and I've seen it before." Then, noticing the curious looks around him, he slipped back into easy Texas twang. "Damn war," he said. "Sometimes now I talk funny."

Boswell had counted the coins. Now he locked them into a strongbox and dipped a steel pen to write a money draft, as "Austin" had instructed. The teller's hand shook slightly, but there was a mean grin on his old face. "Them fellers not. goin' to like this." He chuckled. "Not the least bit."

Beyond the door, in the street, there were raised voices and the sounds of scuffling. Boswell looked up and said, "Some of you younger fellers, shut that door, will you? Hate to have too many people in here all at one time."

Ripples of laughter sounded as the bank's door was firmly closed in the faces of several badged men.

With his bank draft put away, Bodie-Austin headed for the door. "I got business at the courthouse now," he said casually. "Any of you witnesses want to come along, just be my guests."

When he opened the door and stepped out, hard hands grabbed at his arms. Tried to grab, and missed, and a pair of badge-wearers tumbled backward, one sprawling in the street, one doubling over a hitch rail.

"You wouldn't know how to do that, without me," Bodie muttered to himself. "You still need me, Reb."

If anyone nearby heard him, they shrugged it off. A man that went to war and came home talking funny might talk that way to himself, too.

With men crowding out behind him, all wanting to see what happened next, Bodie stepped into the dusty street, and stopped. Vince Terrell and several "deputies" stood in midstreet, facing him.

"What did you do to my men, Austin?" the sheriff demanded.

"Not a thing," Austin's drawl said. "They prob'ly stumbled over each other. You picked some pretty clumsy hands, I'd say."

"What's going on here? Why are you in town?"

Eyes as hard and cold as city streets bored into Terrell, and a voice that was down-home country said, "Why, don't you remember? You delivered a

269

tax bill to me, out at my place. So I'm here to pay my taxes."

Terrell's weathered face went dark at the rippling laughter around him. "You're here to . . ."

"And while you were out there, *Sheriff* Terrell," Bodie-Austin raised his voice so everyone would hear it, "you shot down a youngster in cold blood. Murdered him, just out of spite. So after I settle my taxes, then I've got some settling to do with you. That boy you murdered is my brother."

Terrell gaped at him. "You're crazy! That was some damned Indian kid. I never seen your brother. Your brother died in the war."

"Well, you sure know who you murdered, don't you, *Sheriff?*" He glanced around, making sure everybody was hearing it all. "No, that Indian kid wasn't my brother, before you killed him. He is now, though. Now get out of my way. I have legal business over at the courthouse."

Terrell's hand poised, quivering, above his gun butt, and some of the other badges were thinking about drawing, too. But the big man with the scarred face made no move toward his own gun, though the eyes of him spoke of death and promises. In the clipped, nasal voice of city streets, he said. "You think you could kill me, yokel? *Me?* Not on your best day."

Terrell's confusion was visible, and Bodie-Austin pushed past him, not bothering to look back. After a moment, two dozen or more townsmen followed him, walking around and past the badge-wearers as though they weren't there.

"You're gonna get me killed," the scar-faced man muttered to himself. Then, "Not you, though.

270

You already died." He strode across the streets and up the courthouse steps. "You need me," he muttered.

Upstairs, minutes later, an ashen-faced Reuben Blaes accepted payment of the Austin taxes, by notarized bank draft, and started to make out a receipt.

"Not one," the man standing over him said. "Separate receipts, for the two places. David Austin's and the Tom Austin estate."

The room was full of people, watching, and others were crowding in as word spread. If nothing else, for the citizens, it was the best entertainment since the time years before when Sam Austin and his friends ran the riffraff out of old Catsprings, and out of the county.

Blaes was sweating and muttering as he wrote out the receipts. Several of Terrell's deputies were in the room, but seemed to have no idea what—if anything—they should do. Terrell was, noticeably, not there.

"You'll never get away with this, Austin," Blaes hissed as he handed over the tax receipts.

Bodie-Austin put the papers away and raised a hand above his head. Immediately, the clamor of voices was hushed. "What?" he demanded. "What did you say?"

Blaes's cheeks went ashen again. His lower lip quivered, "I just said, you can't do this."

"I can't pay my taxes? You made out the invoice, didn't you, Blaes? It has your name on it."

"The superintendent . . ."

"Carlile? I didn't see his name there. Just yours. These are legal taxes, aren't they, Blaes?"

271

"Of course they're legal!"

Bodie-Austin put two more pieces of paper in front of Blaes. "Sign these, while you're at it. I just sold Tom's place, and this is to record the transfer."

Shaking, Blaes scrawled his signature on the papers. His tormentor took them and put them away. "Now," he said. "You say the taxes I paid are legal taxes? Then I want to see the appraisal."

"The what?"

"The property appraisal, that these taxes are based on. You can't determine property taxes without an appraisal. That isn't legal even in the north."

"I don't . . ."

"Where is the appraisal, Blaes? Show it to me."

"It . . . it isn't here. The superintendent personally ordered the taxes. He told me to . . ."

"Blaes, shut up!" The voice came from the doorway.

Bodie—or Austin—turned and gazed at the richly tailored man who had just entered. A slim, wiry-looking man in his thirties or early forties, he had a sallow face with a trimmed mustache, and dark eyes that glittered with anger.

Bodie's hard eyes sized him up, and Austin's laconic voice drawled, "Well, well. I expect this is the Provisional Superintendent himself. The chief looter in charge. Carlile, you're every bit the snake your daddy was, an' he wasn't fit to hide in a hole."

The dark eyes blazed at him. "And you're David Austin. What do you want here, Austin?"

"Why, I'm here conductin' legal business with

272

this county, *Mister* Carlile. Business by your own rules."

"What business?"

"Well, let's see . . ." Elaborately, holding "Bodie" in check, Austin raised a hand and started counting off on his fingers. ". . . first, I paid my taxes, by a legal bank draft that's as good as gold except that you're goin' to have a hell of a time lining your pockets with it. Second, I have protested the taxes I just paid, and requested to see the appraisal on which they were based, and have been refused. In front of witnesses. Also, in front of those same witnesses, I recorded a property sale—tax paid—and laid claim to an abandoned property in this county, in accordance with the procedures issued by *your* provisional government, Carlile."

Carlile's voice was a hiss. "What property?"

"It used to be called Catsprings, before the decent folks around here ran the varmints out of it and burned it down."

Blazing outrage and ugly hatred shone from Carlile's eyes. "Catsprings? You can't . . ."

"I sure enough can. What's the matter, Thad? You forget about Catsprings while you were makin' up your property list? You and yours don't own that place anymore. It's abandoned, and I just claimed it. Not only that, but Mr. Blaes here signed the record document for me. All done and legal."

Laughter rippled among the "witnesses," and somewhere in the crowd a man asked, "What for you want Catsprings, Davey? Ain't anything down there anymore."

The hard eyes in the scarred face didn't waver from Thad Carlile's eyes. "We're gonna need a graveyard around here," David Austin said levelly. "Someplace where varmints can be planted, so they won't be side by side with decent folks. I figure Catsprings is just the place."

Chapter Twenty-three

Beat 'em at their own game, that would be David Austin's way. It would appeal to him — *did* appeal to him, Bodie knew, to put on a show like that right there in the critters' own snake den, the courthouse. Grab them by their precious rules and twist until it hurt. Rub their noses in their own corruption. Poetic justice, wisdoms that were not his own told him. An eye for an eye, a tooth for a tooth, a claim for a claim.

Somewhere within him, somebody was howling with glee at the irony of it all.

And that irritated him no end. Such was David Allen Austin's way, not Hands Bodie's. It was the way of a damned reb who should have died a long time ago in a rain-drenched shell crater on a battlefield far away. Who should have died, but somehow didn't. He had known that for a long time now, known that he wasn't alone — that something had happened on that silent battlefield, and there was a rainbow and somehow two men came away that morning, even though one had died there.

At first it had all been dim and senseless, disjointed images in a clouded mind. But he had known, after a while, that he was not alone.

The more Bodie became aware of that—the more he remembered about things he had never known, the more he saw as though through the eyes of another man—the bleaker he felt. Of late, a nameless dread had come alive within him.

The more aware of David Allen Austin he became, it seemed, the less there was of Hands Bodie. It was as though he were being pushed aside by the reb, whittled away with each new recollection. What had begun with rainbows seemed a torrent now, slowly eroding him. As though he were nothing more than a suit of clothes for another man to wear, to don piece by piece so that each piece became a part of him.

"I matter, damn it," he told himself—and the ghost within him. "Me, Callahan Bodie. *I matter!*" And in the silence a voice inside him seemed to say, "Of course you matter, Yankee. I'd never have made it home without you."

And the echoes of the voice went on and on—echoes in many voices saying, hurry now. Hurry. There isn't much time.

Austin's way. Bodie snorted in impatience as he ran his mind over the things he—or the Austin part of him—had done earlier in the day, on his visit to Greenville. "Paid taxes and claimed land," were Austin's words for it. Now Hands Bodie muttered, "just as well if you died when you did, reb. You don't know the first thing about handling gangs."

Paid taxes and made a claim? What he had actually done—and Hands Bodie understood it very well—was spit in the eye of the gang boss himself.

It would have been better to take them one at a time, the tax collector, the badge bull, and maybe the top gun among Carlile's hired hands. Take them one at a time, separate them out, divide them, and then put them down one at a time. Without them, the top boss, Carlile, would be nothing. With all his bulls and bullies out of the way, Carlile would be simply the final step. Shoot him and hang his body from a windmill tower or something.

But Austin had it his way. Beat them at their own game. Beat them? Bodie snorted again. Humiliated them, maybe, so now the entire gang's attention was focused—all at the same time—on him.

"I do it my way from here on," he said, reining in on a cleared rise to look all around. Someone was following him, he knew. Some of them, likely. He had sensed it—had felt someone behind him, from the time he dropped off the receipts and claim papers at Austin's place. They were after him, right enough. But he didn't know where they were. "It's my turn now, reb, and you better hope I'm as good at what I do as I think I am, or you're gonna die again, and me with you this time."

For the first time, there seemed to be no argument. The reb was there, all right, still right there in his mind, stronger than ever, knowing the lay of the land, knowing things that Hands Bodie couldn't have known, giving him directions at every turn, but now he seemed relaxed. Relaxed, confident, and content to let Bodie handle the things that were Bodie's specialties.

The game was on now—or, as Austin thought it, the fat was in the fire. The rug had been pulled and the challenge laid down. It was killing time.

It was the old man who had told him—them—about Catsprings. Old Moss Jackson, pained by his broken bones and rambling on about what was going on in the county.

Bodie hadn't understood—or even cared very much—about what the old man said. About how Old Man Ty Carlile had tried years ago to build up a cattle business by stealing cows and putting them on grass around Catsprings and not letting anybody close enough to read their brands until the calving was done. Talk like that, it didn't mean much to Bodie. "Rustling," the old man said. David Austin knew that out here, that meant stealing livestock. To Bodie it meant petty swindling, like sleight of hand with marked cards. Or politics, like buying votes for an alderman's job.

But Austin listened to it, and made him ask questions. Had anything been going on around old Catsprings lately? Had Carlile moved back onto the place? Had anybody?

There were some cattle on graze yonder, the old man said. He didn't know whose cattle they were. And no, there wasn't anybody staying around there, that he'd heard about. Last he'd heard, none of it had been rebuilt.

Austin heard and understood, and in a way Bodie understood, too, because Austin did. And that was why Austin had done what he had done. Because Thad Carlile hadn't gone to the trouble to

278

reclaim the old place—probably it had never crossed his mind that somebody else might step in and claim it, since it would never occur to Carlile that anybody else was as smart as he was. And because Austin knew what Carlile was up to. On top of getting even with a lot of decent people, and just throwing his weight around for the fun of it, Thad Carlile was out to do what his daddy had tried.

He wanted land, and he was bringing in cattle. Before anybody even knew what he was up to, Thad Carlile intended to have himself a land-and-cattle company that could run things in the county even after a real occupation government was established.

And David Austin had cut him off right at the stump, by claiming Catsprings.

If the claim held up.

Which meant, if "Austin" lived long enough to establish his claim.

Which meant, if they didn't kill Hands Bodie first. Because Austin was dead. Bodie reassured himself of that, pushing away the gnawing dread that clung where the dimmest memories were. Austin had died. He was still here—somehow he was with Bodie—but he was dead.

"Wasn't for me," he muttered, easing his mount down a blackjack slope, "you'd be all the way dead. Only way you stayed alive, was by me. You needed me. You still do. I matter."

Two more miles and he looked down at a section of the Sabine bottoms and knew where he was. Old slab foundations and burned-over timbers were nearly hidden by brush and young thickets. Rutted tracks had once been a pair of roads, and here and there were bits of debris. The fallen shaft of a windmill. A broken-down old wagon sitting out on the clear slope. Trash and debris, barely visible now under years of overgrowth. And on the low slopes, little bunches of grazing cattle.

Old Catsprings.

He turned again to look back the way he had come. Stronger than before, now, was the feeling that he was followed, but still he saw no one. The hills rolled away, like ragged domes of gray and green, rising from their shadows on the late afternoon sun. Clear slopes, brushy stretches, stands of blackjack oak and, here and there in the bottoms, thickets of laurel and the apple-green of brooding willows. Miles of distance, shrouded by its own camouflage of contour and growth.

"Sticks," Bodie said, his lip lifting in a sneer. No decent cover anywhere, not a wall or an alley, not a sewer or chimney stack, nothing to which he could relate. Yet he knew, even as his eyes tried to see the secrets of the land, that there was cover . . . everywhere. He was followed, and his instincts told him that there were eyes watching him. They were there, somewhere, and they could see him. But he couldn't see them.

With one more scan of his back trail—which showed him nothing—he flicked the reins to start his horse down-slope, toward the overgrown rubble of Catsprings.

The shot came from behind him then, the angry-bee sound of a bullet drowned by the sharp crack of a rifle's report, and his Colt .36 was in his hand before the first echoes came. He started to turn, then froze in the saddle as a man appeared suddenly ahead of him, rising from a clump of brush, pivoting, to fall facedown.

Behind him a shrill, angry voice yelled, "Man, are you blind? Get down! Move!" and a second rifle-shot sounded. Fifty yards ahead, and to his right, a man pitched from behind a sandstone ledge and fell, twitching.

Bodie was off his horse, then, and running. In the moment of gunfire, he saw movement ahead, and he made for it. Two of them appeared there, rising from concealment, their guns leveled at him and barking. The Colt spoke twice, two shots that sounded like one. One of the figures collapsed like a puppet with its strings cut. "Middle of the neck," Bodie grunted. The second one stood for a moment, staring at him, then fell backward, dead. "Middle of the chest," he said.

He leaped over a body and dived, rolling into the cover they had arisen from, a shallow little cleft angling downhill, its banks ragged with brush. A few feet away a man was crouched, just turning to see what had happened. Bodie's bullet went into his left eye . . . into the middle of his head.

For long moments, then, there was silence. Even the wind had gone still, as though stunned by the ringing gunfire. Bodie raised his head to look around and a bullet ripped through the brush inches from him.

"Keep your head down!" the same angry voice

281

shrilled.

He dropped down, and when he turned Mason Fremont was crouched beside him, feeding hulls into a Spencer carbine. "Didn't you see those people?" the boy rasped. "They were plain as day, and you were ridin' right into 'em." The anger faded then, and the dark, half-Indian eyes went wide. "Lord, I . . . I killed some of them, didn't I?"

"Where did you come from?" Bodie hissed.

"I was right back there, behind you. I thought you saw me. You looked right at me."

"I didn't see anybody." Carefully, he reached out and tugged at the foot of the dead man on the gully bank.

"Stay down," Mason said. "There are at least two more somewhere."

The body slid downward, between them. It was a face Bodie had seen before, one of the "deputies" from the courthouse. But now he wore no badge.

Mason stared at the dead face. "Right in the throat," he said, with awe. "You shot him in the throat."

"Middle of the neck," Bodie corrected. "That's where the spine is. That was you following me? I knew there was somebody back there. How about these, though? How come they were ahead of me?"

"You *couldn't* see them, could you?" Mason shook his head. "They were here waitin'. I guess they knew where you'd go. What is this place?"

"Used to be a settlement. Called Catsprings. I

claimed it this morning."

"Then that's how they knew where to find you." He paused, head up and listening. "Two more," he whispered. "One's in that little thicket yonder . . ."

"Where?"

"Right over there. Use your eyes."

Bodie squinted. "All I see is a bird."

"That's right," Mason said. "Where that bird flew from, that's where he is. The other one is down lower, farther away. He's moving." Again the dark-agate eyes stared around in wonder. "I killed . . . three men. Just a minute ago."

"So did I," Bodie snapped. "So what?"

"I never . . ." Mason shuddered. "I hope one of them was the one who shot Wendell."

"That was Terrell. These aren't him, but they're the same kind. How long have you been following me?"

"Most all day . . . look! Look now, at the thicket!"

Bodie looked, and saw the man there. Among confusing shapes and shadows, the man had moved slightly. His silhouette was clear. Bodie thrust the .36 away and pulled out the bright Army .44 from Pleasant Hill.

"That's better'n a hundred yards," Mason said. "A pistol can't . . ."

The big gun's bark drowned his voice. In the thicket, the silhouette poised for an instant, then jumped straight up, arms waving, body arching backward. He fell and disappeared in the shadows.

"My Lord," Mason breathed.

"Middle of the chest," Bodie rumbled, his words

283

sharp with New York twang. "Where the heart is."

Mason was listening again, and this time Bodie heard what the boy heard. Rustling sounds, as of someone in a hurry, pushing through heavy brush. "That's the other one," Mason said.

"I hear him. Where is he?"

"He's heading for their horses. Down there, past that cliff." Without a sound, the Indian boy melted into shadowed brush and was gone.

"Crap," Bodie breathed. He couldn't see the horses the kid had pointed to, but he could see the cliff, a twenty-foot wall of eroded stone, its silhouette like the corner of a crumbling building.

The fleeing man didn't know there was anybody behind him until a rifle bullet whistled past his ear. He jerked around, saw a glimpse of movement and fired three times, his handgun bucking. Then he ran again. He had been off to one side, and hadn't seen all of what happened, but he had seen enough. The horses were just ahead, just beyond that rock bank. He sprinted toward it, wheeled around its corner, and ran into a fist that doubled him over.

"Clumsy," Hands Bodie muttered, catching the man before he could fall. A hand like a vise grabbed his gun arm and twisted. Bone snapped and the ambusher's pistol rattled down the slope. The man stifled a scream, trying to kick his way free. A grip on his other arm, and bones broke there, too. Then he was on his knees, Bodie's hard fingers digging into his chest, gouging beneath his collarbone.

"Talk to me," Bodie said.

It was several minutes before Mason Fremont arrived, blood seeping from a bullet nick in his shoulder. He stared in fascination at the broken, battered man lying on the ground at Bodie's feet, and asked, "Is he dead?"

"Didn't last long at all." Bodie nodded. "Damned yokel."

"He isn't Vince Terrell, is he?"

"No. That bull's gonna have to be invited, I guess."

Bodie stepped away, reloading his emptied chambers. "Well, the pot's stirred now," he drawled in David Austin's voice. He looked around, counting in his mind. "Eight," he said, thoughtfully. "I don't suppose you brought a spade?"

"No."

"Then we won't bury them. What is that down there, past that busted wagon?"

Mason peered, shading his eyes. "That fence? Nothing much. Just a couple of sections of rail fence still standing. Why?"

"I guess that will do," Bodie decided. "Come on, you can give me a hand."

In last light of evening, they stepped back to look at their work. Like limp, castaway scarecrows, seven bodies lined the rails of an old fence. Each was suspended, more or less upright, from the top rail, each held there by his own belt or shirtsleeves. The eighth one—the one who had been beaten to death—still lay on the shale slope where Bodie had left him.

Mason stared at them, feeling hollow in the pit of his stomach. He had seen dead men before, but never a sight like this. The seven bodies were lined up for display, like cow-killer wolves hung on a fence.

After a judicious glance, Bodie had turned away. He had collected all the ambushers' guns, and folded them into a blanket. Now he was counting the money he had taken from their pockets. "Carlile sure didn't pay these yokels much," he said. "Not near enough to die for. But then, it's prob'ly more than they were worth. Here." He divided the money and held out half of it. "Your share."

Mason backed away, feeling revulsion.

"Take it," Bodie said. "Money's money."

Mason shook his head, backing away another step. Bodie shrugged and put the money in his own belt-pocket. "Why did you follow me, kid?"

"I just . . ."

"Tell me!"

"I . . . I thought that sheriff, Vince Terrell, might find you. Or you him. I want to kill him."

Bodie nodded, glancing again at the seven dead men hung on the fence. "Well, it doesn't hurt to practice," he said.

Above, on the low slopes, little bunches of cattle were gathering, bedding down for the night. Nearer, horses grazed, their own and the ambushers' horses that Mason had found and brought in.

"Do you know anything about cows?" Bodie asked.

"A little." Mason glanced at the sunset sky, wishing he were somewhere else — somewhere without dead men displayed on a fence. "Why did we do those men up like that, Mr. Bodie? What's the use of it?"

"Symbolic," the man said. "Like throwing them off a tower, or pushing them down the sumps in a school sink."

"What?"

"Never mind. Do you know how to get cows from one place to another?"

"Yeah." Mason shrugged. "Drive them."

"Those cows there . . . are they worth anything?"

"Would be if they were penned and branded. Why? Whose are they?"

"They're ours, now. They're on my property. How long to get them over to Austin's place?"

Mason thought about it. "Most of a day, I reckon. You want to take them there?"

"You don't want any of this money, fine. I'll keep it. But the cows are yours. We'll get started in the morning. We ought to be back by then."

"Back from where?"

"From the courthouse. The best way to get Vince Terrell out here where he can see his symbolic shooters, is to leave their horses—and that busted-up yokel—at the courthouse for him."

Chapter Twenty-four

Pete Joslyn, Rudy, and Wilson had put many a mile behind them in the day and a half since leaving Jim and Hank at the abandoned claim spread. They had traveled around half the county, from Lone Oak over to the Sabine bottoms, then back to the Lone Oak Road and the Austin place, where they had stayed the night, bedding down in the barn at the old place after some late-hours conversation with Justine Fremont, Moss Jackson, and Maude Carver.

Circling around the David Austin place in the morning, they had gone up to Greenville, listened around for a while, then headed back to where they started.

Jim and Hank had a fire going in the hearth of the little abandoned house, and a pot of coffee boiling.

"We'll pack up and move out at first light, boys," Pete Joslyn told the youngsters as the three settled themselves in. "We been lookin' and listenin' some, and we agree we made a mistake."

"Yeah," Rudy added, "It's like that jasper told me—that Bodie, or Austin or whoever . . ."

"The crazy one?" Hank poured steaming mugs.

"That one. He said we was in bad company, and it looks like he was right."

"We're on the wrong side," Wilson agreed.

"I think we might be on the losin' side," Joslyn said.

Jim looked at him, confused. "I didn't know there was sides here, Pete. I mean, we're workin' for the man who runs things, ain't we?"

"There's sides now," Joslyn drawled. "War has just been declared in these parts."

Hank replaced the coffee pot on the hearth rung. "So then who *is* the other side?"

"That crazy jasper," Wilson said. "Unless they've killed him by now."

Morning brought drizzling rain to Greenville. It also brought consternation. Eight bone-weary horses were halter-tied at the hitch rails in front of the courthouse, and eight saddles lay in the street behind them. And on the courthouse steps lay the barely recognizable body of Curt Seldin, former cattle thief and murderer and lately one of Sheriff Vince Terrell's provisional deputies.

The people who found the mysteries there were early risers, citizens of the county who had come to the courthouse on business.

Within minutes of the discovery, Sheriff Terrell and the superintendent, Thad Carlile, arrived from opposite directions, both of them disheveled and irritated.

Terrell squatted beside Seldin's body, stunned at the condition of it. It looked as though every long bone in the man's carcass had been broken, and his face was a lumpy mass of battered flesh and broken cartilage.

Terrell looked up. "Who did this?" When no one responded, he stood, glaring around. "Where are the rest of my men? Who's on duty here?" He took a better look at the horses then, and at the saddles flung in the street. Eight horses and eight saddles. One was Seldin's. That left seven. "Where are my deputies?" he demanded.

"You ought to ask the superintendent," a citizen in the crowd suggested. "Seems like I seen him send your bunch off someplace yesterday."

Terrell rounded on Carlile. "What did you do?"

"I had use for them," Carlile said. "They should have been back last night."

"They're my deputies," Terrell growled. "They take orders from me, not you. You got your own men."

"All my men were busy," Carlile snapped. "Yours weren't, and you weren't around, so I hired them."

"You can't hire my deputies!"

"They weren't wearing badges, Terrell. They were on their own time." He stopped, glaring at the crowd of interested faces around them. "You people clear this street," he ordered. "Get out of here."

A few turned away, but most didn't.

"You heard the superintendent!" Terrell roared. "All of you, go home!"

"We got business with the county, Sheriff," someone said. "We're here legal, on legal business."

Carlile frowned. "What business?"

"We got business with the tax collector," another said. "We want to see our appraisals."

"The appraisals are none of your business,"

Carlile snapped. "Now clear out of here. Sheriff, I want this crowd cleared away, immediately."

Terrell's hand went to his gun, and stopped there. At least a half-dozen rifles, cradled casually across the arms of citizens, were pointed his way, and the looks in the eyes of their owners said they were tired of being pushed. "Let's go inside," Terrell told Carlile. "We can talk there. Some of you men, take care of this body here. Get it off these steps."

"Where'll we put the scutter?" a man wondered.

"Out in the street with his saddle, I reckon," another suggested.

"While you're in there," someone shouted at Terrell and Carlile, "tell Reuben Blaes that he's got taxpayers waitin' to have some talk with him."

As the big doors closed behind Carlile and Terrell, a coach rolled up the street, completing a night run from the east. Riding along behind it, wet and tired, were soldiers. At the depot a block from the courthouse, the stage disgorged passengers. Among those getting off was a uniformed Federal officer who stepped aside to peer up the street. "What are those people doing over there by the courthouse?" he asked.

A baggage handler shrugged. "Talkin' about taxes, I reckon."

A civilian passenger, a nondescript young man who seemed to blend with his background, went inside and rapped on the ticket window. When it was opened, he asked, "Can you tell me where the Lone Oak Post Office is?"

"Last time I heard, it was down to Lone Oak," the agent said curtly.

"Is there a stage that goes there?"

291

The agent's lip curled slightly, an involuntary reaction to the abrasive sound of the Yankee's words. "Why would we run a stage to Lone Oak? It's just down the road a piece. Folks generally just ride down there, or hitch on a wagon."

The man turned away, then turned back. There was a smile on his sallow face, but the eyes in it were as cold as death. "Thank you," he said.

Out in front, the Union officer and his escort were collecting their baggage while a squad of mounted soldiers rode northward, toward the bivouac of the superintendent's escort company.

Word was on the street within minutes. The bluebelly colonel was just passing through, but when he went on west he was taking Thad Carlile's soldiers with him. The sheriff had dismissed them, and they were needed to man a new occupation garrison somewhere southwest.

In the courthouse, Vince Terrell was thinking about killing Thad Carlile. Every deputy he had left had been sent off to Old Catsprings, with orders to find and ambush David Austin. Eight deputies, and only one had been seen since, and that one was dead.

"I got to go down there and see what happened," Terrell thundered at Carlile. "I don't have anybody to send, so I got to go, myself! You damned lawyer, I ought to shoot you for messin' things up like you've done!"

"It's that Austin," Carlile spat. "Whatever's messed up, he did it. And if your two-bit gunslingers haven't killed him, then you'd better, because it's you he's after, not me."

"No, he already got you, didn't he? Claimin' that

spread where you got your cows . . . hell!" He turned away, furious. "Don't worry, Carlile. Austin's gonna be dead. Then when he is, maybe I'll do the same for you." He stopped, listening to the sound of angry voices upstairs. Reuben Blaes had showed up, and his "constituents" were filling his office, demanding legal proofs that they knew as well as he, had never existed.

"It's all gone sour," Terrell muttered. "Damn David Austin . . . and damn you, too, Carlile!"

It wasn't a big herd, making its way eastward along the stepped slopes of the Sabine. Seventy or eighty critters at the most, but they were a handful for the two men driving them.

From a rise, Pete Joslyn watched them for a few minutes, then turned to his partners. "It's Bodie and Miss Justine's kid brother," he said. "Let's go give 'em a hand."

Coming down the slopes, they held wide of the herd until they saw Bodie beckon them in. Then they fanned and joined the drive.

Passing Mason Fremont, Joslyn paused. "Heard about your brother," he said. "Miss Justine told us how it was. I'm right sorry."

Mason gazed at the older man with agate eyes that said nothing. "It was that sheriff," he said. "You all still tied in with that bunch?"

"We just came untied," Joslyn said. "Where y'all takin' these critters?"

"Back to the Austin place. They're Mr. Austin's." He pointed.

Joslyn glanced around, then back. "Is he bein'

293

Austin all the time now? Or is he still Bodie?"

"Best I can tell," Mason said thoughtfully, "it seems like he's both. I can't keep up."

"Mighty strange," Joslyn allowed, falling in to herd cattle. A mile farther along, he reined in alongside the New York man. "We're out of work, by our own choosin'," he explained. "Seems like you've done turned this county over an' shook it out some . . . Mr. David Allen Austin."

Bodie glared at him, then ignored him. In his manner now was the New York street thug, not the easygoing Texan.

"Bodie, then," Joslyn said. "What is it with you, anyway? Justine Fremont says she doesn't know whether you're actin' or just plain confused, but there's more to it than that, ain't there?"

"Drop it," Bodie said. "You want to help, then help. But leave me alone."

"Just curious." Joslyn started to rein away, but he couldn't let it go that easily. "Only thing is, there isn't any way you could be David Allen Austin. But Austin's wife says you really are."

The look on Bodie's face then—and it *was* Bodie—made Joslyn's breath catch in his throat. He had never in his life seen such loneliness, such longing . . . such real pain in a man's eyes. He let his breath out in a sigh. "I'm sorry," he said. "I had no right."

"You were right about me," Bodie's voice was thin and strained. "You had me pegged. I'm Hands Bodie. I'm from lower Manhattan, and I'm nothing at all. Just a street tough—and a shooter. But that's back there. Out here, I'm nobody at all. Like you said . . . dust on the wind."

294

"Hell, Bodie . . ." Joslyn could have kicked himself. Somehow he had hurt the man, deeply, and there was no reason for it. "Shoot, everybody's *somebody*. It's all in what you make of yourself, an' from what I've seen lately—and heard—I'd say you're a hell of a man."

Bodie just looked at him, with eyes that were incredibly remote, as though he were at a great distance. "You don't understand," he said. "I thought I knew what happened . . . back there, in the war. I was so sure . . . but I was wrong. The way I remembered it, that wasn't how it was at all. And that means I'm nothing at all. Now get away from me!"

Through the rest of a wet, gray day they pushed cattle along the Sabine crest, and the man who sometimes was David Allen Austin, and sometimes Hands Bodie, kept to himself and said not a word to anyone. He rode alone and stayed alone, and when one or another of them happened near he moved away.

It was late afternoon, and the Lone Oak road was in sight—and beyond it the Austin spread—when Mason rode alongside Pete Joslyn and asked, "Mr. Joslyn, what did you say to Mr. Bodie back yonder?"

"Nothin' that I should have," the man admitted.

"I'm worried about him. He doesn't seem like . . . well, any of the ways he usually is. But he won't talk. I don't know what's wrong."

"I don't, either, son. I surely don't."

Mason looked around, trying to find Bodie. He realized that he had in some way adopted the man. Had come to feel responsible for him because he seemed so lost so much of the time, and because he cared about him. Someplace back along the long trail from the Territories, Mason Fremont had decided that Hands Bodie was going to have a friend whether he wanted one or not. And Mason was it.

He spotted him after a moment, far out beyond the herd, riding alone, heading for the Austin place.

And he spotted something else, too. Angling in from north of west was another rider, a big man on a big horse, moving fast and keeping cover between himself and Bodie. Even at this distance, Mason saw the glint of a bright badge on the man's lapel, and the gun in his hand.

"Oh, God," he breathed, punching hard heels into his horse, bringing it into a haunches-down run. "Mr. Bodie!" He was too far away for the sound to carry, but he shouted anyway. "Use your eyes, for God's sake! Look around! Please, turn and look!"

Bodie was sudden death with a handgun, Mason knew. He had seen. But out in open country, he was like a blind man . . . as though, being raised in a city, he didn't know how to see what was obvious in the country.

"Mr. Bodie!" Mason screamed it, and other riders heard him—heard him, and saw what he saw, and put spurs to their mounts. But it was too late.

Mason saw the sheriff close in, saw him ride out of cover only thirty yards behind and to the left of Bodie. He saw the gun come level, and screamed, "Mr. Bodie!"

As though it carried on the gray wind, it seemed to reach him. In the distance, Bodie started to turn, to look back, then the gun in the sheriff's hand bucked and Bodie pitched sideways, clinging for a moment to his saddle, then falling to the hard ground.

Like one in a trance, Mason hauled in his reins, bringing his horse to a dead stop. Without being aware of anything except what he watched out there, three hundred yards away, he raised the Spencer carbine Hands Bodie had given him and braced his cheek against its cool walnut stock. "Middle of the chest," he muttered. "Where the heart is."

It was an impossible range. He fired, braced, and fired again. Out there, Sheriff Vince Terrell was turning his mount, circling toward the fallen form of Hands Bodie, lowering his gun for a second shot. Then, as though immensely surprised, he sat bolt upright, lowered his head and looked at his chest. And there, just to the right of the badge, blood spread outward in a growing stain on his shirt. He was still looking at it, seeming puzzled, when the second shot hit him, throwing him backward off his saddle . . . a dead man falling to the ground.

They carried the man called Bodie to Mary Austin's house, then by wagon to Lone Oak, where there was a doctor just back from the war.

For a time they thought he was dying. For a little time, they thought he was dead. But the breathing that had stopped began again, at first ragged, then more level, as though a struggle had ended.

For two days he lay unconscious in a narrow bed while fevers came and went, and through it all Mary Austin was beside him. Then on a morning when the rains had passed, and new sun painted a rainbow over the Sabine bottoms, he opened his eyes.

"Mary?" His voice was weak, barely a whisper, but she was close enough to hear it.

"I'm here," she said, stroking his hand with hands that were only half its size. "David, I'm here."

His eyes cleared and he looked up at her. "Mary," he whispered. "Angel, it's all right now. I've come home."

Many things had occurred recently in Hunt County, and it would take time before it was all sorted out—if it ever was, for though the "Provisional Authority" of Thad Carlile had dissolved, there were still hard times to come and people had concerns other than keeping track of what was past.

Men from two towns had backtracked Vince Terrell, from the Lone Oak Road westward to Old Catsprings, and had marveled at what they found there. But all in all, it did seem appropriate, somehow, that seven dead land-rustlers should be displayed like cow-killer wolves on a sagging old rail fence. And on the very site where the Carliles had headquartered when it all began.

By mutual consent, they buried them there, and Vince Terrell along with them, and left space for plenty more graves just in case there was need for such again.

Thad Carlile's death, a day later, was a mystery and would remain so. The same citizens who locked Reuben Blaes up in the county jail to await whatever justice a reformed and occupied State of Texas

298

might create, also went looking for Carlile. But as far as was commonly known, they didn't find him. Not until the second day, when his body was found beside the courthouse steps. It was generally agreed that the superintendent had fallen off the roof. What he was doing up there, nobody knew—or said. But it was agreed that was what had happened.

"Just clumsy, I reckon," became the accepted logic of it.

And in Lone Oak, on that day, David Allen Austin was sitting up in bed, getting ready to go home, when the postmaster stuck his head in at the door. "Feller here's been lookin' for you, Davey," he said. "You want to see him?"

The man he let in was young—about his own age—slender and quick-eyed, but oddly undistinguished in his appearance. He seemed just to blend into the background, and the stiletto in his hand, hidden by his coat sleeve, was invisible to any but himself.

He stepped into the room, closed the door, and stared at Austin, his eyes searching the scarred face. "You . . . you're Austin?" he asked. His voice was clipped, harsh-sounding, and abrasive. "David Allen Austin?"

Austin looked up at him. "Yes. Do I know you?"

"I'm Sullivan," the man said. "Maybe you heard of me? They call me Sully."

Austin shrugged and nodded. "All right, Sully. What can I do for you?"

Sully stared at him oddly. "I'm looking for Hands Bodie. Callahan Bodie. Billy Bean sent me."

Austin's gaze didn't waver, only seemed slightly

299

puzzled. "Yeah, I've heard that name. But he isn't here. He's dead. He died a long time ago. In the war. Didn't you know?"

"I heard maybe he did." Sully nodded, relaxing a bit. "I had to come, though. I had this notion that maybe . . . well, maybe you were him."

Austin started to answer, then paused, and a trace of humor showed at his cheeks. "Well, you've had a good look. Are you sure I'm not him?"

Sully nodded. The stiletto slid away into its arm sheath and his hand was empty. "I'm sure," he said. "I knew Hands Bodie, and you're not him."

Chapter Twenty-five

"I guess you'll be reading this, Justine Fremont. I know you read what I wrote before, and that's all right. I don't care if you read it and I don't care what you do with it, because it doesn't matter. I was right all along about that. Nothing matters.

"But what I was wrong about was what happened, out there on that hillside in the war. I thought I remembered it all, and it seemed like I did, but then things got a little clearer as time went on, and I knew I was wrong. Can you make up pieces of memory, and then think they are real? Like the Dutchman looked at people and saw only targets, can a man look at what he remembers and see only what suits him?

"Maybe so. And maybe it was the head injury.

"You see, teacher, that Johnny Reb did have a head injury. Something had hit him in the head so hard, that there just wasn't anybody in there at all and the only thing keeping him alive was that his heart was still beating.

"Maybe I knew that at the time. If I did, though, it only came clear to me later.

"I remembered him, crushed in the bottom of a shell crater, all broken and dying. I remembered it like that. But that wasn't how it was. It wasn't him. It was me. His horse had thrown him . . . and rolled on me.

"I guess there was just enough of him left in his head that when I said something, he knew it, and it was like he and I were all the people there were left in the world, and we were dying. Both of us. He was dying of a head wound that he couldn't come back from because it would take too long and he'd be dead before he could ever begin to heal. I was dying because the only part of me that was left — that was any good — was my head.

"We were the only people left in the world, and it was cold and wet and it was raining, and I tried to hang on because it didn't seem right. And then, somehow, we were the only *person* left. Him and me. We were the same person, and between us we could make it.

"It didn't seem possible. It didn't seem like a thing like that could be. But then there was that rainbow, teacher, and all of a sudden I knew I would live. But not . . . me.

"He wasn't the one who died on that battlefield, Justine. David Allen Austin didn't die. I was the one who died. Hands Bodie. I never got out of that shell crater . . . but in his head, I did, and for as long as it took him to come back to life inside his head, it was me that kept him — kept us — going. He had the reason, and I had the means.

"He couldn't have made it back without me. I matter to him. I matter.

"But it won't last long. He's coming back now, he's here just as much as I am and even if either of us wanted it that way, there can't be both of us here. There can only be one person.

302

"There isn't anything I can do about that. But that's why I wanted to write all this down. I wanted *somebody* to know. When Hands Bodie is gone, it won't matter. I never mattered, ever at all. But maybe, if this is written down, maybe you will read it. Do whatever you want with it then, or nothing at all if that seems best. You decide.

"I knew when I saw his home, and his wife and his baby—I started knowing then that I won't be here much longer. Where does a person go, this long after he died? When he isn't here anymore, then where is he?

"Do what you like with this, Justine. It's for you.

"I think I had a friend once, in New York City. Her name was Mrs. Jessup. I don't know if she was my friend, but I guess she came as close as anybody I remember from back then. I think about her sometimes now, because you remind me of her, just a little.

"Maybe you're my friend, too.

"I guess that is all of it. There is still so much to do, so much that David Allen Austin needs to do, and that he can't get done without me.

"I won't write anymore. But whatever happens, Justine Fremont, I'll think of you as my friend.

"The friend of Hands Bodie."

On the front porch of the old Austin place—her place now—Justine Fremont folded the papers on her lap and gazed out across the meadows, off into distances.

After a time Pete Joslyn tipped his chair back, looked at her, and said, "Finished?"

"Finished." She nodded. "All finished."

"Does it explain anything to you?"

She thought about it, then shook her head. "Not

303

really. Not in any way I find it easy to accept. Do you want to read it?"

Joslyn looked away. "Maybe some day," he said.